ALASKA'S MAMA

Cheryle Coapstick

Several churches, missions, schools, and business entities in Alaska's Mama are historical and may still exist. They are used in a fictional way in this novel. Some historical figures are also mentioned, and they are also used in a fictional way. All other characters, except those based on certain family members, are entirely fictional and any resemblance to known persons, living or dead, is unintentional.

First paperback edition August 2022

Paperback: ISBN 978-1-7366706-2-0
eBook: ISBN 978-1-7366706-3-7

Cover design and interior formatting by Andy Towler
www.aplusscreative.com

Published by Biorka Books
chercoaps@gmail.com

Acknowledgments

Three women have encouraged, supported, and lent their expertise in the production of this novel. Vicki Karlsson, Patty Huey, and Maureen Harlan. Your help is more valuable than you know. I appreciate you.

My sincere gratitude to all who have read Alaska's Firy, About Miss Ruth, and now Alaska's Mama.

I am indebted to my designer and formatter, Andy Towler of Aplusscreative. His cover designs give the reader a hint and a promise of what's to come.

And always, always my eternal gratitude to the Lord Jesus. I write for Him.

Series:
MY MAMA'S MAMA

Alaska's Firy

About Miss Ruth

Alaska's Mama

"Miss Ruth,
You have given me an
unintended legacy."

—Cora May Matthews

PROLOGUE

Sitka, Alaska 1907

"Lemuel, come back here!" The young mother shifted her toddler to her other hip and hurried after her five-year-old son.

The boy elbowed, bumped, and jostled the crowds as he ran along Sitka's wooden sidewalks. Jeers and curses followed him, but Lemuel laughed and lifted his head to the mocking gulls that led him toward the wharf. A steamship's incoming whistle blew and he ran faster.

His frustrated mother pushed past those in her way. "Lemuel, stay away from the docks." She threw a hurried "Sorry" to the tall, bushy-bearded man as she thrust past him, pushing him into the, almost as tall, woman in front of him.

"Excuse me," the man grabbed the woman's arm to steady her. "Miss?"

"Quite all right—Miss Ruth, and you are?"

Miss Ruth stumbled again, and he placed his hand under her elbow. "Where are you going?"

He had unexpected manners for a prospector, and she gave him a second look. Over the years, she had given an extra stare to every man who appeared near her father's age but never saw one who resembled his portrait— an image she had seen every day back on the ranch. Today that portrait would not come into focus. She sighed and pushed the effort away. "Just across the street to the mercantile," she answered, lifting her empty shopping basket. "I'm on a mission. Coffee. Sugar. Bacon. It's been a long time since I've had bacon."

"I'm afraid there will be scant supplies on the shelves. There have been too many people here ever since gold was discovered on Chichagof a couple of years ago. Rumors of a new vein are bringing even more."

"A steamship arrived late yesterday from Seattle with foodstuffs and hard goods, and another has just docked."

The bearded man chuckled and said, "Everyone heard today's whistle, including young Lemuel."

She laughed and gazed at the congested streets, clogged sidewalks, and crowded entrance to the store.

"Let me escort you." He offered his arm as if he were an elegant gentleman rather than a somewhat scruffy prospector. He maneuvered them across the street efficiently, without mishap.

"Are you one of those seeking your fortune, Mister...?"

His sad eyes betrayed him, "Everyone is seeking something, Miss Ruth."

"There he is!"

"I see him."

Two obvious would-be prospectors, one young, fresh-faced and freckled, the other wiry, leathered, who looked and smelled as if he hadn't had his spring bath, rushed across the street and blocked their way.

"Boss wants to leave before anyone hears the rumors," the older of the two said.

"Yeah, the boat won't wait."

"It will wait; I'm the only one who knows where we're going."

"Boss wants you on board before anybody figures out you found the mother lode." The wiry one spit tobacco juice out of the side of his mouth.

The younger one grinned, "We're going to be rich."

"Shut up! Don't say that out loud," his partner hissed, then awkwardly attempted to tip his hat to Miss Ruth. "Beg pardon, Miss."

Known in Alaska only as Denver Dan, Robert John Merritt bowed to the striking woman. As she said goodbye and turned to enter the store, he gasped, and his heart throbbed.

Her profile and the few tendrils of hair peeking from under her hat were like his dear wife Emma's. Before he could speak, his two companions grabbed his arms and pulled him toward the docks, babbling about their forthcoming riches. He cricked his neck for one last look at Miss Ruth, but she was gone.

The trip up the outer edge of Chichagof Island was uneventful, the currents treacherous and the tides strong, as usual. They anchored in a secluded cove Merritt had discovered weeks ago. It was well away from other claims and mines on the island.

As they unloaded their supplies and set up camp, the Boss said, "You seem distracted, Denver. What's the problem?"

"Nothing."

"You sure you know where the gold is?"

"I found a creek that showed color and a parallel one with a lot of placer gold. The cave where the water bubbles from an underground spring seemed promising."

The Boss thrust a cup of coffee into his hands and said, "You sure you're okay, man?"

"Yeah. Just glimpsed a face from the past, I think." He gulped the brew, threw the dregs from his cup into the fire, grabbed his pick and lantern, and led them upstream and deep into the woods. At the cave's entrance, he ordered them to wait.

"So you can grab all the gold for yourself?" The youngest of the group growled.

"I need to see if the cave needs shoring up before we go very far; this part of Alaska is prone to earthquakes."

"That's what you say." He sniffed and ran his sleeve under his nose.

The Boss put his hand on his holster and stared at the excitable young man. "Denver Dan is the leader of this here expedition. Besides, you idiot, this isn't placer gold like you pick up from the streams. It's embedded in the rock. That's why we have picks and shovels, so shut your yap."

Denver Dan lit the lantern and disappeared into the cave.

"It's been over an hour. He should have reported back by now. I'm going in," The freckled would-be prospector said.

"We'll all go. You got any matches? It will be dark in there."

Fifteen feet into the cave, they heard a faint rumble that slowly increased in volume, and the ground beneath their feet started to vibrate. They barely made it out before rocks and debris fell and collapsed the cave's entrance.

"Get a load of those boulders! There's no way we can move them." The Boss swore and reached for his tobacco pouch. The three men stared at the cave's mouth.

"He's a goner!"

"What about the gold, Boss?"

"Don't worry, I got it all figured out. Sad about old Denver, though."

They packed up their camp and headed back to Sitka after stacking a pile of rocks to stake their claim— one at the collapsed entrance to the cave and another by the two streams.

"We'll record our claims at the assay office. After we get all the gold out of the creeks, I'll get us some dynamite, and we'll blast our way into the cave. By then, Denver Dan will be a skeleton of an unknown sourdough. We'll never utter his name again. Agreed?"

"Agreed."

"Right."

Robert Merritt wiped his face with his bandana, held the lantern high, and surveyed the rocks that barred his way. Some were bigger than steamer trunks, impossible for him to move. The dust created by the cave-in lined his nostrils and coated his mouth. He spat, blew his nose, and wiped his face again.

No escape. He knew it and the mouse on top of the debris pile knew it, but she didn't give up. She hurried back and forth, squealed, and finally squeezed herself through the tiniest crack. "Godspeed, little mouse." Who would wish him Godspeed when he breathed his last?

He checked the lantern and saw the kerosene level was at the halfway mark. There was even less liquid in his canteen. How long could a man live without water? Five days? Six? Seven? He lifted the canteen to his mouth and drank it all. What was the point of conserving the cool liquid? It would just delay the inevitable. He threw the canteen across the cave, then felt for his pocket watch. He opened the watch's cover and gazed at his wife's portrait. The time had stopped at 4:15. Was that minutes or hours ago? Her profile and hair color matched the woman on Sitka's sidewalk; she also had Emma's same build and walk. He shook his head and pushed the images away.

He didn't know how much time had passed when the lantern sputtered, and the light ultimately died. Robert Merritt lay his head against the boulder. Sleep eluded him as he saw every wrong decision of his life wash over him. Memories, unbidden, unwanted, filled the cavern that would soon be his tomb.

I shouldn't have left you, Emma. Maybe if I had stayed, you and the baby would have lived. You understand, don't you? I wanted a better life for us, a good life.

His times of sleeping, dreaming, and talking to himself merged together, and he had no idea how long he had been interred in what was sure to be his grave. He had no faith that his three partners would try to rescue him.

It could have been a day later; it could have been two or three when he lit the first of the three matches he had found next to his pocket watch. Alone in the dark, time did not exist.

The flame's golden glow rested on Emma's face. He rubbed his thumb over her picture, the face of an angel. The match burned down to his fingers; he yelped and dropped it. It sputtered in the dust, and darkness covered him again. He imagined his wife's sweet face and gentle words encouraging him to come to God. She made it sound easy, but it wasn't, not for him. He turned his mind away from such oppressive thoughts and slept.

The cold woke him, or maybe it was his thirst. The ache behind his eyes, the stiffness in his joints, the condition of his dehydrated body, and the confusion in his mind let him know it wouldn't be long, a day or two at most.

He lit the second match and groped for the watch that had fallen from his lap. He brushed the dust from Emma's face and stared at her likeness; he seemed to hear her voice, "I beg you, Robert, let God love you. Admit you are nothing without Him and everything with Him."

She was correct; he had always been nothing, never good enough. Perhaps, that's why he was always ready to run, move on to the next thing, and leave before anyone found out.

He had discovered silver and gold several times, but what did it matter? It didn't buy him peace. He had lived with different tribes and studied their languages, but to what end? It didn't give him a purpose. He had nothing to show for his life—no progeny—no legacy.

He would die in the dark, cold and alone. His tongue, dry and thick, clung to the roof of his mouth. He tried to speak but wasn't sure what he wanted to say or to whom. He couldn't approach God, not after the life he'd lived and the choices he'd made. He would breathe his last in this cold crypt.

He heard Emma's voice tell him it wasn't too late. He could almost see her standing before him. "The thief on the cross looked at Jesus and said, 'Remember me,' you can do the same, dear husband."

He struck his last match, opened his watch, and gazed at Emma for the last time.

ONE

Seattle, Washington1942

Dear Kamalei,

You might be surprised by the Seattle postmark. I am at the Northwest Plaza Hotel. As I mentioned in my last letter, I'm taking my father's remains back to the ranch. He'll be buried in the family plot next to my mother. I wish Grandpa John were there, but I'm glad you put flowers on his grave every season.

I am thankful your last letter stated you are all well despite the Japanese attack. War is such a horrible thing. I pray for all of you every day. Please give my love to everyone and write soon. I want to know everything happening in Hawaii and the Pacific.

Last night, I noticed a young man in the lobby, half-hidden by an ornate potted palm. He casually lit a cigar.

"Foul things, how can Dad stand them?" He winced, pulled his fedora low on his forehead, rubbed his knee, and stretched his leg out. After recognizing him, I turned away lest he see me in my city clothes.

I looked at my ivory silk shirt and chocolate rayon trousers—pure Hepburn. I've often been compared to that glamorous movie star, although I'm at least fifteen years older than she. I have excellent posture, better bone structure, and good skin, for which I give Sitka's misty weather full credit. Other than that, I don't see the resemblance.

However, I did have her dark caramel-colored hair once upon a time. My western boots peeked out from my trousers. No glamour there.

My musings were interrupted by his voice. "It is you."

"Sammy Mitchell! I thought you were in the Army."

"I got booted out. Busted my leg during training," he cursed and rubbed the offending leg.

I laid my hand on his arm until he looked me in the eye. "They wouldn't discharge you for a simple break. It was more than that, wasn't it?"

"Sepsis. I spent several weeks in the station hospital at Fort Lewis. Healing too slow." He swore again, rubbed his leg, and said, "Sorry, Miss Ruth. Language."

"I've heard worse." I wanted to put him at ease.

"But you!" He indicated my clothes. "You don't look like yourself."

"You found out my secret, Sam, but let's not tell anybody back home."

"But why? You're quite a sight."

"For a woman of a certain age?"

He sputtered, red-faced.

"An old spinster?" I couldn't resist.

He ignored my teasing, although his face still flamed. "Why do you wear that old-fashioned get-up in Alaska?" he asked.

"In 1890, I met the Reverend Mrs. Monroe. Hence the black."

"Good grief! That was fifty years ago. What's the story?"

"I'll tell you Sam, but it's off the record."

(You know Kamalei, no newspaper journalist wants to hear those words, but I knew young Sam would honor my request.)

"Tell me over dinner, Miss Ruth."

"Lovely. But only if we pool our ration cards."

"I have a request of my own," he said, "you must wear what you have on. I'm taking a movie star out to dinner, not Sitka's Lady in Black."

We agreed to meet in the lobby in an hour. Sam whistled and heads turned when I exited the elevator wearing a camel-colored coat tied at the waist and a ridiculous hat with two pheasant feathers that jutted from its brim.

I stopped mid-stride, struck a movie star pose, and threw Sam a kiss with pouty red lips. Bellhops tipped their caps, servicemen saluted, and older gentlemen smiled behind their newspapers.

Young Sam blushed again, but he took my arm and escorted me out of the hotel. We walked a few blocks to a quiet restaurant. The longer we walked, the more pronounced his limp. He grimaced a few times, but I knew better than to comment. I decided that after dinner, I would be a tired old lady who needed a taxi.

The restaurant specialized in seafood, but Sam and I ordered pot roast, mashed potatoes with gravy, and glazed carrots. Two inhabitants from a small town who didn't really know each other, but like all small-town folk, we thought we did.

"Tell me about the Lady in Black," he said.

I explained how the Reverend Mrs. Monroe thought it a woman's duty to protect men from their base natures. Sam's jaw dropped; he closed it abruptly, then said, "Surely, there is no need to continue."

"You mean now that I'm gray and wrinkled and unable to tempt all you base and wicked men."

Sam stammered, "Yes, er, no." He studied me intently, "If I had to describe you for a newspaper article, I would say something about your silver, not gray hair. Your face has very few wrinkles for a woman your age...." He sputtered and lowered his eyes, shoving another bite of mashed potatoes into his mouth. His red face told me he was embarrassed. Poor boy.

"I was just out of my teens when I arrived in Alaska, and that was over half a century ago. You do the math, Sam."

I saw him mentally calculate, and he seemed startled. I had always been told I looked twenty years younger. Perhaps it was true.

"This is now, and that get-up is so..." The word ugly hung in the air.

Finally, I took pity on this uncomfortable young man. "At first, it was a job requirement, then a habit, then a convenience. Whenever anyone in Sitka needed help, they called for the Lady in Black."

"I agree you were easy to find. Everybody knew you."

"Really? Did you know me?" I felt my eyes twinkle but could see he took the question seriously.

He ate several bites of his pot roast while thinking, then shook his head. "No, Miss Ruth. But as you say, you were noticeable."

"It was almost like a nun's habit, and people reacted to me similarly. Some ran to me for help. Some ran in the opposite direction, afraid I might preach or judge them. Few saw beyond my 'black get-up,' as you called it."

"And that hideous hat you always wore."

I laughed, "Don't disparage my hat, Sam. It was given to me many years ago by an ancient mariner who wore it around the Horn."

"Tell me about it and why you're in Seattle. I want to hear all about Miss Ruth."

"There's not much you need to know, dear boy. Although, I once had a lovely nutmeg dress." I stared into the flame of the table's single candle.

"Nutmeg dress?"

I waved my fork at him and smiled, "It's at the bottom of the Pacific Ocean somewhere between San Francisco and Oahu."

"Hawaii? When were you ever in Hawaii? Tell me!"

I shook my head, "We've talked about me throughout dinner. What will you do now that you're out of the Army?"

He struggled but allowed himself to be distracted. "I'm scrounging for ink and newsprint for Dad until classes at the University begin, although Mom has hinted she wants me home. She's still worried about me."

While I kept Sam talking about his future, our bread pudding with maple walnut sauce arrived. Degrees in journalism and writing, jobs at big-city newspapers, the desire to be an international correspondent, and writing the Great American Novel were at the top of his list. I told him he had lofty dreams.

"I'll make them all come true."

As we took a taxi back to the hotel, I said, "A college education is important to you, isn't it?"

"Of course, it's step one in achieving my dreams."

"I'm old enough to be your grandmother, so I'll speak frankly. If you want to be the best newspaperman in Alaska or even the world, go home."

"But..."

"Learn from your father."

"But..."

"I'm not telling you what to do, of course, but listen whenever anyone comes into the office. See how your father interviews and crafts the story, learn how he keeps his articles objective and only offers an opinion in his editorials. See how he lives with integrity. Sit at his feet, Sam."

"But..."

"Notice how he respects people and offers those with opposing views an opportunity to express their opinions. If I were you, Sam, I'd go home."

"Yes, but..."

"Live and breathe the newspaper. Let your dad mentor you." I could see Sam trying to think this through. He didn't know how to respond to my blatant suggestions. I yawned. "My train leaves in the morning."

"Where are you going?"

"I'm tired, Sam."

"I'll meet you for breakfast," he said.

I smiled but didn't answer. We said good night and went to our rooms. I made several phone calls before retiring. I had a promise to keep.

TWO

SAM

Sitka, Alaska, 1962

Sam Mitchell, Jr., editor of the Sitka Sentinel, raced through the letter the stranger from Hawaii had given him just minutes ago. He gazed at the pages in his hand but saw the evening he had spent with Miss Ruth.

He closed his eyes as her image hit him with the force of a stormy incoming tide. They had said good-night that warm summer night of 1942 and gone to their respective hotel rooms. He put the key in the lock of his room and then kicked the door. The slam felt satisfying.

He had cursed himself for being a lousy reporter. If his time with her had been an interview, he could say that she looked like a movie star and had a nutmeg dress at the bottom of the Pacific Ocean. He didn't even know what that was, a color, style, or type of fabric? He had always thought nutmeg was a spice.

Sam leaned back in his chair and thought about the intervening years. He hadn't gone to college, never worked for a big-city newspaper, or been a foreign correspondent, and no, he hadn't written the Great American Novel.

Sam rubbed his eyes and reached for the telephone. Alice would help him figure this out—something Miss Ruth said about dreams and destiny. It had been a long time since he thought about his dreams.

He let the handset fall back into its cradle when he saw the open suitcase full of Kamalei's letters.

Margaret Mary filled slugs into the tray of the linotype, but there was no sign of the aged Hawaiian.

Sam heard the drone of the floatplane overhead and knew Kamalei had gone. He grabbed the suitcase, ensured the latches were secure, bolted out of the Sentinel, bypassed the Café, and barely nodded at the passersby.

He slammed the kitchen door and spread the letters on the table.

Feeling richer than any miner on the Klondike, Sam's eyes glistened. He now understood those who had been afflicted with gold fever. This was the mother lode! Miss Ruth's life in her own words. Her Spencerian script—elegant; the onion-skin paper and envelopes—delicate.

He arranged over seventy stacks on the table by year, with around fifty letters in each pile. He felt like dancing a jig but saw Sadsack in the living room doorway. The disdain on the feline's face stopped him, and Sam growled, "It's just like you to deflate my balloon, Sad. Not this time. I've struck it rich!"

Sam grabbed handful after handful of the letters, threw them in the air with glee, and they fell like Sitka's plentiful rain.

The cat put his nose in the air and walked away. Sam's eyes swept the small kitchen now decorated with thousands of pieces of mail. He moaned and fell to his knees. The years 1936 and 1947 were tossed in the corner, the 1950s scattered across the counter, and a couple of 1890s and a 1961 were draped over Sadsack's water bowl.

Sam snatched them and blotted each with a dishtowel. Miss Ruth had obviously used a fountain pen, and the cat's water caused the ink to leach and smear. How could he have been so foolish?

Peeking out from under the refrigerator were a 1904, a 1932, and several 1953s. He gathered the letters and piled them on the table, berating his half-witted actions.

Sadsack returned and rubbed himself around Sam's leg. "I'd like to blame you for this, you lousy cat, but I let my enthusiasm get away from me."

The cat blinked, and Sam picked him up. "Just look at the chaos in this kitchen. I've mixed them up, decade after decade." Sam scratched Sadsack under his chin. "Never mind, I can fix this."

The cat dug his claws into Sam's chest. "Okay, you don't have to get nasty." He dumped a can of food into the cat's dish and threw the can opener into the sink. "Well, are you going to eat?"

The large tabby blinked twice and turned away.

"I know it's not people food, but you're not people."

Sadsack twitched his tail and retreated to the living room.

"I'm not going to telephone the Café. Your food's in the bowl; take it or leave it," Sam called after him.

Sam pulled the letter out of his vest pocket that Kamalei had given him earlier. He turned it over, then placed it under the book he was currently reading, and picked up a letter from the table, 1897. He read the first sentence, and then his eye caught the postmark of another letter—1916. What was in that one? Sam started reading several letters but couldn't focus on them.

Disgusted, he made himself a sandwich, put on a pot of coffee, and laid a fire in the old stone fireplace while the coffee perked. Mug in hand, Sam settled in his well-worn leather chair. An hour later, his burning stomach told him he should ease off the caffeine and eat the sandwich.

His racing mind told him to calm himself. The letters were massive, and Sam, unable to focus, picked up his book. The letter came with it. Sam reread it, slowly this time.

"I'm going to tell you a story, Sadsack. If you pay attention, I'll call the Café and have them deliver dinner."

The aged cat, still somewhat spry, jumped into his lap.

"I was in Seattle during the summer of '42. Miss Ruth and I had dinner and agreed to meet the following morning for breakfast. I got to the hotel dining room early. It was nearly full; I guess the war made early risers of us all. The mood was somber, anxious. Through the double doors that led to the lobby, I saw Miss Ruth leave the elevator with an older couple. She kissed the woman on the cheek and hugged the old man. A soldier rushed to her side, they spoke for several minutes, and unnoticed, she slipped some cash into his pocket then quickly turned with familiar affection to greet a bellhop. She seemed to know just about everyone, and I began to think she was more than who I had seen in Sitka, and I admit I was curious."

Sam's grip tightened, and Sadsack hissed, "Sorry." Sam felt, rather than heard, the cat purr as he absent-mindedly rubbed Sadsack's ears.

"During our dinner, Miss Ruth told me to go home and made it sound easy, but I had plans, and they didn't include life in a small fishing village on an island off the Southeast coast of Alaska." The wind blew and rattled the windows, but Sam didn't notice.

"The waitress served my breakfast and placed an envelope next to my coffee. Inside was a note and a bus ticket to Boeing Field. Bob Nelles had come to Seattle to pick up parts for one of his planes and was scheduled to fly back to Sitka that morning. I scrambled from my table, but Miss Ruth was nowhere to be found."

The cat gazed at him with unblinking eyes. Sam scratched him under the chin.

"I still don't know why I took that bus; I barely made the flight." Sam smirked and said, "Later, Bob told me he had orders from Miss Ruth to wait for me."

Sadsack jumped from Sam's lap and crouched on the side table next to the phone. Sam ordered dinner for both of them and ignored Mick's complaints about delivering in the rain and the wind. He continued to share his memories with the cat.

"We had an uneventful flight, and when I entered the Sentinel unannounced, Margaret Mary had me in a bear hug before I had time to notice Dad wasn't there." Sam's fingers stilled as he replayed the scene in his mind.

He remembered how he had extracted himself from her embrace, threw his fedora towards the hat rack, and missed.

"He comes in most mornings." Margaret Mary said, "On good days, he stops at the Café before going home."

"What do you mean, good days? Is something wrong with him?"

"His heart and something respiratory."

"Not tuberculosis?" Sam took a step back.

Margaret Mary shook her head. "Thank God, no. It's something I can't pronounce."

"Why didn't anyone let me know?"

Margaret Mary, tears in her eyes, sniffed and said, "That was your Dad's decision."

"Mom should have told me anyway, or you should have," Sam growled, leaned against the file cabinet, and took deep, slow breaths. "I'm glad it's not TB. How is he handling it? I can't ever remember him being sick."

"He's full of energy some days and seems like his old self. Other times he's moody and drags himself around. Your Mom is beside herself. She'll be glad you're home, Sam."

"Dad will have a word or two for me about that," Sam sighed and ran his hand through his hair.

"Just blame Miss Ruth."

"What?" Sam's eyebrows elevated.

Margaret Mary shrugged and said, "She had personal business in the States but promised she'd send you home." Margaret Mary picked up the phone's handset. "I'm going to call your mom."

"I'll just go to the house." Sam retrieved his fedora from the corner.

Margaret Mary shook her head as she dialed, "Trust me, she'll need to cry and won't want to do that in front of your father."

Sam tossed his hat and missed the hook again. He reached for the percolator on the windowsill. "Okay. I'll make a fresh pot of coffee."

Margaret Mary finished the call and shrugged into her coat. "You know your mother doesn't like coffee. I'll get tea and fry bread from the Café."

That Miss Ruth! The memories still tugged at him, but Sam pushed them away. "Did you hear all that, Sadsack? I wonder what Miss Ruth would've done if I hadn't used that bus ticket?"

But Sadsack didn't hear. He sat on the windowsill and watched for Mick through the rain. He hoped his dinner included halibut cheeks.

THREE

SAM 1962

As was her habit, the linotype operator arrived for work thirty minutes before the Sentinel's office opened. Sam was usually there. The past two days, she entered a cold, dark building with no coffee and no Sam. She telephoned his home, and he mumbled he hadn't slept well. Margaret Mary had no doubt he spoke the truth, and she knew why.

This morning she put on the coffee, turned up the thermostat, switched on the lights, then sat down at the linotype. Just like yesterday, her inbox was empty. She threw the wire basket across the room and stomped out.

A misty drizzle reflected her mood. She ducked into the Café and hailed Agrefena. "Did Sam pick up dinner last night?"

"No, and I'm a bit worried. If he doesn't show tonight, I'll send Mick over."

"Cook all his breakfast favorites and Sadsack's, too," Margaret Mary tapped her fingers on the counter. "Never mind, just give me whatever's ready."

Sam answered his door, unkempt and unshaven. His disheveled pajamas and coffee-stained bathrobe did not indicate a good night's rest.

She brushed past him and set the bag of food on the counter. Sadsack rushed in. Margaret Mary hugged the old feline. "Feed yourself, Sam. I'll tend to Sadsack. By the way, you look terrible."

"You talking to me or the cat?"

Margaret Mary glared and turned her back.

He moderated his tone, "I must admit I've been living on black coffee." He rummaged through the bag. "Thanks for the food; it sure smells good."

"You're a mess, and look at this chaos, stacks of letters everywhere."

"Don't touch anything! I've got a system."

"So you say, I don't see it."

"The 1920s are on the counter. The thirties and forties are on the table."

She wandered through to the living room and saw the 1950s on the couch and the '60s on the coffee table. "Where are the 1910s?"

"Bathroom."

"And the 1890s? That's when Miss Ruth came to Alaska, right?"

"By the bed."

Margaret Mary saw notebooks and tablets scattered among the letters, "I see you've been making notes. What are you going to do with all this information?"

Sam had already demolished Agrefena's bacon and eggs; now, he brought the coffee and fry bread into the living room. "There are thousands of letters, most of them several pages long. It's too much. I'm drowning in the details. And I don't know if I should devote a whole issue to Miss Ruth or write a series of articles. I don't know how interested people would be." He ran his hand over his head and sank into his chair. "I don't even know why I'm interested. I wish I could forget the whole thing."

"We both know that's not going to happen, but right now, your responsibility is to the citizens of Sitka. The paper goes to press soon, and I don't have any stories. We can't have an issue with just advertisements."

Sam slammed his mug on the side table and searched for his watch, "What time is it?"

"You mean, what day is it?" Margaret Mary started gathering the letters.

Sam jumped up and swore, "I told you, hands off the letters!"

"Don't you yell at me! Go, take a shower and get to the Sentinel! The news won't wait!"

"You know Margaret Mary if you weren't old enough to be my mother..."

"Well, I am, and since she was my best friend, I think I know what she'd say about this mess."

Sam laughed, "I give up, but please don't touch the letters."

"All right, Sam, but I don't like it. You're obsessed."

Sadsack followed Sam as far as the hallway, then turned back to Margaret Mary and meowed.

"You're right, Sad; this is not good."

Sam appeared at the office well after lunchtime.

"I expected you earlier. You look like something the cat dragged in," Margaret Mary grated, "and I don't mean Sadsack."

"I spent most of the day reading more of Miss Ruth's letters."

"Get it together, Sam. You can't ignore what's going on in Sitka."

Sam poured himself a cup of coffee. "What is going on?"

"That's for you to find out." Margaret Mary pointed to the sign above her beloved linotype machine, FIRST, THE NEWS.

Sam settled behind his desk. He lit his cigar and attacked his inbox. Two hours later, he picked up the last item, a single piece of unlined paper folded in half. "What's this?"

"You rushed out of here so fast last week you didn't notice it was under the old Hawaiian's suitcase."

"Why didn't you bring it to me?" Sam dropped his cigar into one of several large ashtrays on his desk.

Margaret Mary shrugged and peered over his shoulder. "What does it say?"

Dear Sam,

I'm glad I made the trip to Sitka. You are everything Miss Ruth said you were. Although you never attended a university or worked for a big-city newspaper, much less became a foreign correspondent, there's still time for you to write a great novel. The letters should help.

Kamalei

Stunned, Sam sank into his chair and reached for another cigar, "Apparently, he thinks I should write a book about Miss Ruth," he glanced at Margaret Mary, "Don't grin at me like a Cheshire cat."

"She must have written to Kamalei about you. I could have told her a thing or two. Him too, if he had asked."

Sam's eyebrows quirked, and he laughed out loud. "I'll have to scan the other letters and see what she said about me."

Margaret Mary stood before the editor with crossed arms and tapped her foot on the bare wooden floor. She took a deep breath and blew it out, "I know I will regret this, but I can hold down the fort one day a week while you work on the book."

Sam grabbed his hat, kissed the linotype operator on the cheek, and yelled as he raced out the door, "It's almost closing time. I might as well go home and read a few letters."

He had enough foresight to stop at the Café and pick up something he could warm up later. He didn't want Sadsack to distract him. He'd read until his eyes were full of grit, and then he'd read some more.

Sam opened his unlocked door; nobody in this small town ever locked their houses. Every available surface was covered with Miss Ruth's letters. He decided to start with the last letter she wrote and worked backward. If that didn't work out, he could always change his mind.

FOUR

Dear Kamalei,

Remember Sam Mitchell, Jr.? I've written about him several times, even interfered in his life a time or two.

He tried to interview Our Firy and me immediately after the murder trial, but it wasn't the right time. Our Firy was still in shock.

I'll be in Sitka in a few weeks. Perhaps, I will stop by the Sentinel and answer his questions.

I had a couple of adventures with Sam's parents before he was born. I wonder if his father ever told young Sam?

Anyway, he's a good man. There is a depth to him even he doesn't realize.

I've much to say to you, but I haven't packed yet. Yelena will mail this note for me, and I'll write more on the plane...

—MISS RUTH'S LETTERS 1962

"Adventures with my parents? Why didn't I know anything about that?" He scanned the pages. Nothing. "Hey, Sadsack, apparently Miss Ruth thought I was all right."

The cat blinked twice and walked away. "Just because you don't value anyone's good opinion doesn't mean the rest of us don't. Lousy cat." But he said it with affection.

Sam stuffed the letter back in the envelope and reached for one with an earlier postmark. He forced himself to read about the trial when he wanted to scan the letters to see what she had written about him. He reached for his percolator and then made sure he had a fresh supply of cigars.

FIVE

Dear Kamalei,

Anna Marie's murder trial is over. Guilty, of course. We await the sentencing. As you know from my previous letters, I did not allow Our Firy to attend, but I knew everything that happened in the courtroom. My heart goes out to the defendant. He was thirteen years old when he killed Our Firy's dear sister.

Sixteen years later, his sins have caught up with him. I dread visiting him but know I must...

—MISS RUTH'S LETTERS 1962

The defendant had refused all visitors, including his lawyer and the jail chaplain. The crazy old lady sitting outside his cell in a straight-backed chair, silent and staring, caused him to curse.

He banged on the iron bars with his tin cup. The guard stormed in and laughed when the prisoner motioned he wanted the woman gone.

"Judge Cooper says this here lady has complete access to you any time, day or night," he turned to Miss Ruth and said, "You give a holler, ma'am if this murderer gets riled up." He left, jingling his keys and muttering, "Dirty, no good..."

Miss Ruth folded her hands. Her scuffed and worn cowboy boots rested under the frayed hem of her long black skirt. The prisoner took one look at her and flung himself on the cot.

"Tell me about Anna Marie," she said.*

He stuck his fingers in his ears. Spat. Paced. Squatted in the farthest corner of his cell. Finally, he stood at the cell's door and gripped the iron bars. With dull, empty eyes, he stared at her through the bars and bit the inside of his cheek.

"I will sit here until you speak."

After a few minutes, his voice low and flat, the words came, "I watched the girl and the dog for months. Riding her bike, playing baseball. I never had a bike or a dog. I only knew about baseball when my drunk old man picked up a bat and came after me." He fell silent, and his knuckles whitened as he gripped the bars.

"Go on."

"She asked me to join their ballgames, but I didn't." He grabbed the bars tighter and clenched his jaw. "I watched them all the time, and one day I put up my hands, not to catch the ball, but to protect my face. They laughed. She got the ball, stood next to me, and ordered them to leave me alone."

"Did they?" Miss Ruth asked.

"They jeered and said I needed a girl to protect me. I knocked her down, snatched the ball, and threw it down our well."

"Then what?"

"It was their only ball, so their games ended. The others wanted to come after me, teach me a lesson, but she talked them out of it. I hated her."

***My Mama's Mama: Book One: Alaska's Firy*

"Tell me about the day she died."

He turned away and threw himself on the cot once more. He scratched his ear and turned his face to the wall, hoping she would leave. She didn't. He put the pillow over his head.

"I can stay here all day and night," the white-haired lady said.

He sighed and dragged himself back to the iron bars. Perhaps, if he told her everything, she would go away. "One day, I skipped school and caught the dog. I tethered him to a tree deep in the woods. I tried to play with him, but he strained against the rope, always whining. He wouldn't eat, even when I gave him fresh fish heads."

"Why didn't you let him go?"

The young man gazed at her with dull eyes. "He was my dog now, even though he wanted the girl." His lip curled, and his eyes glinted before they dulled again, "I watched as his blood stained the ground. I wiped the blade of my knife on my pant leg. Stupid dog. Stupid girl. I told myself I would get her too."

He raised his arm as if holding the weapon. "The blade was sharp and long. It made me strong."

Miss Ruth shivered but kept her voice low. "Tell me more about Anna Marie."

His voice was low and flat as he described how the blood flowed out of the girl as it had from her dog.

Miss Ruth fisted her hands, her knuckles lost all their color, but she remained still. "The life is in the blood," she said. "Let me tell you about One who gave His blood for you so that you might live after you die."

He put his hands over his ears. "Go away."

SIX

SAM, 1962

Sam put his head in his hands. The trial had lasted several days, and Sam sat in the gallery with his pen and pad. He had watched the defendant for hours. The young man remained still with no expression on his face.

Sam wanted to stride to the defendant's table, jerk him out of his chair and shake him. Do you know what you did? Do you have any idea of the pain, the hurt you caused the family, to the entire town?

Sam berated himself. For some reason, he couldn't remain the detached observer, the reporter. This young girl, Anna Marie, had slipped beneath the hedge Sam built around his emotions and captured his heart.

He knew how much Miss Ruth loved this family, so how could she have visited this murderer and offered him the comfort of her religion? Sam wanted to rip out the man's heart.

SEVEN

Dear Kamalei.

As you know, Our Firy has always been the child of my heart. After the trial, I said farewell to her with a deep sense of satisfaction. I am thankful that the tundra of her soul has been exposed to Bozhe's light and love — echoes of Eden. I cannot say the same for Judge Nathan Cooper. My heart hurts for him.

—MISS RUTH'S LETTERS 1962

Miss Ruth spent the next few days enjoying Firy's cousin Yelena and her boys. It was always lovely to stay with friends rather than in a hotel. They would have enjoyed the visit more if it weren't for the trial.

Tomorrow morning, Robert Nelson was scheduled to deliver medical supplies to Hoonah, Tenakee, and Pelican Cove. They'd leave for Nome after he returned to Juneau and refueled, so she must see Judge Nathan Cooper today.

Even though it was illegal for the Judge to have given her the trial's daily transcripts, she was not sorry she had pressured him. She tried to think of it as holy intimidation and righteous manipulation.

This morning she entered the stately courthouse amid its hustle and bustle. She found a sign listing the day's sessions, and according to the calendar, Nathan was not in court, so she assumed he would be in his chambers doing whatever judges do when not presiding over trials.

Even though the young woman sitting behind the desk said the Judge was not in, Miss Ruth sat and made herself comfortable. Several minutes later, she said, "Does Nathan's office have a back door?"

"No, ma'am." The young woman's fingers paused on the typewriter keys.

Miss Ruth considered the young secretary, "And although the Judge is not in his office, he will have to use that door to leave?" Miss Ruth pointed to the solid oak door next to the file cabinet.

Miss White nodded.

"I will wait until he appears."

"Oh, no, ma'am, I can't let you do that."

"Can't?" Miss Ruth straightened her shoulders.

Miss White came around her desk and knelt before Miss Ruth. She regarded the closed door and then the older woman. "You see, it's like this," she whispered, " I'm not his usual secretary. She's sick. I drew the short straw and had to fill in for her. I'd rather be back in the typing pool." She shuddered, "You know he's in there, and I know he's there." She took Miss Ruth's hands in her own. "We both know he's not coming out until you're gone. We also know you're not leaving until he comes out. You do understand what a terrible position this puts me in?"

Miss Ruth rather liked this intense young woman. Eyes twinkling, she said, "I can see you have a plan. What is it?"

"There is an empty meeting room down the hall. With the door ajar, you can see the entire hallway. You leave, and I'll tell the Judge he can escape. Whatever happens in the hallway is out of my control." Miss White squeezed Miss Ruth's hands. "You get what you want, and more importantly, I stay on the Judge's good side."

Miss Ruth shook her head and whispered, "He'll never believe I left." She checked her watch. "It has only been ninety minutes; he knows I'm more stubborn than that."

Miss White sat back on her heels, pulled her brows together, and said, "I suppose I could always pull the fire alarm."

"No, I wouldn't want you to get in trouble. I'll do it."

"It's a federal offense."

Miss Ruth's eyes twinkled. "Would you turn me in?" Miss Ruth headed to the door. Miss White, who still knelt on the floor, shook her head.

Miss Ruth turned and said, "Get up, dear. Sit at your desk and shuffle some papers or something."

"I was joking," Miss White muttered to Miss Ruth's back.

The fire alarm sounded throughout the courthouse. Judges, jurors, bailiffs, and lawyers scrambled out of the building. Clerks, secretaries, defendants, and witnesses made it safely out of Alaska's Superior Courthouse—all but one hapless, irritated Judge who was locked in a room with a determined old lady. The meeting did not go well.

"It was you, wasn't it? There is no fire."

"Nathan, you refused to see me. I had to do something."

"And you came up with that? Why didn't you go ahead and set fire to the place?"

"Now, Nathan, you know I would never do anything that might cause someone harm."

"No, you just inconvenience and embarrass them," he glared at her. "I am a judge. The first Yupik to reach the Superior Court. I have my own courtroom."

"That's what I came to talk to you about, Nathan; the disturbance I caused in your courtroom."

"It was undignified and embarrassing."

"Yes," Miss Ruth agreed.

"It didn't put me in a good light."

"I thought you handled it quite well, Nathan."

The Judge shook his head as Miss Ruth continued. "I wanted to assure you that when that reporter from the Anchorage Daily News asked me for an interview, I started preaching, and he walked away. I even refused the Sitka Sentinel's editor, and I know him."

Miss Ruth noticed Judge Cooper's pale face. His dignity is so important to him. *I suppose it's not so bad for a judge. He must possess a certain amount of decorum, but honestly.* She shook her head. "I didn't tell them the first time you went on a whale hunt; you asked the elders to throw you overboard to see if the whale would swallow you."

"When I go back to the village to see my grandmother, the elders call me Judge Jonah. No respect."

Miss Ruth bit her lip to keep from laughing.

"Not dignified at all." He scrutinized his hands.

"And I didn't tell them you ate skunk cabbage because the kids told you it was corn on the cob. Nathan, you were so gullible." Miss Ruth hazarded a smile but quickly erased it when he glared at her.

He squirmed in his chair, his face mottled, but he remained silent.

"I didn't mention anything about your teenage years. All your escapades and misadventures are safe with me."

Judge Cooper pulled his favorite gavel from his suit pocket. He sighed and put it down. "You manipulated me into illegal activity, giving you a copy of those transcripts."

"It was the right thing to do, but let's not talk about that now. I came to tell you I'm going home."

The relief was visible on his face, although he did not voice it. She was silent for a moment, then chose her words carefully, "Before I go, I wanted to tell you about Bozhe one last time. I want your heart to live."

Nathan winced and picked up his gavel again. To Miss Ruth, it looked like he wanted to bang on the table and shout, 'Court adjourned.'

"Now, Miss Ruth, I've outgrown all those stories you used to tell. If I were going to become religious, which I'm not, I would embrace my ancestors' beliefs. They make more sense to me than your stories of Bozhe and his Great Son, as you call him."

Miss Ruth bit the inside of her cheek as a great sadness settled in her soul. His reply was disheartening but not unexpected. She could never interest him in spiritual things. "Oh, Nathan, it's not a religion. It's knowing and trusting the Creator of the universe."

Nathan scowled past her and stared at a crack in the wall. His eyes glazed over, and he muttered, "I'm going to cross you off my Christmas card list."

She ignored the remark and said, "Bozhe loves you, Nathan."

He shrugged his shoulders and continued playing with his gavel, the symbol of his power and worth.

This pioneer woman who had served in Native villages and small Alaskan towns for over seventy years rose stiffly to her feet and said softly, "I will pray for you."

Again, the Judge shrugged, "I don't believe in such things, but if it makes you happy."

"I love you, Nathan."

He didn't respond.

EIGHT

SAM, 1962

Sam watched the flames dance in his fireplace and wondered what Miss Ruth meant, *echoes of Eden.* He scratched his head and thought it must be religious, something to do with Firy's strange encounter on the beach. He should place a phone call to her in Washington State. Although he'd be embarrassed to ask something so personal. Some journalist he was. He knew there was more to Firy's story.

Gather the information about Miss Ruth, Sammy Boy. See where the story takes you. Don't get side-tracked by anyone else's story. Stay focused. His dad's advice had a habit of surfacing just when he needed it. "It's almost as if he's here talking to us. Isn't that right, Sadsack?"

Sam chuckled to himself as he imagined Miss Ruth manipulating a Superior Court Judge of Alaska. Imagine him giving her the daily transcripts of a murder trial.

NINE

Miss Ruth
THE FLIGHT HOME, Juneau, 1962

The next day Yelena's boys, Ed and Ted, skipped school and carried Miss Ruth's bags to the dock where Robert Nelson had his floatplane moored. They hoped to convince him a ride over Mendenhall Glacier was in order.

Miss Ruth saw Robbie shake his head. She snapped her fingers and exclaimed, "I have a book I must return to the Bishop before we leave. It will give you time to give the boys a ride."

Robert inspected the older woman and demanded, "Does anyone ever refuse you, Miss Ruth?"

"You'd be surprised," she thought briefly of Nathan, and pain pierced her heart. Miss Ruth nodded in the boys' direction as they scrambled aboard the blue and yellow floatplane. "Thank you, Robbie."

"Don't you think it's time you called me Rob or Robert?"

"I'll try," she reached up and patted his cheek.

She was waiting on the dock when the small plane returned half an hour later. The brothers hugged her and told her about their adventure. They were both determined to become bush pilots. "I hope Alaska doesn't become too civilized before we get out of school and into the sky," Ted said.

"What do you think, Miss Ruth?" Ed asked.

She told the boys Alaska had changed in the last seven decades and saw their faces fall but then brighten when she said, "No matter how civilized Alaska becomes, boys, she will always be rugged and wild. You both will have many adventures."

"For sure?" they cried in unison.

"I've seen it," Miss Ruth laughed.

Both boys whooped and hollered, then ran to their mother's beauty shop. If Miss Ruth proclaimed it, it must be true.

The distance from Juneau to Nome was just over a thousand miles. The small plane touched down near several villages to deliver and pick up the mail. In one isolated community, Miss Ruth stretched her legs and visited the tiny church. Although she had intended to write to Kamalei, she spent her time looking out the window and sharing her thoughts with Bozhe.

Miss Ruth had been praying since Firy was a child; her mind knew Bozhe's timing was perfect, even if her heart sometimes struggled to agree. Now that Firy was safe, Miss Ruth had one last request.

The plane took off, and she stared out its side window. The Alaskan summer was awash in wildflowers. Her soul whispered to her Lord, "It's beautiful, Bozhe, but I want to go home."

"You are."

The small airplane hit a thermal and lost a hundred feet of altitude.

Miss Ruth clutched her stomach as the plane lurched again. "I don't mean to Nome. I want to come home to you."

"You are."

More turbulence. Robert's knuckles showed white as he gripped the controls.

Miss Ruth whooped, "Hallelujah!" while Robbie yelled, "It's okay, just a few thermals."

Miss Ruth knew it would be more than a few thermals. She frowned when she remembered Robbie didn't know the Lord. Bozhe leaned close and whispered. "My angels will bring him into my realm as you leave yours."

Before the plane hit the ground, Miss Ruth's heart stopped beating.

Alaska Air Rescue scrambled into action as soon as they received the mayday. They spotted the wreckage strewn across a small meadow exactly where the pilot radioed it would be.

Robert Nelson held Miss Ruth's body and moaned, "Oh, Lord God!"

The rescue workers could not explain how he had survived the crash without a mark on him and why Miss Ruth looked like she was napping. The autopsy revealed no apparent reason for her death, so the medical examiner wrote 'natural causes' on the death certificate.

The investigation into the cause of the crash cited a fluke mechanical problem. Robert knew better; he had found a note clutched in Miss Ruth's hand.

Dear Robbie,

You will always be Robbie to me, and I call you that with great affection. Whenever I flew with you, Bozhe's angels soared with us. They are here now and will keep you from perishing.

Bozhe has told me you'll fly all over Alaska and describe how you fell out of the sky and into His arms. Welcome to the Kingdom.

Miss Ruth

TEN

Sam's letter to the old Hawaiian, 1962

Dear Kamalei,

I enjoyed meeting you and appreciate you bringing Miss Ruth's letters to Sitka. Your excellent suggestion to write a book about her has inspired me, and I am seriously considering it.

Miss Ruth left me a note wrapped in a piece of lambswool hidden in a judge's metal box (long story) and asked that I tell you about the Shortys and how her letters had affected their lives.

It's an odd story, and of course, she didn't know its conclusion. I am a little perplexed by her request to send it to you, but I believe it reveals her character and heart, which I know you are well acquainted with.

Sincerely,
Sam Mitchell, Jr.
Editor, Sitka Sentinel

The linotype machine had been clacking in Margaret Mary's ears for decades, yet she still heard everything. "Sam. Phone."

She yelled again, turned off the machine, and walked to Sean Connor's wooden leg. It leaned against the file cabinet where it had rested for the last twenty years. She remembered the day Sam carried it in and said the old sourdough had bequeathed it to him. All those who entered the newspaper office remembered Sean Connor.

"Connor, me boy-o, if only I had a boss that paid attention to me, if only...."

The telephone's shrill ring sounded again. Sam grabbed the handset and motioned for Margaret Mary to hush. He covered the receiver and said, "Can you sweep the filings and melt some lead or do something quiet? I can't hear over that infernal machine's clacking."

Margaret Mary glared at him as she picked up the broom. Sam had been working amid the clatter and chaos for decades. "It must be important if the linotype's noise is interfering with his concentration," she muttered to herself.

Connor's leg glistened in the sunlight streaming through the window. The sun reflected off the metal hinge at the knee. It was as if Connor winked at her. "I know. I know. Sam's almost as good an editor as his father. It's been a joy to watch him grow up here."

She threw another glance at the leg. "And if you ever let him know I said so, I'll grind you down to sawdust."

"What?" Sam yelled into the phone. "Haines and Skagway? Slow down, Rob, start from the beginning." Sam pleaded as he grabbed a pencil and paper, scribbled, and mumbled, "Uh-huh, uh-huh."

He hung up and turned toward Margaret Mary. "Rob Nelson is on his way to Skagway, and he sent that new bush pilot, Jim Alison, to Haines."

"And?"

Sam grinned, "They're picking up the Shortys."

"Both of them?"

"Rob and Jim are bringing them to the office to meet with me."

"Both of them? To meet with you?" She fell into the chair near his desk.

"Rob said it was something about Miss Ruth."

"As far as I know, the Shortys haven't talked to each other since the strike on Porcupine Creek, and I didn't know they were acquainted with Miss Ruth."

"Everybody knew Miss Ruth."

Margaret Mary rubbed her forehead, "Did you know Short Shorty hightailed it to Skagway so Long Shorty wouldn't kill him?"

Sam grabbed a blank sheet of paper and licked the end of his pencil. He poured himself a cup of coffee and one for Margaret Mary. "Tell me everything you know."

"But, Sam, how was Miss Ruth involved with the Shortys?" Margaret Mary cradled the cup of coffee.

"I guess we will find out tonight. Now, what do you know?"

"Before my time, but my dad told the story often enough. The brothers were twins but didn't resemble each other in looks, height, or weight. One tall and fair, the other short and dark. Their real name? Bigelow, I think.

"Once they arrived in Alaska, the tall one was called Long Shorty, the other Short Shorty. He was the older of the two by several minutes and hated the name."

Sam stopped scribbling and looked up, "But I thought...."

"Who's telling the story, Sam?" Margaret Mary asked. "One thing your dad always did was let people ramble. When they ran out of steam, that's when he asked another question." She gave him an eyeful over the rim of her coffee cup and winked. "You should remember that."

"Yes, ma'am." Margaret Mary often talked to him as if he was still a schoolboy.

"Haines was the departure point for strikes on Kicking Horse Creek, the Chilkat, and Porcupine Creek. There were about 500 miners up the Porcupine when Short Shorty left Haines with his sled dogs. Long Shorty wanted to wait until spring and refused to go. I guess Short resented it."

She got up, refilled her coffee cup, and held the pot toward him. He shook his head no.

"There was about five feet of snow when he got to Porcupine Creek, so prospecting and cabin building were limited. But Short Shorty persevered and eventually found a 3-ounce gold nugget.

"That's when the trouble started. Short Shorty filed the claim under his name alone. "

Sam shook his head. Death and destruction in the goldfields had started with less provocation than that. "What did Long do?"

"Together, the Shortys owned nearly every saloon and bawdy house in Haines. Long put them all in his own name and threatened to kill his brother. Short Shorty hired others to work his claim and headed off to Skagway. That's all I know."

A trip to the Sitka Cafe was in order. Sam had almost earned a permanent spot at the round table; this should clinch the deal.

Sam got his coffee and hesitated a few feet from the table as was his custom. Ade, Ivan, and Jake were there. Too many empty chairs. Too many old-timers gone.

Ivan motioned him over. Sam shared his news, and the reactions were just what he had expected.

"I not believe," Ivan said.

"Are you sure it was Long and Short? Maybe other Shortys are running around Haines and Skagway," Ade said.

Sam winked at Ade, "That sounds like something Ivan would say."

They all laughed harder when Ivan said, "What funny?"

Jake was silent. He leaned back in his chair and stared at the ceiling.

"What are you thinking, Jake?" Sam asked.

"Miss Ruth tried for years to get the Shortys together. And now they're both going to meet with you?"

Once again, Sam scratched his head and said, "Rob told me they each received a letter from her lawyer."

"But she walked into the forest weeks ago," Ade said,

Sam pictured a gravestone; S. MITCHELL, Jr. WALKED INTO THE FOREST, a beautiful way to describe death.

"Sam!" Ade punched him on the arm.

Sam jerked his thoughts back to the conversation. "The lawyer made arrangements to have the brothers flown to Sitka."

"They don't know the other is coming?" Ade asked.

Ivan leaned over his coffee cup and stared at the editor. "Each will be death of other."

Chuck came into the Cafe and rushed over to Sam. "Boss, there's a Judge from Juneau waiting in your office. He said to give you this." Sam opened the note.

"This odd situation has just gotten stranger." The others around the table stared at the note in his hand. "I'm to have dinner for four delivered to my office at 7 PM. We'll have dinner with the Judge, and he'll preside over the meeting."

"Pilots stay?" Ivan asked.

Sam checked the note. "Just four dinners. The Shortys, the Judge, and me, I presume."

"Gentlemen," Jake said, "I suggest we meet later. Excepting Sam, of course."

Jake nodded to the newspaper editor, "Send Rob and Jim over once they deliver the Shortys. Tell them dinner's on us."

Stormy Durand heard the tail end of the conversation as he seated himself at the table, "The Shortys in the same room? They'll come to fisticuffs for sure. Glad I'm retired."

Chairs scraped and cups clattered as they made their exit, leaving Stormy alone with Sam. "Hang around...trouble," Sam said.

"How much trouble can those two old coots be? They must be in their nineties?" Stormy said, "You do know I'm retired?"

"Just be there."

Stormy nodded, and Sam ordered halibut cheeks, pan-fried potatoes, and shortcakes made with Haines strawberries. Mick promised to make the delivery on time.

Sam let the Judge wait, walked to the Pioneer's Home, and told Alice about the evening activities.

"Why did so many sourdoughs have monikers and nicknames?"

"That's Alaska," Sam laughed.

Margaret Mary, ensconced in the storeroom with the dinner she made Sam buy for her, left the door ajar, determined to hear every word.

The brothers sat in silence and refused to address each other.

Sam tried to make small talk and failed. He hoped the strawberries would sweeten the old sourdoughs who had left most of their food untouched.

He gathered the dishes, stacked them on the counter, and then contemplated the Judge. What was going on in the man's mind?

He seemed agitated and uncomfortable. Sam's fingers twitched, so he knew there must be a story behind the Judge's discomfort.

Nathan Cooper reached into his briefcase and pulled out a file. "Let's get this over with. I have court tomorrow. I believe you have received something from Miss Ruth's lawyer."

The two old men pulled a few strips of paper out of their pockets. Sam opened his top drawer and reached for the tape. He handed it to the Judge, who pulled several more strips from his file. He laid them on the desk and fit them together like a puzzle. The brothers stared, silent.

Judge Cooper cleared his throat and waved the taped strips in their direction, "This is a letter for both of you from Miss Ruth. She has instructed me to read it aloud."

"Does he get to listen?" Long Shorty asked and pointed to Sam.

The Judge smiled, "As the owner of Sean Connor's wooden leg, Sam is allowed to be here."

Sam eyeballed the leg. Others' heads swung in the same direction. Margaret Mary put her hand over her mouth and stifled her gasp.

Judge Cooper put on his reading glasses and picked up the carefully taped paper, and read:

Dear Ones:

Words cannot convey what each of you has meant to me. Each time I was in Haines, I stayed with you, Wilbur. I appreciated your hospitality and dry wit.

When I was in Skagway, William, you opened your home and amused me with your cheerful laughter.

You boys may not look alike, but you are two peas in a pod…

Sam thought he sensed a slight softening in each brother but couldn't be sure.

The letter continued:

I have corresponded with both of you for over 50 years. Now I have walked into the forest, but I have a final request.

Wilbur, I want you to read a selection of letters William has written to me.

The blood drained from William's face, and he shouted, "No!"

"No talking!" Judge Cooper yelled, held up the paper, and pointed, "That was Miss Ruth. She wrote NO TALKING in capital letters." He continued as the two brothers glared at each other:

William, I want you to read Wilbur's letters. Sam and Nathan can move to the back of the room.

The Judge folded the paper and slipped it into his file. After a second or two, Sam whispered to the Judge, "Do you have the letters?"

"Do you have Miss Ruth's prayer journal?"

"What? Not with me."

"We'll wait."

Sam dashed out of the office and ran across the street.

"It's been in my purse this past month. Whenever I have a break, I study it. We need to talk about it soon. I…" Alice looked at him with a question in her eyes.

Sam shuffled from one foot to the other as she retrieved her purse. He snatched the small book and yelled over his shoulder as he ran out the door, "I'll tell you everything later."

The Judge slit the book's cover with a small knife and pulled out a brass key which he then inserted into a metal box he pulled from his briefcase. He pulled out three packets wrapped in lamb's wool. He gave a packet to each brother and the third to Sam. The Judge told him to leave it unopened.

Sam and Nathan leaned against the linotype machine and watched the older men read. Finally, Sam whispered, "Can I interview you about the trial when this is over?"

"I never discuss my cases, especially with journalists."

"What's the name of Miss Ruth's lawyer?"

"Not your business."

Sam's eye's flashed, but he kept his voice neutral, "Do you have any idea why Miss Ruth kept the journal in Sean's leg?"

Nathan frowned, "She was an odd duck."

"Why not just leave everything with the lawyer?"

Judge Nathan Cooper shot back, "I gave up inquiring about how Miss Ruth conducted her business long ago."

"But the leg...?"

Judge Cooper snapped, "When Miss Ruth settled Connor at the Home, she left instructions to have the leg's location sent to me when he died."

"What if they buried it with him?" Sam asked.

Nathan shrugged and fingered the gavel in his vest pocket. He studied Sam over his glasses and said, "I am a judge."

"You would have had the body exhumed?"

Nathan clutched the gavel tightly and said through gritted teeth, "I have learned to do Miss Ruth's bidding sooner rather than later. I will say no more."

Sam considered Judge Cooper and his willingness to fulfill Miss Ruth's wishes even after her demise. He seemed irritated and reluctant, but he did it. Sam's fingers tingled, and he knew there was a story there. He also knew the Judge would never tell it.

He turned his attention to the two ancient sourdoughs sitting at his worktable. Big red bandannas stuffed in fists were wiped across eyes and under noses as the Shortys wept quietly.

"Gentlemen, Miss Ruth left me one more paper."

My boys,

Two more stubborn, old coots I have never met. Neither of you married. All you have is each other, but pride was a mountain neither of you were willing to climb. Now that you know your brother's heart...

Alaska gave you riches, but she did not provide you with life. Only God can do that. We talked about it often.

If you love your brother more than your riches, I ask you to liquidate your holdings and give everything away, reserving only enough to live a simple life.

If you do, I have a small cabin near Totem Park. I bequeath it to you both.

Love,

Miss Ruth.

The men studied each other across the table, silent, wary. After a time, one brother spoke to the other. "You mean what you wrote in them letters, Billy?"

William wiped the tears from his eyes, "What about you, Willie? You mean it?"

Willie coughed, glanced out the window, shrugged, and cleared his throat. "Yeah, I did."

"Me, too."

They stared long at each other.

Sam and Nathan remained silent, holding their breaths. Finally, Sam asked, "Does this mean you're both moving to Sitka?"

The brothers reached across the table and clasped hands. They nodded. "Happy birthday, Willie."

"Happy birthday, Billy."

"That's why Miss Ruth chose this day," Sam whispered.

Nathan Cooper, Superior Court Judge of Alaska, wiped his brow and gathered his papers. "I have a plane to catch. And hopefully, this is the last time I have anything to do with Miss Ruth." He threw the cabin's keys on the table and left without saying goodbye.

Sam pocketed the keys and told the Shortys he'd prepare the cabin. He made reservations at the Sitka Hotel and motioned for Stormy Durand to escort them there. "Thanks for leaving the window cracked, Sam. I heard everything."

"You can report to the guys at the Café, so I won't have to."

Margaret Mary added her dirty dishes to the pile and said, "So when are we searching Miss Ruth's cabin?'

Sam's face blanched, and Margaret Mary laughed, "I know you, my boy, but you won't find anything. Whatever was important, she put in Connor's leg. Whatever was personal, she wrote to Kamalei."

ELEVEN
SAM, 1962

Sam rubbed the back of his neck as a wave of grief for this woman he barely knew flooded over him. Why hadn't he paid more attention to Sitka's Lady in Black when he was a teenager? Like most boys, he was self-absorbed and callow. He and his friends searched Sitka's watery horizons and talked about getting off the island and having adventures. When they weren't hunting, fishing, playing sports, or thinking about girls, that is.

He rubbed the grit out of his eyes and let his cigar smolder in the overflowing ashtray. What was Miss Ruth like when she was his age or when she arrived in Alaska? How had she handled the lack of civilization and lawlessness, not to mention the weather?

He abandoned his plan to read backward chronologically and looked for a postmark near Miss Ruth's arrival.

TWELVE

Dear Kamalei,

Oh, how I miss the sunshine and warmth from all those I love in dear Hawaii. The weather here is gray and dismal, cold and rainy. I am afraid my mood is the same. I cry myself to sleep every night. My first month in this place has been the most difficult of my life. I desperately need a day off, preferably with sunshine. And I need to find my father...

—MISS RUTH'S LETTERS 1890

The long room was barely wide enough for the twin rows of single cots lining each side. The unadorned, faded beige walls added to the room's gloomy atmosphere.

The clock in the hall chimed midnight, time for another bed check. Miss Ruth had a tally sheet for each child and was ordered to note who was still awake or crying or had a feather or tiny totem under their pillow.

Miss Ruth sighed, held the lantern high, and surveyed the room. She could tell many of the children remained awake though they acted otherwise. The stillness of their bodies was unnatural. She ambled between the row of cots, her pen and pencil still in the large pocket of her apron. She left them there.

Many of the little girls' faces were streaked with tears. Miss Ruth sighed and said a silent prayer. In the last cot, she saw the covers pulled over the head of the youngest student.

As Miss Ruth came closer, she heard the muted sobs. She turned the lantern's flame to a soft glow, set it on the bare wooden floor, and lay down on the covers.

She cradled the quivering form. Soon the shaking slowed, then stopped. Miss Ruth rubbed the little girl's back and sang 'Jesus Loves Me.' The girl immediately stiffened.

"I'm sorry little one. I didn't mean to add to your misery." She sang again, this time in Hawaiian. After a time, the body next to her relaxed. When she sang in Cherokee, the little head popped out and turned toward her. The slight smile turned to horror when the child saw the woman on the bed was white.

Miss Ruth put her finger to her lips in the universal sign for quiet and continued her soft singing. She even sang in a fake French accent that had no resemblance to English. The child seemed comforted as long as Miss Ruth did not sing in English.

Miss Ruth's heart ached for the loneliness these children suffered. She could only imagine how they felt—separated from their parents, forbidden to speak unless it was English, which they didn't know, and forced to eat foods they had never tasted before.

Miss Ruth heard her stomach protest. The thick yet slimy oatmeal she had choked down for breakfast and dinner threatened to return. She remembered her childhood breakfasts in the ranch house kitchen, Aunt Ellie's hearty oatmeal stuffed with walnuts, chunks of apple, and cinnamon. It bore little resemblance to the abomination served in the dining hall.

There had been macadamia nuts and coconut added to the oats in Hawaii. Sometimes she had sliced bananas or mangoes on top. Her stomach growled. Miss Ruth didn't know if it was from hunger or memory.

She often thought about skipping meals but felt duty-bound to be a good example. If they did not eat every spoonful and in silence, they suffered the consequences.

Miss Ruth caught herself drifting off to sleep and roused herself. She couldn't imagine the consequences if she were caught. She pushed herself from the bed and reached for her lantern.

The little girl, whose name had been changed to Eleanor, had fallen asleep with her thumb in her mouth— also forbidden. Miss Ruth kissed the little brown cheek and returned to her small room with a sad smile and a heavy heart.

Morning would come soon enough. Each student, fully clothed, face washed, and teeth brushed, stood beside their made bed at six. The inspector ripped the bed apart for the smallest of wrinkles, and the student was punished and had to remake the bed. Once everyone had passed the inspection, they could march to the dining hall.

As Miss Ruth entered the dining hall, she saw several posters on the wall—

Attention

Breakfast: 6:30-6:50
Chores: 7:00-7:50
School: 8:00-11:50
Lunch: 12:00-12:30
School: 12:30-4:50
Dinner: 5:00-5:50
School: 6:00-8:45
Bed: 9:00-

Other posters admonished the children not to talk during meals, in the hallways, or in classrooms.

The grueling schedule was challenging for Miss Ruth to follow. She couldn't imagine how difficult it was for the little ones. Children needed to walk in the woods or play on the beach. Both were adjacent to the school grounds, but no time was built into the schedule. No time to play or dream or imagine.

This was not the kind of school Miss Ruth thought she would find in the North. She hoped she could comfort these dear ones and bring them a little joy.

She reached deep into her apron pocket, past the dreaded tally sheets, and found her last lemon drop. *Excellent idea, Lord. I will write to Maureen and ask her to send me a large bag of lemon drops. I will slip them to the children when no one is around.*

THIRTEEN

Dear Kamalei,

The past year has been one of adjustment, and I find I am not as submissive and obedient to the powers-that-be as I ought. Remember how encouraging Sister Agnes's classroom atmosphere was? The school here has some good teachers, but they are ruled with an iron rod by the Reverend Mrs. Monroe.

She often reminds me that I am only twenty-one, inexperienced, and desperately need her guidance. I bite my lips and refuse to agree.

Detours and delays have complicated my journey to Alaska, and they are still active as I seek my father's whereabouts. I am also learning the necessity of hanging on and letting go...

—MISS RUTH'S LETTERS 1891

Miss Ruth plaited her nearly waist-length hair and plunked Silas' hat atop her head. She glanced in the mirror and smiled as she saw memories of the old mariner rather than her own reflection.

It was a beautiful summer day in Sitka, and the temperature promised a warmth unlike what she had experienced in Hawaii, but pleasant nevertheless.

She dug deep into the closet for her brightly colored shawl, a going away present from Iolana. Miss Ruth stroked the soft fabric and was warmed by the memory of the Hawaiian woman's farewell embrace.

Even though it was her day off, Miss Ruth hurried through the school grounds. The Reverend Mrs. Monroe often found extra tasks that needed to be done immediately and only by Miss Ruth.

Freedom! Miss Ruth wondered how the children coped with their lives. So many came from small, isolated villages with far less structure and scheduling. Several parents had sent their children willingly to learn white ways. Other families were bribed by school officials or bullied by threats of arrest. She heard rumors that a few children had even been kidnapped.

She shuddered and surveyed the sky. *I will enjoy this day of freedom and give no more thought to the school.*

She strolled through downtown and, as was her habit, scrutinized every man near her father's age and eavesdropped on as many conversations as possible, even asking several folks if they knew the name Denver Dan. A shake of the head or a curt no were the only answers.

Miss Ruth passed through Indiantown and returned greetings from several Native families. Some of the elders turned their back on her. She understood they had reasons for their caution and mistrust, but it pierced her heart.

She turned onto Halibut Point Road until she found a peaceful spot. The rocky beach and dark slate water were nothing like Hawaii's sunny skies, tawny sand, and soft blue ocean. The rhythmic sound of the small breaking waves on this beach, ironically called Sandy Beach, was unlike the surging waves crashing on her favorite beach on the North Shore. But it had its own beauty.

Mount Edgecombe jutted out of the southern edge of Kruzof Island across Sitka Sound. A slight haze made the shoreline of Kruzof indistinct, but the volcano rose above it sharp and majestic.

The afternoon sun warmed her, and the chattering seabirds kept her company as she ate. Afterward, she reached into her satchel and retrieved her writing materials.

She leaned against the driftwood log and let her pen and paper lay idle in her lap as she thought about her last days on the sands of Hawaii.

She had walked near the water's edge, carrying her shoes. She told herself she was scouring the sand for shells. Instead, she stared past Diamond Head toward the horizon. She drank the pineapple juice Iolana had sent with her and ate two bananas. The island's floral air warmed her face as she turned her gaze to the North.

The northern horizon beckoned, and thoughts of her father pulled her emotions toward Alaska. Would she ever reach that vast wilderness? Would she ever find her father?

Captain Walker was due in port any day now, and hopefully, they would set sail for Alaska soon.

Behind her, Grandpa John lay in a fresh grave in the city cemetery. She had visited that morning, and the ache in her heart almost doubled her over. Abandoned. Deserted. Dejected.

The waves battered the sands as they had since creation's dawn, the sounds measured and hypnotic. Rachel Ruth Merritt let them lull her into a dull daze, but it did not lessen her grief. Desolate. Forlorn. Forsaken.

No, not forsaken, just terribly alone.

Overhead, seabirds danced in a cloudless sky. Miss Ruth sat on the warm beach, picked up handfuls of sand, and let the grains fall through her fingers.

How much of her strength was Grandpa John's, and how dependent had she been? How much of her confidence and perseverance had she borrowed from him?

Captain Harlan Walker's face flashed before her, and she pictured herself on the deck of The China Doll, gazing through the topsails, creamy white against an azure sky. Dear Silas in the Crow's Nest, Cook in the galley, Abel by her side, and the Captain piloting them over the Seven Seas. Freedom! Adventure!

How easy it would be to depend on the Captain's strength and moral fortitude. She shook the sand out of her skirts and the thought out of her head. She would learn to rely on the Lord. He would give her strength and faith.

She walked to the water and felt the waves roll over her feet and ankles. As the water receded, it pulled the sand from under her feet. She shifted her weight and kept her balance. Whatever life had thrown at Grandpa John, he had kept his bearing and balance. She would learn to do the same.

She knew Iolana and the others grieved with her, but none knew the depth of her pain. Sister Agnes saw her floundering but did not know the breadth of her struggle. *Since I was a little girl, I tied myself to Grandpa John.* She lifted her eyes heavenward. *Now I bind myself to You.*

It was near sunset, and a chorus of conch shells sounded further down the beach. A group of South Sea Islanders had gathered for a ceremony of some kind. The sound reminded her she was not alone.

FOURTEEN

Dear Kamalei,

I have missed you dreadfully these past three years and long to feel close to you. That closeness comes when I write. I'm happy I decided to write to you instead of keeping a journal.

I am pleased you have kept all my letters; maybe one day, when we are wiser and older, we will sit with large mugs of good Kona coffee and reread them. What fun we'll have remembering when we were young.

Captain Walker is due back in Sitka soon, and I am anxious to see him and hear all the news from his travels, especially from his time in Hawaii...

—MISS RUTH'S LETTERS 1893

Captain Walker walked along the edge of Crescent Bay and soon approached the school. The gate was closed, and through the iron bars, he saw two little brown faces, silent and solemn.

"I'm here to see Miss Ruth. Is she available?"

The small boys looked at each other, then back at the Captain. Neither spoke. Someone had cut their hair above their ears and dressed them in dark wool pants and jackets. The Captain had no idea if they were Tlingit, Haida, Yupik, or Aleut. The younger boy shoved both thumbs in his mouth.

He squatted and looked them in the eyes, "Tell me, do you fellows know where Miss Ruth is?"

Two pairs of shoulders rose and fell. Two pairs of eyes stared until Captain Walker reached into his jacket pocket and pulled out a bag of lemon drops. "Miss Ruth?" he said and shook the bag above them.

The boys peeked at each other and jabbered in a language the Captain did not recognize, then they threw their hands over their mouths and swiveled their heads. Seeing no one, they opened the gate. The older boy snatched the bag, and the younger grabbed the Captain's hand, leading him to a small chapel not far from the school's main building.

Captain Walker put his ear to the door. Silence. He glanced at the boys and saw they were dividing the candy. Some went into their pockets, most into their mouths, forming chipmunk cheeks. Captain Walker winked at them and opened the door.

Her hair strained against the coil at the nape of her neck. She whispered an amen, pulled out the pins, and let her hair swing free. She massaged her head and neck. "Oh, that feels good."

His fingers itched to do the massaging for her. He shoved his hands into his pockets and crushed the thought. "Ahem," he cleared his throat.

She jerked around, wide-eyed, then laughed when she saw it was him. "You caught me. I'm having a moment."

He put his hand on his heart and took a step back in mock horror. "What? You?" They laughed together, and then he said, "Why is your hair not stuffed under Skookum's hat?"

"Poor Silas, his hat isn't allowed here."

He frowned, then said, "I've come to say goodbye. We sail at dawn".

"Sail?"

"It doesn't seem right to say we steam away at sunrise."

"Your time here has been so short. I'm sorry we didn't have a proper visit. You have my letters for the Connors?"

He patted his jacket pocket. "I will deliver them myself."

"Thank you. The postal service is so erratic." She wrung her hands, and the corners of her mouth turned down a fraction. "I wish I were going with you, at least as far as Juneau."

The Captain shared her sentiments; what he would give for them to sail the seven seas on his old clipper ship, The China Doll. He closed his eyes and focused on the situation in front of him.

She seemed frazzled, unlike herself. She had been on her own the past three years, and he had not had the opportunity to return to Sitka until now. "Haven't you told me the good Lord knows the end from the beginning?"

"He does. I don't." She raised tear-filled eyes to his. "There has been no news of my father."

Captain Walker took a step forward, then stopped himself from pulling her into his arms. "Alaska is vast. Many men have disappeared into the interior, some by choice." He kept his voice soft and gentle.

"There is that possibility, but I will continue to search for him." She glanced at her plain black attire. "In the meantime, I will continue to dress like a sea witch and be kind to the children I teach."

"They have all fallen in love with you, I'm sure."

She continued speaking as if she hadn't heard him. "The rules are harsh, and I often refuse to enforce them. The Reverend Mrs. Monroe has routinely scolded me, and as I said, I've had few opportunities to inquire about my father." Even to herself, she sounded uncertain, anxious. "I apologize, Captain. I know how much

I've always leaned on Grandpa John. He helped me think things through, clarify my feelings, and determine the correct course of action. I'm determined to lean on the Lord and not Grandpa John's memory. I believe it will be a long and difficult process."

He took her hands, rubbed her knuckles with his thumb, and whispered, "Everything will work out."

"What nonsense is this?" A shrill voice shattered the stillness of the chapel.

They sprang apart. "Nothing," they both said.

"I can see it's not nothing!" The Reverend Mrs. Monroe shrieked, "I will not tolerate this behavior!"

"Really, ma'am," the Captain scowled at the short, stout woman from his six-foot, two-inch frame.

"Ma'am?" Her face flooded with color.

Miss Ruth stepped between them, "He means no disrespect, Reverend Mrs..."

"But I do." His words tickled her ears, and he poked her between her shoulder blades. She shrugged it off, and he did it again.

The Reverend Mrs. Monroe glared at them, sucked in her breath, and said, "I suppose the charitable thing, the Christian thing to do is..." the spittle gathered in the corners of her mouth as she stumbled over the word, "forgive."

"Please do, Reverend Mrs. Monroe." Miss Ruth lowered her eyes and bowed her head.

Another poke and Miss Ruth stepped to the side. The movement caused the light from the stained-glass windows to dance off her hair.

The Reverend Mrs. Monroe gasped and stomped her cane on the wooden floor. "Why is your hair down? I repeat, what is going on here? This is a fireable offense."

"The Captain came to say goodbye. He leaves tomorrow."

"You should not have returned to Sitka, especially not to this school." She waved her walking stick in his direction, "Go."

"But..." Red-faced and clearly agitated, Miss Ruth defended him. The Reverend Mrs. Monroe stomped her walking stick on the wooden floor. "Silence!"

Captain Walker bowed and bid Miss Ruth farewell, but he did not move.

"Go!" The Reverend Mrs. Monroe commanded again, "And you, put your hair up and follow me."

Miss Ruth complied. As she passed Captain Walker, she tapped him on the arm and whispered, "Next time you're in Sitka, send a message through the hotel's clerk. He has a boy who delivers that sort of thing."

"Yes, ma'am," he tipped his cap. He smiled at Miss Ruth, then glared at the Reverend Mrs. Sea Hag's back.

Captain Harlan Walker marched through Sitka on his way to The Aloha. He hated to leave Miss Ruth in the clutches of that woman. Still, he was confident Miss Ruth could hold her own if only she chose to. The school's constricting environment seemed to be stripping her of her spunk and spirit.

When he delivered his cargo of mining tools and foodstuffs to Juneau, along with the letters, he would urge the Connors to somehow rescue Miss Ruth from the obnoxious Reverend Mrs. Monroe.

He had contracts with merchants and traders in San Francisco, Cartagena, Honolulu, Hong Kong, and Canton. He sighed and rubbed the back of his neck. It would be at least a year before he returned to Sitka.

FIFTEEN

SAM, 1962

Amber sunlight streaked over the mountains and across Sitka Sound. A clear sky promised a pleasant day. Sam folded the letter, then raced to the bathroom as the coffee he had downed through the night demanded release.

Sadsack, that ancient feline, met him outside the bathroom door and led him to the kitchen. Sam fed the cat, put on another pot of coffee, and foraged through the cupboards—nothing exciting. He dropped two pieces of rye into the toaster and reached for the peanut butter.

"What do you think, Sadsack? Was our good Captain tempted to sell his steamship and head for the goldfields?"

The arthritic feline didn't bother to lift his head from the food bowl.

"You're right, Sad. He was too intelligent for that. From what I read earlier in her grandfather's journal, Captain Walker was in love with Miss Ruth."

Sadsack twitched his ears, and his green eyes met Sam's.

"She thought of him as a dear friend. But if you read between the lines, she loved him, too. I'm sure of it."

Sam poured himself a cup of coffee, took a drink, then dumped the rest down the sink. The acid burning his stomach told him he wasn't as young as he used to be. The toast popped up, but he ignored it.

He picked up the letter again, but his thoughts were of Alice. "Should I call her," he asked the cat? "She'd want to know if there was a romance. I imagine women like that sort of thing."

Sadsack licked his paws, and Sam yawned. He should grab a couple of hours of sleep before heading to the office. Instead, he settled in his favorite chair, and the cat jumped into his lap.

"You know, Sadsack, I'd be more comfortable if you slept somewhere else."

The cat dug his claws into Sam's thighs.

"You mangy animal."

The cat hissed.

"Settle down. You can nap for the both of us." Sam scratched Sadsack under the chin and behind his ears and listened for the feline's rhythmic purr. He leaned back in the chair and thought about the past several months.

When Sean Connor died, he bequeathed his wooden leg to Sam and wanted it displayed in the newspaper's office. He also requested his nurse, Alice Blakely, visit that leg weekly, and she honored that request. He was grateful that those visits now occurred almost daily.

He pushed the sleeping cat off of his lap. "What should we do about Alice?"

The cat put his nose in the air and turned away.

Sam shrugged into his hat and coat. His thoughts were on Alice as he walked the few blocks to his office. She had never given him any indication she was interested in anything other than coffee and crullers, and Miss Ruth, of course.

Besides, he was old, well, middle-aged. Losing his hair, set in his ways. Getting a little thick around the middle. No woman in her right mind would be interested in him. He was in a foul mood when he reached the Sentinel.

Margaret Mary took one look at his face and said, "What's wrong? Where's the coffee and crullers? Alice will be here any minute."

He cursed, and the door slammed behind him. His negative thoughts marched alongside him all the way to the Café. The men at the round table had noticed Sam's frequent appearances and standing order.

Why so many pastries and so often, who were they for? They asked politely, then questioned, inquired, cajoled, and demanded. Purchases in hand, Sam left without a glance in their direction.

"This will take some detective work," Stormy Durand drawled and twirled his jailhouse keys.

Ade shook his head. "I can't believe you still have keys to the jail."

Stormy laughed, "I had them made special. You never know..."

Ivan eyed the keys. "Is good. Lock Sam behind bar. Soon he talk."

Stormy stood and patted Ivan on the shoulder. "That's exactly what I'm going to do." He winked at the others who hid behind their coffee mugs or shoved more food into their mouths.

The next day Stormy reported that a particular nurse from the Pioneer's Home had regular meetings with Sam at his office.

Sam ignored the whistles, taunts, and good-natured jibes coming from the round table on subsequent visits to the Café. He made pleasant chit-chat with Agrefena and took no notice of anyone else.

"I think we're losing our touch. We couldn't even get a rise out of him," Ade said.

"It's not us; it's him," Jake insisted, "He's got it bad for that cheechako."

"Who is this Alice Blakely anyway? Where is she from? Why did she come to Sitka?" Stormy wondered.

"Leg tell Alice, see Sam." Ivan forked eggs followed by toast into his mouth.

The others looked askance. "It's true. I heard that old sourdough Sean Connor left his wooden leg to Sam, don't know why, but he wanted this nurse to visit it every week." Mick poured more coffee.

"Is good leg," Ivan said.

"I say we need to find out everything about this nurse, see if she's good enough for our Sammy," Stormy said.

"Is good leg," Ivan said again.

"Yes, Ivan, the leg is good. Now we need to see if the woman is good." Agrefena wiped her hands on her apron and glared at each occupant of the round table. "Ollyanna and I will do that. You fellows stay out of it."

And so it was decided, and so it was done.

Sam growled at passers-by as he walked back to his office. Even the smell of fresh crullers crawling up the side of the bag and assaulting his nose didn't cheer him.

Not only was he feeling his age and lack of good looks, he now knew the entire town was aware of him and Alice. He cursed the men at the Café, cursed his receding hairline, and if a dog crossed his path, he would condemn it, too.

He ate a cruller on the way; it didn't make him feel better. Alice waved to him from across the street. "Morning, Sam."

Her face, fresh and dewy, immediately lifted his spirits, and that cute nurse's uniform! Sam took a deep breath and waved.

He loved Alice's way of focusing all her attention on him. She had an inquiring mind and asked intelligent questions. When she rested her elbows on the edge of his desk, cupped her chin in her hands, and leaned forward, his heart soared like Sitka's ever-present eagles.

Whenever she said, "Tell me more, Sam," the sparkle in her eyes made his chest swell, and the words poured out of him. Afterward, he couldn't remember what he said but felt like he could climb mountains.

He waited for her at the end of the block, and they walked to his office together. Sam hoped she didn't notice the effort it took to hold in his stomach.

SIXTEEN

Dear Kamalei,

Once again, I have been summoned by the Reverend Mrs. Monroe. Scripture commands us to live at peace with everyone as much as we can. I have tried, oh how I have tried. I'm beginning to think it is impossible to be at peace with that woman...

—MISS RUTH'S LETTERS 1894

The school's principal finished the prayer for the evening meal. Miss Ruth anticipated the children's excitement when they saw their dinner. But before it was served, she was handed a note commanding her presence at the Monroes' living quarters. She scraped her chair back and placed her napkin next to her plate. As she made her way to the door, she noticed bowls of gluey oatmeal set before the children. No excitement there.

She hurried across the school grounds and knocked on the door. Miss Ruth gazed at the gilded furniture and ostentatious bric-a-brac, so different from the barren school rooms and unadorned dormitories. She sat stiffly on the horsehair settee. She smiled at the Tlingit girl who poured tea and retreated to the corner of the room; the smile was not returned.

The Reverend Mrs. Monroe entered, settled her bulk in an ornate Victorian chair, and ignored the delicate Chinese porcelain cup and saucer. The soothing aroma of the light oolong tea tempted Miss Ruth, but she dared not reach for the teapot or the plate of scones.

"This will not do, Miss Ruth. Once again, you've usurped my authority and injured the integrity of the school. I have tried my best to help you these past few years."

"Yes, Reverend Mrs. Monroe."

"I find you difficult, obstinate, of questionable moral character, simply unmold-able."

The silence stretched, and Miss Ruth fingered the lemon drops deep in her skirt pocket. She pictured herself offering one to the sour woman sitting across the tea table.

"Smiling and grinning was not the response I expected, especially from a subordinate."

"What were you hoping for, Reverend Mrs. Monroe?"

"I assumed you would show some respect for my wisdom and years of experience once enlightened. I've been working with uncivilized tribes since before you were born."

Miss Ruth folded her hands in her lap and wondered how many young lives this woman had damaged. She bit her lip.

"My dear girl, aside from your inappropriate behavior with that obnoxious sea captain, did you not allow a heathen Indian into the school's kitchen, and did he not bring in a foul animal?"

"No, ma'am."

The older woman raised her eyebrows and frowned.

"On my way back from town the other day, I met a Tlingit elder, Petrov Bravebird. He had killed a seal and wanted to donate it, so I invited him to show us how to cook it. I knew the children would be excited to have a meal that reminded them of home."

The Reverend Mrs. Monroe's back was ramrod straight. Her piercing eyes flashed. "Precisely! We do not want the children reminded of home. The sooner they forget, the easier it will be to civilize them."

"But Reverend Mrs. Monroe, they will never forget. Don't you think...?"

"The quicker they learn our way—the white way— the better. Hygiene, literacy, good Christian values."

"It's just food."

The Reverend Mrs. Monroe held up her hand. "This is not up for debate, Miss Ruth. You are in no position to offer your ignorant opinion."

"I appreciate your years of service; I do. However, we seem to have a fundamental difference of opinions about what these children need."

Face mottled, eyes blazing, the Reverend Mrs. Monroe spat out the words, "Such impertinence. I have never—" She signaled for the Tlingit servant girl to leave the room.

Miss Ruth smiled at the young teen and saw her leave the door open just a crack. She imagined this conversation would be repeated throughout the institution.

"These Indians are ignorant and primitive," The Reverend Mrs. Monroe snapped, "and..."

"With all due respect, their customs and culture may differ vastly from ours, but it does not mean the people have less value."

"It certainly does, don't interrupt me." The Reverend Mrs. Monroe licked at the spittle that gathered at the corner of her mouth. "I will hear no more of your outlandish views."

Miss Ruth's shoulders stiffened, and she bit the inside of her cheek as the Reverend Mrs. Monroe continued, "I've also received reports you visited the dormitories at night, in addition to the required bed checks."

Miss Ruth leaned toward the older woman and tried to make her voice as gentle as possible, "So many younger children have trouble sleeping. They are dreadfully homesick and need comforting. Their tears break my heart. I sing to them, pray, and encourage them to talk about home."

"Exactly! Your interference is doing more harm than good. These children are not to be coddled or reminded of their homes."

"Some of them haven't seen their parents for years. They're lonesome and afraid."

"Nonsense, there's nothing to be afraid of, and how can they be lonely? There are so many of them."

Miss Ruth sat on her hands and regarded the other woman without speaking; her body quivered with the effort. She glanced toward the door and saw the Tlingit girl still listening.

The Reverend Mrs. Monroe did not soften her tone, "If it were up to me, you would be terminated immediately."

"The Reverend Jackson hired me. I imagine he's the only one who could fire me." Miss Ruth kept her voice low but firm.

"He hired you sight unseen, and he's not here to see your blatant disregard for me and my authority."

"Still, he has the authority," Miss Ruth struggled to soften her voice.

"You will stay in your room until tomorrow at two o'clock, when my husband will take you to meet the Lutheran clergyman in town. I am lending you to him for a year. Perhaps when you return, you will be more pliable."

"What?"

"You are dismissed."

"But—"

"Dismissed!"

❧

On the way to her room, Miss Ruth stopped at the Reverend Mr. Monroe's office. He sat behind his simple cedar desk. Miss Ruth entered and was invited to sit. The Reverend shuffled several papers and then observed her over his wire-rimmed spectacles. "What's to be done with you, Miss Ruth?"

"I'm sure you know Reverend Mr. Monroe."

He left his desk, opened the door a crack, glanced down the hallway, then returned to his chair. "Are you aware my wife and I have worked for the Bureau of Indian Affairs for over three decades, mostly with the Plains Indians?"

She nodded and again felt sorry for the Indian children of the Western Plains.

He paused for a moment, frowned, and spoke softly. "I don't disagree with many of your ways, Miss Ruth. Neither Reverend Jackson nor I favor boarding schools for Alaska Natives or eradicating their culture. In fact, he is trying to establish day schools in as many outlying towns and remote villages as possible, so the children don't have to be boarded. Unfortunately, Alaska is too big, and his budget is too small. Children from all areas must be educated. It's a government mandate."

"There should be a kinder way to go about it, and their culture should be respected."

He shook his head and threw his pen onto his desk. "The government also mandates these children be civilized as they are educated. That means they must leave everything behind." His Adam's apple bobbed.

"It breaks my heart that they are torn from their families, language, and environment. How lost they must feel."

He blinked several times and adjusted his spectacles. "I'm afraid there's nothing to be done, no matter how much one longs to. At least, the Reverend Jackson contracted with Protestant churches and raised money to build even more day schools. He has established them in some of the most inaccessible places."

Miss Ruth nodded, not sure what this had to do with her.

He took off his spectacles, wiped them with a handkerchief, and sighed, "I understand that my wife removed you from the classroom and set you to work in the laundry and then the kitchen."

"Yes, Sir."

"Neither of which has worked out?"

"I found a locker full of the children's Native clothing and returned it to them. I didn't realize it was forbidden."

"Oh, dear." He cleared his throat and looked everywhere except at the young woman sitting across from him, "Well, The Reverend Mrs. Monroe is rather set in her ways." He seemed to want to say more but rustled his papers. "And the kitchen?"

"I cooked a seal."

The corner of his mouth twitched, but he turned it into a frown and said, "Yes, I heard. We had better remove you from her field of vision."

"She said something about lending me to the Lutherans."

"Perhaps it's for the best."

SEVENTEEN

Dear Kamalei,

My heart is heavy as I write. I found a boy on the beach, as intelligent and proud as you but hostile and afraid. Unlike you, he has not had a secure and safe childhood, which has marked him. I hope I can become his friend. I've also learned that Lutheran women can be mighty gossipers, although kind-hearted and industrious. Their children are delightful...

—*MISS RUTH'S LETTERS 1894*

The Reverend Mr. Monroe accompanied Miss Ruth to the Lutheran Church and introduced her to Pastor Hansen.

"If you are willing, I would like you to take over the ministries to our women and children."

"I assure you, Pastor Hansen, I've had no experience working with women, and you might have heard that the Reverend Mrs. Monroe won't have me in any of her classrooms."

"Precisely," he needled his fellow minister, who grimaced. Mrs. Hansen entered the study with a tray of lefse and strong Norwegian coffee.

"My dear, you should be in bed," Pastor Hansen said, taking the tray from her and setting it on his desk.

"Nonsense, I wanted to see my replacement."

She handed Miss Ruth a china cup half full of coffee and a piece of the lefse. "It's a thin bread made from mashed potatoes, smeared with butter, sprinkled with cinnamon sugar, and rolled up like a cigar. I usually make it at Christmas, but I'll be at my mother's, and I know she won't let me, so I've made a couple of batches now."

Miss Ruth took a bite and grinned, "I could eat this every day. Thank you."

"Dear, really, you need to go back to bed." Pastor Hansen discretely admired his wife's very pregnant form.

She smiled at Miss Ruth. "We've heard stories about you, Miss Ruth, how you tried to comfort homesick students. Reverend Monroe assures us your heart is kind and your character solid."

Miss Ruth flashed a smile toward the Reverend. "I try. Children are easy, but I haven't known many women."

"They are like very tall children—often spoiled, raucous children." Pastor Hansen took his wife's hand, led her to the door, pushed her through it, and said, "Go to bed."

"Yes, husband." She turned and winked at Miss Ruth.

Pastor Hansen shrugged and picked up the coffee pot. "What was I saying about spoiled children?" He poured himself another cup and gestured with the pot. Both Reverend Monroe and Miss Ruth shook their heads.

"My wife says she's fine, but I'm determined to take her to her mother's in Seattle. We lost the last one, miscarriage." His voice broke, "We will stay until this baby's ready to travel."

Miss Ruth voiced her sympathies, cleared her throat, and asked, "Who will take over your duties, sir?"

"No one, I'm sad to say. Most of my parishioners are fishers and only attend during the off-season. It's their wives and children who are faithful. That's why I need you. If you could take over the children's Sunday School classes, Bible Clubs, Catechism Class...."

"Catechism?"

"I have a book; the lessons are written out. You'll be fine. Oh, and there's the Women's Missionary Circle."

"What's that?"

Pastor Hansen grimaced, "I'm not too sure. They drink coffee, eat pastry, and sew for foreign missions. According to my wife, your most important task will be to keep a lid on the gossip and backbiting."

"Oh dear, I'm sure I don't know how to do that."

"I'm hoping the women will be on their best behavior since you will be a stranger to them." He reached into his vest pocket, "Here's a key to our house and one for the church. We leave in three days. Please see yourselves out; I need to check on my wife." The harried man grabbed his pipe and tobacco pouch and hurried out of the room.

And so, Miss Ruth settled into the Hansen's small cabin behind the Lutheran church. The children were a delight, as she knew they would be. The women were cooperative and enthused during the Christmas season. They cheerfully shared their customs and festivities with her. There was a bit of competition between the Swedish, Norwegian, and Finnish women and some grousing when Miss Ruth refused to say which customs were the best.

Now that the holidays were over and the January doldrums had settled over the island, they were not enthused. The constant fog and dank, dark weather added to their gloom.

Still, over the last several days, Miss Ruth had developed a workable schedule she hoped would bring the ladies out of their malaise. She suggested they plan a Valentine's party, and after that, there would be Easter activities to prepare for and celebrate. Maybe they could put on a Passion play or have a musical program. Week by week, they became more cheerful, especially when it didn't rain or snow.

Miss Ruth was unfamiliar with Shrove Tuesday and Lent, and the women delighted in teaching her. The Swedish women were most excited about Waffle Day, March 25th.

Miss Ruth hoped these festivities would turn their attention away from their gossip and extreme interest in everyone's business.

Light from the midnight moon streamed through the window. Miss Ruth punched the pillow for the fourth time and gave up any notion of sleep.

She pulled on Pastor Hansen's sealskin coat, tugged his boots on over a pair of thick socks, and tucked her braid under dear Silas's hat.

The aroma of Pastor Hansen's pipe lingered in his clothing. Miss Ruth took a deep breath as she left the cabin and walked down to the beach.

She had never seen so much wet weather in her life; would she ever become accustomed to it? Fog, mist, drizzle, hail, sleet. From showers to downpours and cloudbursts, Southeast Alaska had it all. There were many more rainy days than sunny, but how glorious and golden Alaska's light was when the sun reflected off the waters surrounding Sitka.

Tonight's midnight mist swirled and spiraled over Crescent Bay. The moon glistened off its waters, and the tide finished its ebb. A curtain of fog accompanied the incoming waves.

She snuggled deeper into the Pastor's coat. His oversized boots pushed in the wet sand and left prints like some large forest creature or Tlingit spirit animal. She turned when she reached the bay's curve and followed her footsteps back.

A quiet moan disturbed her. She stopped, unsure of its source or if she had heard anything. Again, there was a sniff, a groan, a quiet cry.

Miss Ruth found the boy huddled behind a large driftwood log wedged between two boulders. His eyes, blackened and swollen, were full of fear and hostility. He glared at her and then for a way of escape.

"Don't be afraid," she said.

No answer.

"I just want to help you."

Again, no answer.

"Do you speak English?"

He spat; she ignored the spittle on Pastor Hansen's boots. "I can see you're hurt. Those cuts and scrapes need attending."

He shrugged.

"I'm Miss Ruth."

"You are one of them," he said in English.

She followed his gaze toward the boarding school. "Do you need help back to the school?"

"I'm not going back," he snarled, then moaned again.

"Me either."

"What?"

"I was a teacher, but they sent me away."

"Why?"

"I visited the children's quarters at night, tried to learn your language, and cooked a seal for dinner, but the Reverend Mrs. Monroe threw it away."

He scowled and rubbed his side. "I think I remember."

"I don't remember you, but I only worked with the younger children."

He lifted his head and glared at her, "I refused to speak their language or eat their food. They beat me for that. They didn't send me away. I ran."

Miss Ruth sat on the log near him. Silent minutes passed, and the fog rolled toward them. "I don't blame you."

He rubbed his eyes. His stomach growled, and he moaned again.

"Come. I will feed you and clean your wounds. You can stay or go. Your choice." Miss Ruth walked away with tiny steps and hoped the boy followed. She did not turn around until she left the beach to cross the road. Through the wispy fog, she saw he was twenty paces behind. She pointed to the cabin.

He stood inside the cabin door—silent, watchful. She indicated the chair near the table and asked, "How old are you?"

"My mother thinks I have thirteen summers."

"Only thirteen?"

For the first time, he smiled, "I am only thirteen summers, but as tall as a man, grown."

Miss Ruth smiled back, "Sit down, Boy of Thirteen Summers. Eat."

"That's white man's food," he snorted.

"It's fish chowder."

"Fish?"

"Salmon."

He choked it down and made a face. "White man's cooking ruined it."

She reached into a Mason jar in the middle of the table, "Here's some smoked salmon."

"Better."

"What is your name, Boy of Thirteen Summers?"

"My mother saw a white-water otter in the Chilkat river when she carried me. She knew the freshwater otter would be my spirit animal."

Miss Ruth didn't know much about spirit animals and now was not the time to ask, "So your name is?"

"I just told you, but you won't be able to say it in my language. Call me Ott."

Miss Ruth calmly dressed his cuts and scrapes. Some bruises were fresh, some older. She could imagine the cause but didn't inquire. She tore one of her nightgowns into strips and wrapped his ribs; he bit his lips but did not cry out.

"Boy of Thirteen Summers, I predict we will be great friends. And one day, I will say your name in your language." She handed him one of Pastor Hansen's nightshirts and pointed to the bedroom.

"I cannot stay in a white woman's house." He threw the nightshirt on the floor and kicked it away.

Miss Ruth gathered several blankets and pointed to the woodshed. "Promise me you will be here in the morning, Boy of Thirteen Summers."

He had a child's eyes for a moment but hardened them. "I cannot promise."

She took a step closer. "If you are here in the morning, I promise on the life of my father I will help you return to your family, and I will not tell anyone you are here."

"Promise on the life of your mother."

"I have no mother."

Pain flickered in his eyes, and he whispered, "Promise on her spirit."

She promised. He stayed.

EIGHTEEN

Dear Kam,

The Boy of Thirteen Summers sleeps most of the day; I don't know what he does at night—roams the streets of Sitka, I suppose. I'm sure my Lutheran ladies suspect I have a man friend. The gossip has started, and I need to stamp it out before it spreads beyond the Missionary Circle. Of course, the Sunday School children have discovered Ott and think it's a delicious secret. They bring him small treats and beg him for stories...

—MISS RUTH'S LETTERS 1895

"I want to go home, Miss Ruth."

"The weather is not good, and the seas are too wild. We can go in the spring."

"I want my Mama," his voice broke, and he sounded like the boy he was, not the man he appeared to be.

"I know, Boy of Thirteen Summers. Come, finish your lessons. When your mother sees how much you have learned, she will be proud of you."

"White man's ways, white men's knowledge." His eyes narrowed, and he spat.

She wiped the spittle from the bare wood floor, took his hands, and looked deep into his eyes. "Ott, your mother sent you here to learn these ways. White men have been in this land a long time and are here to stay."

"Whites are evil."

"Yes, many are – but some of your people are as well."

He pulled his hands away and protested. Miss Ruth raised her eyebrows. "Didn't you tell me the Haidas raided your village, killed your father, and took your mother as a slave? Were you not born into slavery shortly after?"

"Yes, but our Chilkat Chief ransomed us. It took many months and much fur."

"Your chief was a good man. We must learn to live together no matter the shade of our skin."

Ott bit the end of his pencil and worked on his lessons while Miss Ruth bustled around the kitchen and fixed their supper. He pulled up his sleeve and looked at his arm, then down the neck of his shirt. "I've seen you when you put your hair on the top. The back of your neck is lighter than the rest of you."

Miss Ruth thought of the burning sun of the Western Plains and the hot, humid land of the South Pacific. "Whenever the sun is shining, I try to go outside and let the rays darken me, but all the parts of me the sun doesn't see are lighter."

"How can that be? I am the same all over."

She laughed and said, "Back to your lessons."

Ott had refused to speak or eat over the last several days. This morning, resolve etched his features. "You have been good to me, but I will go home now."

"It's too dangerous. Wait until spring."

"I will go."

"Boy of Thirteen Summers, Pastor Hansen will be back in Sitka in a few days. If you wait, I will go with you."

"Even on dangerous waters?"

"Yes, but we must have a plan."

"I have a plan."

Ott explained he had been working at the saloon and the hotel at night, sweeping floors, washing dishes. He did whatever chores the bosses ordered. He had spent hours sifting through the dirt and dust of Sitka's streets outside the saloon when the weather was dry. He had collected a small cache of gold. Tiny flakes, too small to be called nuggets. He also had several American dollars.

The Boy of Thirteen Summers had gone to Indiantown and hired a canoe and paddlers. He planned to buy a sled and dog team when they reached Haines since his village was further up the Chilkat.

"You have planned well, Ott, but I would feel safer with an engine."

He smirked and let it morph into a slight smile, "My people are canoe people. We have paddled these waters for thousands of years. How old is your engine?"

Miss Ruth laughed, "As I said, you have planned well."

Huddled in the thirty-foot canoe between eight Tlingit paddlers fore and aft, Miss Ruth shivered and thought about her trip from Hawaii. Cornflower blue skies and balmy trade winds were far from today's freezing gray drizzle.

She had loved Captain Harlan Walker's clipper ship, The China Doll, and enjoyed standing in the Crow's Nest with Silas or strolling the deck with the Captain. She appreciated the speed and safety of his steamship, The Aloha.

What a contrast the rich teal Hawaiian waters were to today's dark gray-green of Sitka Sound.

She shivered as she met Ott and the Tlingits at the edge of Indiantown before dawn. They loaded the canoe with more than enough provisions for a journey that could take several days or perhaps, weeks. The time frame depended on the weather, the smoothness of the waves, and how many hours a day they paddled.

The eldest native gave her a large bundle tied with thick string made of bear gut. She got in the canoe and placed it at her feet. He frowned, shook his head, and turned away.

They left Sitka as the dull morning light crawled over the mountains. The overcast sky and low clouds kept the sun from showing itself all day. The soft drizzle soon turned brutal. Ott passed her a seal skin. She wore it like a shawl to protect herself from the cold and the rain.

Jagged mountains, steep crags, and rocky cliffs hemmed them in as they journeyed north. The wind rushed around those peaks and cliffs and assaulted the canoe from every direction. The Tlingits paddled through narrow passageways of erratic tides, vile currents, and pounding rain.

Several hours later, they pulled into a sheltered cove and maneuvered around the waves breaking over several offshore reefs. The booming surf smashed over the rocks and soaked them. Miss Ruth shivered, and her teeth chattered.

One of the Tlingits built a small fire; another pulled smoked salmon, chokeberries, and fry bread from a cedar basket. The others disappeared into the forest.

Ott was anxious to get back on the water, but the Tlingits refused. The winds had pushed the waves ashore with great anger. The sky spirits said a storm had gathered behind the moon and would soon plunge to earth. The swirling waters and thick black sky did indeed appear menacing. The paddlers would not resume the journey until the storm passed, no matter how many days it lasted.

The three youngest Tlingits pulled Red Cedar and Mountain Hemlock branches into the campsite as the clouds spewed a hard rain. They built a lean-to shelter.

Silent, sodden, and soggy, Miss Ruth caught Ott's eyes and winked. As miserable as she was, she knew the boy felt worse, "Boy of Thirteen Summers, have a lemon drop."

"It won't make me feel better."

Miss Ruth laughed, "It won't make you feel worse." She passed out the little yellow balls of goodness to everyone.

The rain stopped near sunset three days later, and they prepared to resume their journey.

"Isn't it dangerous to travel in the dark?" Miss Ruth asked.

Ott pointed to the sky. "The Big Bear leads. The stars shine. The moon glows. These Tlingits know the way, besides the night is much longer than the day during these months."

Miss Ruth bit her lip and nodded. She had already decided to trust the Boy of Thirteen Summers, but she wasn't happy. She prayed for continued clear skies and calm seas.

The answer was no.

Between Peril Strait's unpredictable, treacherous waters and the storms they had encountered in Chatham Strait, it took them twice as long as they expected to arrive at the southern end of the Lynn Canal.

The freezing rain had pelted them mercilessly for days. The large tidal exchanges and the winds gusting inside the breakwater pushed them back. The temperature dropped, and the canoe iced up. They found a small inlet and paddled as far as they could away from the canal as the ice on their paddles grew thicker.

A small cove near the end of the inlet gave them a little protection from the winds rushing down the mountains. Its freezing sleet collided with winds of equal force that rushed up the canal, which was not a canal at all, but a ninety-mile-long fjord.

Although it was mid-winter, the Natives said the wind spirit would soon rest. While he slept, they would continue their journey. For now, they would camp.

Miss Ruth had never been so saturated with cold. The wet wool of her skirt had no occasion to dry itself. The wind sliced through it and her woolen jacket as well. The only part of her that didn't feel icy were her hands and feet, thanks to the mukluks and sealskin gloves Ott had made.

The older Tlingit, who had given her the bundle before they left Sitka, now threw it at her feet and growled.

"What did he say, Boy of Thirteen Summers?"

Ott shrugged.

Miss Ruth glared at him.

The boy shrugged again and replied, "He said you are a stupid white woman who refused his gift, but you must take it now for your life."

As Ott spoke, Miss Ruth untied the bundle and pulled out an oversized pair of pants and a hooded pullover made of fish skin and bear intestines. They were sewn together in four-inch squares like a quilt. She saw each square was stuffed with something she assumed was moss.

She apologized for her ignorance and lack of grace. She repeatedly thanked the elder Tlingit for his kindness and cautioned Ott to forcefully translate her gratitude.

She retreated to the lean-to and struggled to remove the soaked wool skirt, heavy and wet. The Levi's and long johns she wore underneath her skirt were also soaked and challenging to do away with. After changing into the Native garments, she hung her own clothes on long sticks over the fire.

Now that she was clothed with the Native pants and pullover, she no longer felt the wind pushing through to her skin. Bliss.

After her clothes dried, she decided to wear her long johns and shirt under her Native clothes. They smelled of wood smoke but were warm and dry; she packed the rest and tied the bundle with the bear gut string.

After they broke camp, she waddled to the water's edge and again expressed her thanks for the clothing. The elder Tlingit picked up his paddle, brushed past her, and settled in the canoe.

The Tlingits pulled on the paddles with deep strokes from dawn to dusk without a break, reaching Haines four days later. The ground had about a foot of snow, and the heavy, low-hanging clouds promised more.

Ott and Miss Ruth said goodbye to the Tlingits at the edge of Haines, where a small cluster of large wooden structures designated the clan houses.

Miss Ruth sat on a fallen log and waited while Ott sought out the chief. The clouds, thick and full, released the large white flakes they held. Miss Ruth pulled Ott's seal skin around herself and waited.

She felt like a snowman by the time he returned. Miss Ruth admired the sled and dog team. She threw off the sealskin and bent to hug the lead dog. It growled and snapped, and she jumped back.

"They are not pets! Stay away from them, Miss Ruth," Ott shouted.

He settled her in the sled and wrapped the fur blankets tightly around her, then laced her in like she was a papoose. The snowflakes fell faster, and the wind chapped her face. She wrapped her long scarf around her neck, covering her face. The extra length was tucked into her parka. She pulled the frozen scarf several inches every few minutes to find a warm spot and keep her face from freezing. She kept her eyes closed against the biting wind.

They entered the forest several hours later. The wind died, and the overhanging branches dissipated the falling snow. A stillness settled over them, and she opened her eyes to its wonder.

That evening, starlight and moonlight filtered through the trees and reflected off the snow. Ethereal. She swallowed several times and felt like crying at the beauty of it all.

Ott called out orders to the dogs, and they ran toward the Chilkat River. They heard the water tumble over the rocks.

"Keep the river on your right when you return, and it will lead you back to town."

Miss Ruth, warm under the furs Ott had tucked around her, barely heard. The soft light, diffused by the canopy of branches, the delicately falling snow, and the gliding motion of the dog sled lulled her.

It was near nightfall when they reached Ott's village. He paid his respects to the chief and asked about his mother.

"She has the breathing sickness. We built a shelter close by but away from us. Someone takes wood and food every third day and leaves it outside her hut," the chief said.

Ott's face lost all color as he stumbled from the clan house. Miss Ruth followed. Ott's mother lay under many furs; her eyes glistened when she saw her son. She whispered to him and frowned.

Miss Ruth could not follow the conversation even though Ott had spent much time teaching her his language. They talked so rapidly that she could only recognize a word or two. However, she could detect the emotions: his mother's pleadings and Ott's stubbornness.

After several minutes Ott motioned Miss Ruth outside, but not before they saw his mother cough up blood and mucus.

"Ott, we must take your mother to a doctor, although I fear it's tuberculosis. There is no medicine—no cure."

"Our shaman told her it is the white man's disease, and she must not go to a white man for help. He said the spirits punished her." His voice broke as he pounded his fist on the door frame. "They punished her for sending me to the white man."

"That's not true."

He did not meet her eyes or argue with her. "I will stay and care for her."

"This disease is highly contagious and deadly. I'm so sorry, but it seems as if it has progressed, and your mother will probably die, if not in a few days, then a few weeks." She put her arm around his shoulder, but he remained stiff and silent. "I will help you, but it's perilous."

"The sick spirit will not leave my mother if you remain."

Ott rejected her pleas and refused to let her back in the hut. He walked her back to the clan house and arranged for her to spend the night. He inspected the sky and frowned. "You must leave early in the morning. I sense there will be a change in the weather. Just follow the river back to Haines."

Ott bought salmon for the dogs and paid the chief's son to feed and harness them in the morning. He quickly taught Miss Ruth how to use the brake, throw her weight to the left and right when turning, and what commands to give the dogs.

Dawnlight. The stars faded, and the moonlight waned. Miss Ruth scanned the sky. Sunlight glowed behind the mountains and would soon crawl over the ridges and flow into the valley.

She laced her mukluks tightly, put on her gloves and hat, and approached the dog sled. She gave the orders, and the dogs obeyed, lunging forward. At the edge of the village, she smiled, relieved to see Ott one more time. Perhaps he had changed his mind, and she could stay. He had not.

She waved, then yelled at the dogs and braked. The dogs obeyed instantly. *I can do this.*

"I have news about the man you seek—this Denver Dan. The Chief said he captured our words with a stick that made little scratches. The shaman said that if they allowed this white man to take their words, he would also take their spirits. They banished him."

"When was he here?"

"Four years ago. I am sorry, Miss Ruth. They do not know where he went."

Miss Ruth nodded, "I will miss you, White Water Otter," she pronounced his name perfectly in his language.

His smile almost broke his face, "I am honored to think of you as another mother, even though you are white."

"The honor is mine, Boy of Thirteen Summers."

NINETEEN

SAM, 1962

It was a quiet Saturday morning in Sitka. Blue skies were shared by gulls, eagles, and ravens. Peaceful and serene, but Sam didn't feel it. He hadn't slept well. There were too many letters to read, and he couldn't get those he had read out of his mind.

Sitka to Haines, in a canoe, in winter! Impossible! It was about one hundred and fifty nautical miles to that small town at the far end of the Lynn Canal. Peril Strait was well named, and Chatham Strait was deceptive. Both were dangerous.

Lynn Canal, Alaska's longest fjord, was more than treacherous, especially in winter. He'd flown over those waters many times and traveled over them in a large fishing vessel and the Alaska Ferry. He wouldn't want to make the trip in anything smaller.

"It's no use talking to you, Sadsack. I'll just give Alice a call. I know it's her day off, but maybe she'll meet me at the office." The cat put his nose in the air and turned away.

"I've never been here without Margaret Mary pounding on that linotype machine. It's so quiet," Alice said.

"It does make it hard to think." Sam opened the bag of crullers and handed one to Alice.

"Your tribute issue about Miss Ruth was wonderful. Everyone in town thought so."

"There's so much more." He poured them each a cup of coffee.

"Perhaps it's time for you to write that book."

"I haven't vetted all the Letters to the Editor or organized Miss Ruth's letters to Kamalei. There are so many facts to verify."

"You don't have to, Sam. People were sharing their hearts and memories, not necessarily the facts."

Sam shuddered. "I'm a newspaperman. I deal in facts."

Alice paused, took a sip of her coffee, and then spoke slowly, "What if the facts don't matter?"

His head jerked up. "Blasphemy!"

"I'm going to tell you something about facts, Sam. They're not all they're cracked up to be."

"Now, you are going against the bedrock of my existence."

"My father was a cop, a detective. He'd rather have forensic evidence than witnesses."

"Hmmm. I've been to crime scenes and accidents where bystanders are eager to tell me what happened. It was hard to know whose version was true."

"So now it's the truth you want, not just the facts." Alice smiled at him over the rim of her coffee cup.

Sam ran his hand over his head and patted his pockets, groping for a cigar. "I want to be as accurate as possible, do Miss Ruth justice. She was important to so many people. I need to do more research, see how her letters to Kamalei slot into Alaska's history."

"You don't need any more information, Sam. Write with your heart, not your mind."

"I don't know if I can."

TWENTY

Dear Kamalei,

I left the Boy of Thirteen Summers with his dying mother. I fear I will never see him again. On my journey back to Haines, I received a marriage proposal and taught a young girl how to sew and bake bread. She was a tender little thing and crept into my heart. I am afraid I will leave pieces of my heart scattered all over Alaska...

—MISS RUTH'S LETTER'S 1895

She hoped the barking dogs would alert those in the cabin to her presence. She set the brake on the sled and stumbled toward the door, guided by the light from the small window. She didn't make it. With a small cry, she grabbed the stair rail but still stumbled. Exhausted, frozen, she could not rise.

The door opened, and she heard a voice, "Son, attend to the dogs. Cora May, heat water and bring the copper tub in from the lean-to."

The teenage boy took his time with the sled dogs. Ten-year-old Cora May, thin and lanky, struggled with the copper tub. Her father lay the woman on the bed in the corner of the room and helped his young daughter. He added more wood to the stove and poured pots of steaming water into the tub.

"What's your name?" he called over his shoulder.

"Miss Ruth," she followed him with her eyes.

"It's not smart to travel alone."

She heard the irritation in his voice, "It couldn't be helped." She sneezed and sniffed.

He hung a blanket around the tub, came to the bed, and averted his eyes, "You do realize we're going to have to get you out of those wet clothes and into the tub?"

Miss Ruth wished she had taken Ott's advice and worn the Tlingit clothes instead of her own, but the weather appeared stable when she left. Would she never learn? Once on the trail, it took all her concentration and energy to control the dogs; she couldn't stop to change.

"Miss Ruth?"

She shook the memory of the rough trip away and answered him, "Cora May will help me."

"She's a skinny thing, sickly, never been much help, should have been a boy." His tone was matter-of-fact, and he didn't see the hurt on his daughter's face, but Miss Ruth did.

She bit her lip, frowned, and then turned to the girl, "Will you help me, Cora May? Women are strong when they stick together, and I need you."

The girl clasped her hand, and the two disappeared behind the blanket.

Caught by the wind, the cabin's door slammed open, "Pa, it's the worst storm I've ever seen."

"Did you settle her dogs away from ours and out of the wind?"

"Of course I did. They're on the other side of the shed. She had salmon among her things but not much else. It looks like she tried to lighten the load."

"Any more clothes?"

"Outer garments. Indian," the boy replied to his father.

"Why didn't you wear those Indian clothes? Don't you know Alaska's storms can appear out of nowhere in an instant?" The man growled in Miss Ruth's direction.

Miss Ruth, glad the blanket hid her from view, bit her lip and said, "The weather was fine when I left, but I've lived here long enough to know better. It was foolish of me. It was my first time driving a sled. Good thing the dogs knew what to do."

He turned away and muttered, "Stupid woman. You could have died."

"How close is Haines?"

"Three miles." He peered out of the window. "It might as well be three hundred. Nobody is going anywhere in this weather."

The hot water stung, tingled, then soothed and warmed Miss Ruth's cold body. She lay back and let the water seep into every pore. She could have stayed in the tub longer, but the water had cooled.

"We're done, Pa," Cora May called.

The man turned his head away and thrust his arm around the blanket, "Here, this was my wife's nightdress."

"It's lovely. Thank you. I'm sure my clothes will dry soon, and I can return this."

"It doesn't matter. The wife died last spring."

Cora May hung her head and sniffed.

Miss Ruth whispered to the girl, "You miss her, don't you?"

Miss Ruth slipped into the pink nightgown with darker pink rosebuds and leaned toward the little girl. Cora May nodded, hiccupped, and buried her face in Miss Ruth's shoulder.

"I think it's painful for your Papa to talk about her, is that right?"

The young girl shrugged.

"I'll be here until the storm blows over. Will you tell me all about your mama?"

The girl hugged Miss Ruth even tighter.

Miss Ruth, uncomfortable wearing just the nightgown, asked to borrow the boy's extra shirt. She might've appeared odd in pink rosebuds and red flannel, but she felt more modest.

The man of the house hung her clothes near the fireplace and the cookstove, turning them every half-hour. Soon the smell of wet wool permeated the room.

Miss Ruth and Cora May huddled on the bed. The girl whispered incessantly about her mother. The teenage boy constantly poked at the fire and blushed whenever he met Miss Ruth's eyes. The man shot quiet, thoughtful looks at her while cooking supper, but he didn't say much.

After a silent, awkward meal, the boy checked on the dogs, the man cleared the table, and Miss Ruth asked the girl if she could brush and braid her hair.

Cora May squealed, "French?"

"French or Dutch?"

"I never heard of a Dutch braid."

"It's just like French, but you go under instead of over."

Miss Ruth took her time brushing out the girl's tangles, then braided her hair.

"Now it's your turn," Cora May said.

Miss Ruth sat on the chair and took down her hair. The girl brushed, counting to a hundred. Miss Ruth relaxed and closed her eyes. She didn't notice when the father came and took the brush from his daughter.

Miss Ruth rubbed the side of her neck. "Cora May, I think I have a kink."

The man rubbed Miss Ruth's neck and shoulders. Cora May stood in front of Miss Ruth and took her hand. Miss Ruth's eyes flew open, and she peeked over her shoulder.

The man's hands stilled, but he didn't remove them, "You fit here. You could stay. Be my wife, their mother."

Cora May squealed and jumped into Miss Ruth's lap, "Say yes! Say yes!"

Cora May's father searched Miss Ruth's face with no expression on his own. "You're alone; I assume you have no family or husband. Women were meant to be wives and mothers. You're good with the girl."

"Please, Miss Ruth, please be my mama."

Miss Ruth put her palms on her cheeks and closed her eyes.

"We don't have much. A little gold from the creek keeps us going, and we run trap lines in winter. Whatever I've got is yours."

Cora May squeezed Miss Ruth around the neck and whispered, "I love you already."

For a moment, Miss Ruth entertained the idea of motherhood, family, and husband. When she did, a certain sea captain's image pierced her heart. If any man could have tempted her toward matrimony, it would have been Captain Harlan Walker of The China Doll. Miss Ruth blinked his image away.

As gently as she could, she pulled Cora May's arms from around her neck and said, "I cannot be your mama, but we will be great friends. I love you too."

Miss Ruth did not look in the man's direction.

After a moment, he put on his gloves and parka, "I need to help the boy attend to the dogs."

The storm lasted for twelve days. It should have been uncomfortable inside the cabin, but Cora May was constantly at Miss Ruth's side, a buffer between Miss Ruth and the girl's father. Miss Ruth focused all of her attention on the young girl.

Cora May wanted Miss Ruth to braid her hair, teach her to bake bread, and do motherly things for her.

"Cora May, your mother's nightgown is pretty. Did she have any other clothes?"

"There is a trunk in the loft, next to my bed. Mama had two blouses, a skirt, and a dress."

After talking to the girl's father, Miss Ruth asked Cora May to get the clothes. "We are going to resew them to fit you."

"I don't know how."

"I will teach you." Miss Ruth cut a handkerchief-sized square and said, "Fold the edge over twice like this and then run the needle up and down, in and out. Try to make the stitches all the same size."

"Like this?"

Miss Ruth nodded, "I'm glad your mother had a sewing kit. It's yours now. Take good care of it."

"She seems like a different girl, growing up too fast." Cora May's father sighed, put another log on the fire, yelled at his son to fill both wood boxes, then stoked the woodstove. With the fireplace and wood stove roaring, the cabin remained warm.

Miss Ruth poured him a cup of coffee and asked him to sit at the table. "I want to talk to you about her future. She's almost eleven and can't read. She can barely write her name.

"My wife taught the boy. The sickness took her before she could teach the girl."

"Cora May needs an education."

He shrugged his shoulders and stared into his coffee.

"In the next few years, she will begin her womanly time. Who's going to help her through that? Have you thought about her future at all?"

"Never thought about any of it until you came."

"I'm sorry, but I can't be a part of your future. What about Cora May's grandmothers?"

"My mother's dead and my wife's mother lives in Vancouver. She didn't want us to marry. She doesn't know her daughter has passed or that she has grandchildren."

Miss Ruth sucked in her breath and bit her lip. *Honestly! Some people!* "Do you have her address?"

"My wife had some papers in the bottom of her sewing kit."

Miss Ruth emptied the basket and found the address. As she put the sewing supplies back, she asked, "If her grandmother is willing to take her, will you let her go?"

"I can't leave the boy alone on our claim."

"If her grandmother can't come to Haines, I'll take Cora May to Vancouver."

He got up from the table and reached for the coffee pot; his hand stilled on the handle, "The wind has died down, the sky is clear, best to take her in the morning."

"But I haven't written...."

The man shoved his hands in his pockets, "You're right. This is no life for her. If her grandmother refuses, find a place for my daughter—a good place."

He loosened a brick from the fireplace and pulled out a small pouch of gold, "This should cover your expenses." He lifted his jacket off its peg near the door. With a long gaze at Cora May, he opened the door and yelled, "Boy, leave those dogs. We best check the trap line."

TWENTY-ONE

SAM, 1962

Sam reread the letter, folded the thin paper, and replaced it in the envelope.

He lay on the couch and stared at the ceiling. Did Miss Ruth take the young girl all the way to Vancouver? Did Cora May's grandmother accept her?

What did Ott do after his mother died? Did he make his way back to Miss Ruth or stay with his tribe?

Were Ott and Cora May still alive? Would they appear in future letters? He made a mental note to have Chuck scour Miss Ruth's letters and search for Cora May's name. He wasn't sure if Ott had an Americanized name. He'd inquire at the state's Department of Vital Statistics, although, without their surnames, it would be impossible to track them. He groaned in frustration, reached for a cigar, and then let his hand fall back.

He glanced at the letters strewn around the room. His reading plans had fallen apart. Initially, he started in 1890 and read a few letters chronologically. But then he wanted to know what Miss Ruth had to say about critical historical dates; the World Wars, the stock market crash, Spanish influenza, so he pulled out the letters postmarked close to those historical events.

Overall, he found himself drawn to Miss Ruth's random people, like Ott and Cora May. They may have seemed random, but they were not ordinary.

His father had always told him every life was a story. Through the letters, Sam had found that to be true. It made him wonder about everyone he saw on Sitka's sidewalks. What were their stories?

Sam ran his hand over his unshaven face. Once again, he had read until near dawn. He needed a shower and a shave. He yawned, put his hands behind his head, and counted the ceiling tiles.

He saw himself in that humble cabin near the Chilkat River several miles beyond Haines. The wind beat against the shuttered windows, howling as fierce as a wolf pack. The cookstove and fireplace crackled with numerous logs, and the smell of woodsmoke and stew permeated the room.

The odor of wet wool from Miss Ruth's snow-soaked clothes hanging in front of the fireplace filled Sam's nostrils, and he breathed deeply and stretched, knocking the sofa pillows off the couch.

He wondered what motivated this trapper's proposal. Was he attracted to Miss Ruth, or did he just want a mother for Cora May? Sam closed his eyes and felt drawn into the scene. He could almost see his hand take the brush from the girl. The light glistened on the woman's silky hair as he slowly pulled the brush through it. Rhythmic. Hypnotic. It seemed to Sam that he brushed that tawny hair for hours, but when the woman turned to look at him, it was Alice's face he saw.

Sam bolted off the couch. "What was that about?"

Sadsack lay on the footstool, fast asleep. "You are no help at all." Sam patted his pockets, no cigar.

Every drawer pulled open and slammed shut, every cupboard door swung on its hinges and bounced back, and every pocket turned inside out. Not a single stogie to be found.

The racket woke Sadsack, and he followed Sam as the man pillaged each room. "Aha!" Sam reached behind his bedside table and pulled out a tattered cigar of indeterminate age. The dry, crumbling thing flaked in his hand. He cursed and threw it in the trash.

He reached for his wallet and his jacket. Sadsack meowed, and Sam said, "I'll be right back. Don't worry. I'll get you a can of sardines."

Sam left the grocery store loaded with stogies and cat treats and took a slight detour down Biorka Street. He stopped in front of a small house surrounded by a white picket fence with peeling paint. Sam felt safe leaning against the fence and staring at the house. Alice was the night duty nurse all this month. She would be asleep and unaware of him. Perhaps, she'd dream about him—silly old fool!

There were flowers on the table in the front window—yellow roses—her favorite. How did he know that? He told himself he was a journalist trained to notice details.

Sam ran his hand over his thinning hair and cursed himself for forgetting his hat. Sitka's ubiquitous rain fell and not just a drizzle. He turned up his collar, but the rain continued to drip down his neck. Still, he kept vigil in front of the house. Old fool!

Sam smiled to himself. It was a good thing Stormy Durand was retired. Along with his mastiff, Bull, he had regularly patrolled Sitka's neighborhoods on foot. Stormy might not arrest him for lurking or trespassing or acting like a dang fool, but he would relish informing the guys at the Café. Sam puffed on his cigar and surveyed the short block that was Biorka Street.

From the corner of his eye, Sam saw a light shining through her upstairs window. Alice must be awake. He hurried away; the image of her soft, silky hair accompanied him.

❧

Alice Blakely took one last gander into her hallway mirror, grabbed her jacket, and closed the door to her little house on Biorka Street. The paint on the white picket fence begged for a new coat. Chipped and flaking, it projected sad neglect, and she wondered if she could imitate Tom Sawyer. There were lots of kids in the neighborhood. They might be able to scrape and sand the flaking fence. Of course, she'd pay them, or maybe she should ask Sam to paint the fence with her.

She frowned. Besides a couple of leisurely walks, they couldn't be called hikes; she had never seen Sam do any strenuous physical labor. He was approaching middle age and would become portly if he didn't watch out.

Maybe she should encourage him to take more walks and only have one cruller instead of two or three during their morning visits. No, that would be too forward.

She slammed the gate, and it bounced back without latching. She stilled her irritation and closed it softly. Sam had not shown her that she meant anything to him beyond a sounding board about Miss Ruth, his grand passion and project. If she was honest with herself, she'd have to admit she didn't even qualify as a friend. It was Miss Ruth he loved, not her.

The word love stopped her in the middle of crossing Baranof Street. She put her hands to her hot face. A pickup truck's horn blared, and she jumped out of the way.

Alice had already resigned herself to an old-fashioned spinsterhood. The passion to be someone's wife and mother had cooled long ago. Had her visits with Sam caused some of those embers to ignite?

She turned right onto Lincoln Street and passed the Russian Bishop's House. A few blocks later, she came to St. Michael's Russian Orthodox Church and saw Sam, farther down the street, coming out of the Cafe.

They had agreed she'd visit before starting her evening shift. She could hail him or increase her pace to catch him, but she didn't. The word love still hung in the air and confused her.

Alice gnawed on her lower lip. She was a woman in her mid-30s who should be over this nonsense. She had a cute little house with a white picket fence. True, she only rented, and the fence needed paint. It was half the dream, wasn't it?

Still, no husband or child. Perhaps she should get a cat. Sam seemed satisfied with one.

Alice smoothed her starched white uniform and thought about her patients at the Pioneer's Home as she continued walking. She gave herself to them, and they loved her. It should be enough. She would make it be enough. She didn't need romance. She didn't need Sam.

She marched past the Sentinel with a determined step and knew she hadn't convinced herself of anything. She went to her job without stopping for coffee and crullers. She didn't know if she could ever face Sam again. What if he could see her feelings on her face?

What exactly were those feelings?

Sam ate all the crullers but didn't taste them. He reached for the telephone several times but never dialed.

Margaret Mary shut off the linotype machine and pulled a chair close to Sam's desk. "What is going on? You are as cranky as a bear shaken out of hibernation," she said.

"Nothing." Sam stubbed out his cigar and put a fresh sheet of paper in the typewriter.

"It's Alice, isn't it? She didn't show up today."

Sam didn't answer. His fingers flew over the typewriter's keys, but the sentence was undecipherable. The coffee was cold, and he had eaten all the crullers.

He sniffed, and all he smelled was newsprint. Alice made the place smell like springtime. Fresh. Cheerful. The woman brought the sunshine with her, even on the grayest days.

He slammed one drawer after another and swore when he couldn't find any cigars. He ran his hand over his head and berated himself for not bringing some to work.

"Must you swear?" Margaret Mary loaded another tray into the linotype.

"Yes, I think I must." Sam patted his pockets. No luck.

"Do you know what your problem is, my boy?"

"No, and don't tell me. I'm going to Akervik's."

"Better buy some lemon drops." Margaret Mary watched Sam cross the street. Poor, besotted fool. He couldn't see the love story unfolding before him. She rubbed her temples and took two aspirin. If Sam and Alice were ever going to get together and the Sentinel returned to its everyday peaceful chaos, she would have to intervene. *Hold on to your hat, Sammy boy. I am going to put you out of your misery.*

Agrafena and Ollyanna would help her take Alice in hand, but she'd need reinforcements for Sam. She reached for the phone,

"Mick, tell the men at the round table, I need them...yes, Sam and Alice...I know, but we have to do something...Yes, top secret."

Sam returned amid a haze of tobacco smoke. His mood was a bit better, and he settled at his desk and attacked the typewriter keys.

"I saw her earlier," Margaret Mary folded her hands across her chest and goaded Sam, "She almost ran past the window. Her expression was set, and she faced straight ahead."

"Probably an emergency at the Home," Sam said, thinking about how lovely Alice's hair had shined when the sun bounced off its waves. He swallowed and glared at Margaret Mary.

"You must have done something to upset her," his linotype operator accused him.

Sam bit his lower lip and grabbed a file of copy from his inbox. "I didn't do anything; something was going on at her work, that's all. She won't miss our next appointment."

"I wonder." Margaret Mary stared across the street toward the massive building where Alice worked.

"What's that?" Sam's fingers stilled on the keys.

"Nothing, Boss. I just have a couple of errands to run after work."

"Don't forget, tomorrow is my day to concentrate on the book."

A few weeks later, Alice saw fresh crullers and hot coffee on Sam's desk, but no sign of him. She wondered if he had bought the coffee and pastries every week. She picked up the note she saw peeking out from under the pastry bag. *Accident at one of the canneries. Back soon.*

She tried to imagine what Sam would say when he saw her sitting in her usual spot? Was it okay to come without calling? Without explaining her absence? What could she say? How would he respond? Maybe she should leave?

Alice didn't see Margaret Mary and thought she had accompanied the editor. She wandered around the newspaper office and poked at the strange machinery, silent now. She sat in Sam's chair and almost reached for a cruller, then sighed, no sign of him yet.

It had taken Alice three weeks to find the courage to return to the Sentinel for her meetings with Sam. She had spent a lot of time practicing a noncommittal friendly expression in front of her mirror. There was no way Sam would see any sign of love on her face.

She turned her attention to the corner. "Sean," she moved closer to the wooden leg leaning against the file cabinets, "do you think I should keep coming? Sam seems to enjoy my visits, but..."

The brass hinges on Sean Connor's knee glinted in the sun. Alice dabbed at her eyes with a lacy white handkerchief. "They say women can make the first move, ask a man out. It is the 60s, after all, but I could never do that." She patted the smooth wooden leg. "If it hadn't been for your last request, Sam and I would have never had our coffee and crullers. To tell you the truth, Connor, it's the highlight of my week."

"For goodness sakes," Margaret Mary came from the backroom and dumped office supplies on Sam's desk. Two rolls of tape fell behind his chair. She ignored them and said, "You have got to act like a real woman."

"I didn't know you were here."

"I was in the supply room and heard every word."

"Connor and I were having a private conversation."

The old linotype operator squatted before Alice and took hold of her hands. "Now you listen to me, young lady..."

"Young? I'm thirty-five and never had a romance. I don't think I know how. If I can't have Sam," she hiccupped and pulled her hands free.

"You can and will, but only if you listen to me. I've known Sam all his life. I know how to handle him. Connor has done all he can; now it's my turn."

"You mustn't do anything underhanded or sneaky." Alice held her handkerchief to her lips.

Margaret Mary stood and leaned against the window. "I'll come up with a plan."

"Sam is honest. No tricks."

"You want my help or not?" Margaret Mary saw Sam through the window, "Don't say I didn't offer." She scuttled back to the linotype machine. She muttered to herself, thankful the clatter of her machine would cover her voice. "You young people! Although, you're both closer to middle age and set in your ways. It would serve you right if I left you to your own devices."

The bell on the door jingled, and Sam's face brightened when he saw Alice sitting in her usual place.

"Time for coffee and crullers, although the coffee is probably cold. Is everything okay at the cannery?" Alice asked.

"A retort overheated and exploded. Two workers have minor burns. Scores of cans were thrown everywhere. One hit the foreman on the back of the head. He's got a pretty bad concussion. But enough of that."

Alice laid some unused newsprint on the worktable and emptied the bag. She kept her expression passive and hoped Sam followed her lead. Thankfully, he didn't ask about her absence the last several weeks.

"How's Connor's leg today?" Sam gazed fondly in its direction.

Margaret Mary punched out another headline and continued muttering, "First the leg, then the weather. Sam will ask about her patients. Alice will ask about Miss Ruth's letters. Predictable."

She looked over her shoulder at the couple sitting on opposite sides of the worktable. "Sam, you have no idea you're in love with Alice. Some newspaperman you are, unable to see the love story right in front of you."

The linotype machine clacked and clanged. "Alice, you are just as bad; you talk to him like he was an older brother or, worse, an uncle."

Margaret Mary switched off the machine; the sudden quiet enveloped the room. Alice stopped mid-sentence; Sam stopped mid-bite.

Margaret Mary pushed past them and hissed, "I need some air."

As she left, she heard Alice say, "Is Margaret Mary upset about something? What did you do, Sam?"

"Me? I didn't do anything." He pulled a somewhat stale cruller out of the bag, took a bite, then threw it in the trash. "Why do you people always assume I've done something?" He patted his pockets, feeling for his matches.

"What?"

"Nothing." He gave up the search, laid his unlit cigar in the ashtray, and picked up a letter. "I read something about Sean Connor. Listen to this."

TWENTY-TWO

Dear Kam,

I've often told you about the Irish boy, Sean Connor, the fun we had on the ranch, and our adventures when I first came to Alaska. Sean is no longer a boy. In fact, he's in his sixties, about your age if I'm not mistaken. And what I have to tell you is tragic...

—MISS RUTH'S LETTERS 1942

It was nearly midnight, and the pounding on the cabin's door was incessant. Shaken out of a deep sleep, Miss Ruth grabbed her bathrobe and ran for the front door. Sven Anderson panted, out of breath, "They need you... Dorothy... Chichagof."

"Calm down, Sven," she pulled him into the kitchen, pushed him into a chair, and thrust a cup of water in his hand. He gulped, choked, and then sipped it. Slowly his breathing returned to normal.

"I thought you still lived at the See House. The minister's wife told me about your cabin."

"The current Bishop and his wife have many children, and her sister lives with them to help. There was no room for me."

"Oh." Sven gulped his water and held out the glass for more.

"Why are you here and in such a panic."

Sven jumped up wild-eyed. The water sloshed out of the glass. "Short-pants McGee radioed! Accident! Cave-in! Someone's trapped!"

"Injured?"

"Don't know. Agrefena says to bring your medical kit. Doc is out of town."

Miss Ruth headed down the hallway, throwing the words over her shoulder, "Get the blankets out of the bathroom cupboard."

As she dressed and pulled on her cowboy boots, Miss Ruth complained, "The Doc is always out of town. Hunting and fishing seem more important to him than the town's health." She shook the thought away and made a mental list of her medical supplies. "Sven, grab a stack of salt sacks from the back porch; we might need to tear them into bandages. Did you say we were taking the Dorothy? That's the shoreboat that's partly covered, right?"

The boy nodded, relieved to be given directions.

"Is everyone at the Café?"

He shook his head, "Conway's dock. Jake's getting the Dorothy ready, but he said I can't come." Sven hung his head.

Miss Ruth grabbed his chin and lifted it. "You're my assistant. Stay behind me and don't speak. Can you do that?"

"Those old geezers at the Café think I'm still a kid."

"It's that kind of talk that makes them think so."

Sven hung his head again, then smirked, "I'm going to join the Army. That will show them, especially Ivan. He'll have to let me marry Ivana."

"You will do no such thing, Sven Anderson. Your mother and I will march down to the recruiting office with your birth certificate and show them how young you are. Don't hang your head. That's the third time."

He tried to meet her eyes, "With the war and everything, it's so stupid to be stuck in high school. I just want to get on with it."

"Be patient, Sven."

"How?"

Miss Ruth ruffled his hair, "I used to ask myself the very same question, even had a few tantrums in front of God."

"Not you!"

"I could tell you stories that would make your toes curl, but not tonight." She pointed at the stack of blankets and salt sacks.

He pulled his watch cap from his jacket pocket. Miss Ruth laughed, "Between the blankets piled high and your cap pulled low, you're clearly unrecognizable."

Sven started to speak. Miss Ruth shook her finger in his face, "I can't guarantee your passage if you open your mouth. Understood?"

Sven started to speak. Miss Ruth raised a single eyebrow.

TWENTY-THREE

Dear Kamalei,

I think of you and Sean as my brothers. I can't write yet about how we had to amputate his leg. I shudder just thinking about it. We brought him back from the mine and took him to the Pioneer's Home. After several weeks he was released and is back in his little house. Nurse Maddie checks on him daily, and I stop in several times a week. It will take some time for him to return to his usual cheerful self.

I must tell you, poor Sven couldn't keep quiet, and the men wouldn't let him go. It broke his heart and annoyed me, but as you know, I don't always get my way...

—MISS RUTH'S LETTERS 1942

Miss Ruth chopped the vegetables and tossed them into a cast-iron Dutch oven with the venison roast. "You should be able to eat on that for several days."

She let the contents of the heavy pot come to a rolling boil, then pushed it to the back where it would simmer, poured herself a cup of coffee, and sat near Sean. "Are you sure you wouldn't like me to contact your Irish relatives in the Matanuska Valley? I'm sure one of them would come and stay."

"I'm perfectly capable of hobbling around the house by myself. Don't treat me like a baby."

She put her hands on her hips in mock indignation. "Sean, me boy-o."

Sean grinned, and for a moment, she saw the young freckled teenager she had met on the ranch more than half a century ago.

"Don't take that tone with me; it makes me feel like I'm twelve." Sean reached for his now cold coffee and groaned as he felt the pain in a leg no longer there.

"I'm sorry we had to take your leg." Her tone softened, and she sniffed.

He turned his head and wept.

"Better your leg than your life." For once, Miss Ruth felt awkward and didn't know how to comfort her friend. She patted his shoulder and whispered, "I'll make lunch."

"Might have been better if it was my life."

Miss Ruth pursed her lips, threw her dishrag into the sink, and took him by the shoulders, "You wouldn't leave me in the wilds of Alaska all by me-self, now would ye?"

"Whenever you lecture me, you sound like me dear, sainted mother," he tried to use his mother's Irish brogue as Miss Ruth had.

"Imagine the talking to she'd give you. She'd not let you grieve over losing a silly leg when you have another."

Sean felt like cursing but pulled out his tobacco pouch instead. Miss Ruth could do a lot, but she couldn't make his leg grow back. He dropped the bag as he slipped into his own private darkness. He didn't hear her chatter as she dished up the stew.

The fever attacked him in the wee hours of the morning. He

stumbled out of bed and crawled to the phone. They found him passed out on the floor.

Infection! Doc feared septicemia, which could prove fatal. He called the Navy doctors on Japonski Island, and they admitted Sean to the Navy hospital.

Miss Ruth met Doc outside Sean's room. "What can they do for him, Doc.?"

"What they can do and what they are willing to do are two different things," Doc sucked on his pipe, then coughed.

"What do you mean?"

Doc stuck his head in the room. Sean looked like death. He frowned and swore.

"Doc?"

"I know the Navy has some of that new miracle drug—penicillin. But they're saving it for those wounded in battle."

"There haven't been any battles around here."

He swore again, "Excuse my language. I don't know what to do."

Miss Ruth went to the nurse's station. "Please, nurse, who's in charge of this hospital, and who's the base commander?" She borrowed Doc's pen and prescription pad and wrote down their names and phone numbers.

"Don't leave him." Her black skirts fluttered like a pirate flag as she hurried down the hall. Doc scratched his head and sat next to Sean. "I don't know what she's doing, but I'm sure she'll get results."

Several hours later, Miss Ruth returned with the head of the hospital, who administered the penicillin and gave the head nurse dosage instructions for the next few days.

The commander's wife accompanied Miss Ruth and wanted to know about the older woman's adventurous life in Alaska. Miss

Ruth had promised to speak at a tea for officers' wives in return for the penicillin.

Sean spent ten days in the Navy hospital and then was transferred back to the Pioneer's Home to finish his recovery and regain his strength.

Miss Ruth fluffed Sean's pillows and straightened his blankets. She pulled up the shade and opened the window.

"Don't fuss," he said.

"It makes me feel useful."

Sean shut his eyes tight to the reality of his situation. After several moments he appealed to Miss Ruth, "I have to ask, where is it?"

She patted his shoulder and grinned, "Remember? Ivan told you he buried it on Chichagof. But the guys at the Café decided it was just as Irish as the rest of you, and it needed a proper wake. Bill Wall made a small casket while the others went to Chichagof. Ivan guided them right to the spot. He had even made a crude Russian cross for the site."

Sean's lips twitched, but then he groaned.

"They laid the casket on the Café's bar, and your leg was toasted by all who knew you and many who didn't. The next day they escorted it to almost every cemetery in town. Since you were still alive, the military wouldn't permit burial at the National Cemetery; their commander said it was all or nothing. Since your leg was Irish, the Russians said they couldn't sanction its burial in their cemetery. The Lutherans weren't sure what religion your leg was, so they wouldn't take it. Finally, Petrov Bravebird buried it at the Native cemetery. First, he made your leg an honorary member of the Frog house of Eagle clan."

Sean could only imagine the tiny casket being shuttled from one cemetery to another. "I'll have to thank old Petrov."

Sean Connor picked up the wooden leg newly arrived from Seattle and heaved it through the plate glass window. It stood at attention among the budding rosebushes. He crumpled to the floor and cursed the limb that wasn't there.

Nurse Maddie, still as a statue, stood amid the shattered glass and asked herself if she should attend to the broken window or the broken man. Hands-on her hips, she delivered a scathing lecture to her patient, but only in her mind.

"You best clean up this mess," he growled.

"I could get you some medicine."

"It doesn't help the pain when my leg is not here."

"Can I get it for you?" She wrung her hands.

"Not unless you take a shovel to the Native Cemetery."

She stretched her arm toward the window, "I meant—."

He glanced toward the window. "I never want to see that cursed thing again." He pulled himself up, fell back onto the bed, and groaned.

"Mr. Connor, I don't know how to help you."

"You can't. Nobody can."

"What about Miss Ruth?"

"Can she grow me another leg?"

Nurse Maddie fled, wondering why she had become a nurse, why she'd come to Alaska and worked among these cranky old men. She returned with a broom and dustpan and found Sean asleep. She didn't care what he said; she'd make a call to Miss Ruth as soon as possible.

The window, taped with cardboard and tarpaper, gave the institutional room an even gloomier feel.

Miss Ruth forced a cheerful tone to her voice, "Have you been causing trouble again, Sean me-boy-o?"

He reached for his tobacco pouch.

"Aw, Sean." She snatched it and shoved it in a drawer out of his reach.

"Every time you mother me or act like a big sister, you use Ma's Irish brogue. I'm sick of it! You can't baby me or take my smokes. I'm almost sixty-five years old."

"You'll need half a decade to catch me," She took his hand and kissed it. "When Jack and Maureen died, it comforted me to mother you."

"I was in my 30s, didn't need a mother then, and I don't need one now."

She lifted his hand and placed it on her cheek, "Maybe it's me that has the need." Her voice broke, and she sat on the bed and wept.

Sean squeezed his eyes shut and felt a twinge of remorse. He patted Miss Ruth on the back in a jerky, awkward way. "I'm sorry, Ruthie. Each step I take on that wooden monster is agony. Don't confine me to this bed. I'm an Alaskan."

"How many legs has Doc tried?"

"That was third."

"Where do they come from?"

"The first two from some company out of San Francisco. This one was from Seattle."

"So, me-boy-o," she used the brogue deliberately, "what you need is a good Alaska leg."

"Huh?"

"The territory of Alaska took your leg, Sean, so it will provide another." She gathered her things, kissed him on the forehead, then stopped at Nurse Maddie's desk and asked where the chapel was. They didn't have one.

She headed across town to St. Peter's, and her thoughts walked along with her. Should we have tried to save his leg? She shivered as she remembered the blood and bone fragments and the infection oozing out of the open wound.

What if a splintered piece of bone reached his heart or pierced his lung? She put her hands to her temple and forced herself to stop asking such questions. Grandpa John always said you shouldn't dig up in doubt what you planted in faith.

Once she reached the See House, she made tea and forced herself to drink it. She made several phone calls and asked everyone to meet at the Café that evening.

Miss Ruth mumbled to herself as she made her way to the Café. Sometimes she didn't know if she was thinking out loud or praying. Either way, it was a comfort.

If it were anyone but Sean, she wouldn't feel so conflicted. She loved that redheaded boy that wanted to rope and ranch like a real cowboy. Together, they talked about the jokes he played on Aunt Ellie and the skills he learned from Grandpa John. Their last round-up camping under the Texas sky came to mind.

He alone could talk about that dusty piece of Texas she called home. The memories were sweet as the bluebells that burst forth in spring. The present for Sean was bitter.

The following week everyone Miss Ruth had contacted crowded into Sean's room, all talking at once—Petrov Bravebird, three Tlingit women, and the men from the Café.

"What's going on?" Sean tried to push himself up, and they all rushed to help.

"The Alaska Territorial Consortium for the Design and Manufacture of an Official Alaskan leg for Sean Connor Inc. is having its first meeting," Ade said as he swept his fisherman's cap off and bowed.

"The problem with the other legs," Bill said, "is not enough padding on the top and too much weight at the bottom. I suspect the wood was not lathed properly."

"You figure?" Sean's eyes betrayed his skepticism.

"We need the right hardwood, but the leg should be hollowed out some and balanced with the weight of your other," Jake said.

"Where's the Doc? And where's that old Russian?"

"Ivan's in the hallway. He says sick rooms make him nervous."

"Ivan, get in here," Jake yelled.

"Doc says it's not ethical for him to support an unofficial manufacture of a homemade leg," Bill said.

Sean snorted. Ivan hovered just inside the doorway, and the others pretended not to see his ashen face.

"Doc said it with a wink and a drink and gave me all his measurements and notes." Bill patted his shirt pocket.

"Ivan, you cowardly old man, get over here," Jake yelled again.

Petroff Bravebird pulled some moss from the bag at his feet, "The women will make a seal skin pad, fill it with this, soothing herbs, and other medicinal grasses. It will be fitted over your—"

"Go ahead and say it. Over my miserable stump. Half a leg – half a man. I'm an old man. Might as well give up and die now."

"Sean Connor, if you think a man in his sixties is old, I won't even ask what you think of me." Miss Ruth let her frustration show. "You have an extraordinary mind and heart, neither of which you are using right now. I have half a mind to disband this committee and never come here again."

Sean shivered and pulled the covers up to his chin. The flash in her eyes told him she meant it. "Okay, Ruthie."

"Old man, no give up. No die." Ivan hurried to the bed, gulped, and scampered back to the doorway.

"That's me-boy-o. Bill, check those measurements. Petroff, let these wonderful ladies know they can rub their hands over Sean's leg and stump."

Sean opened his mouth to protest, and Miss Ruth whispered, "These women need to feel your leg to determine the shape and size of the pad they are making. Let them do this."

He closed his eyes. The women took several minutes kneading and massaging the muscles from knee to hip, and they were tender with his stump and used some sort of ointment. They also kneaded and patted his good leg. He didn't ask why. Surprisingly, both legs felt better afterward.

Petroff explained that the women would make several seal skin pads to cushion his stump from the wood.

"There are several hardwoods at the mill. And I've got a fine piece of birch on my lathe. We'll have it ready soon," Bill said.

Everyone shuffled out, anxious to begin. They left Sean with nothing to do but continue to grieve.

"Whatever kind of peg leg they make, you'll learn to walk on." Miss Ruth said as she left.

He lay back and reached for his tobacco pouch. Ruthie had

taken it again. Dang it. "Nurse. Nurse," he yelled and threw his pillow at the door.

True to their word, they delivered the leg the following week. It had been designed by the committee. Sean hobbled on it for three days, enough to satisfy the Doc and get out of the Pioneer's Home.

Once settled in his own house, he unstrapped the leg, jammed it into the fireplace, and watched it burn.

That afternoon Miss Ruth let herself in. She raised the blinds and opened the windows to let out the stale tobacco odor. She shook Sean awake. "You didn't answer your phone, and I was worried. Where's your leg?" she asked as she searched the room.

"At the Native cemetery, according to you."

"That's not what I meant, and you know it."

"It didn't fit quite right, Ruthie. Painful."

"Then it's back to the drawing board."

It became a competition open to anyone in town—the prize: a free month of meals at the Café. Over the next week, nine legs were left on Sean's front porch. He tried each one for a week without knowing who had crafted it and then chose the one most comfortable.

To everyone's surprise, Ivan had designed the winning leg. After Bill Wall lathed it, Ivan added a brass hinge at the knee and a secret compartment that went undiscovered for years.

The rest were burned on the beach during a full moon with many speeches and toasts. Budnikov offered to come with his pushcart and sell clam chowder and smoked salmon. They agreed, but only if he changed the menu to hotdogs and potato chips.

TWENTY-FOUR

SAM, 1962

"I'm going to buy some forget-me-nots and put them on Sean's grave this afternoon."

"Alaska's state flower," Sam mumbled and reached for another cruller.

Alice wanted to slap his hand, playfully, of course, but that would embarrass them both. Instead, she reached for her coffee. "Poor Sean. I can only imagine what he went through. What happened immediately after his leg was amputated?"

"What do you mean?"

Alice laughed, "Some journalist you are. The leg was removed under unsanitary conditions without Sean's knowledge or consent. How did he react when he regained consciousness? How long before he forgave everyone, especially Miss Ruth?"

Sam scratched his head. "I'm not sure."

"And what about that infection? Did it reoccur? It can take months to find your balance, to adjust to a new way of walking. How did Sean manage? Did it change his personality? As a nurse, I have more questions."

"When I visited Connor, he was in a wheelchair and rarely wore his leg. I confess I never gave it a thought."

"You are so obsessed with Miss Ruth. It's given you tunnel vision, not a good thing for a newspaperman," she smiled to take the sting out of her words.

Sam ignored the criticism and said, "I'm sure she must have written about all that. I'll find those letters tonight. You'd make a good partner, Alice." Sam leaned back, a satisfied smile on his face. "Yes, a mighty fine partner."

Alice, red-faced, gathered her things, mumbled she was late for work, and rushed out of the office.

Margaret Mary slammed several galley proofs on Sam's desk. Her voice rose a notch, and she said, "Sam, how could you?"

Sam raised confused eyes to his faithful employee. "How could I what?"

"Talk to Alice like that! What kind of partner? Business partner? Tennis partner? Fishing partner?" Margaret Mary's index finger stabbed Sam's chest with each syllable. "What about dance partner, dating partner, marriage partner? Did you ever think of that?" She stomped back to her linotype machine.

Sam slumped in his chair and frowned. No, he hadn't thought about any of that. Perhaps, he should.

Margaret Mary gentled her voice and asked over her shoulder, "When are you going to ask that nice woman out on a date?"

Sam paused in the process of lighting his cigar. He swiveled in his chair, picked up the coffee pot, then slammed it down.

"Dinner? Dancing? The movies?"

He sucked on the stogie and puffed furiously until it gave him a headache. He rubbed his eyes and the back of his neck. Then stubbed out the cigar and lit another.

Should he call Alice? What could he say? How would she react? Various scenarios ran through his head, but he rejected them all. "It's not like that. The only thing she's interested in is Alaska's history, and Miss Ruth, of course."

Margaret Mary snorted, "Ask her out."

"I must be ten or fifteen years older." His sigh was heavy, and his expression bleak.

"Seven years, six months, and four days."

"She looks so much younger, and how do you know that?"

"You call yourself a newspaperman!" A grinning Margaret Mary settled herself in front of the linotype. She glanced at Sam and saw him staring at the telephone.

Sam groaned, pulled the latest article from his inbox, and promised himself he'd call Alice later. As soon as he figured out his approach, as soon as he had the words. As soon as he felt confident. Presently, all thoughts about how lovely she was faded from his thoughts.

TWENTY-FIVE

Dear Kamalei,

It's been several months, but Sean can hobble on his wooden leg without too much discomfort. Now it's time for me to take my father's remains home to the ranch and lay him next to my mother in the family cemetery. Will you please put flowers on Grandpa John's grave for me? You know the ones he likes...

—MISS RUTH'S LETTERS 1942

"I have been so concerned about myself. I never asked about your father," Sean frowned and rubbed his thigh. He really wanted to rub beyond the stump. The phantom pain in his missing leg distracted him.

"I'm taking him to the ranch."

Sean sat up straighter and said, "I'll come with you."

She hugged him, "Bless you, but you still see Nurse Maddie weekly. She's doing wonders for your rehabilitation. I won't interfere with that."

Sean blushed, "She's a slave driver."

"She finally figured out how to manage you, and you love it."

"I guess I do—too old for such dang fool feelings." He ducked his head and sighed. After a moment, he swallowed and said, "I'm sorry I didn't find your father alive. From the looks of it, he was in that mine for decades."

Miss Ruth winced but forced a neutral voice, "Perhaps it was for the best."

"Da loved him even though he didn't understand him. Ma said he never thought he was good enough for your grandfather."

Miss Ruth felt her heart constrict. So many misunderstandings led to so much tragedy. "Grandpa was a man's man, like the film star John Wayne. But he loved his son and forgave him for abandoning my mother and me."

"What about you?"

Rachel Ruth felt a stab near her heart, regret, guilt, anger? "Your mother and I had many long conversations about that. Because of her and Grandpa John, I chose to become better, not bitter. His rejection hurt me deeply. After all these years, I still occasionally struggle with it."

"Then why are you bothering to take his remains back to the ranch? You don't owe him anything; bury him here."

The question brought Miss Ruth back from her musings. "The watch you found was engraved with 'Locked in Holy Matrimony.' It must have meant something since he kept it all those years. My mother's grave is on the ranch, and her husband should lay beside her. It's my duty."

"As I said, you don't owe him anything, Ruthie. He didn't do his duty to you."

Miss Ruth came and sat next to her life-long friend. "It's hard to explain. Maybe I'm doing this for my mother. Even as she lay dying, Grandpa John said she forgave her husband and begged Grandpa to forgive also."

Sean patted her hand awkwardly. "Your mother sounds like a wonderful person. I wish we could have known her. I think John would be pleased you're taking his son to the ranch. You've never been to Hawaii to visit his grave, have you?"

"Fifty years in Alaska passed almost without me noticing, and there is still so much to do, now with the war..." she shrugged. "It seems like I arrived in Sitka yesterday, and fifteen minutes before that, a freckle-faced teenager visited the ranch and wanted to be a cowboy."

"I would have been a good one," Sean crowed, "When I was a little boy, Denver Dan...I'm sorry, Ruthie, I can't think of him as your father. John was a real father to you. Anyway, Denver played with me and told cowboy stories. He made it exciting, but he never said anything about his family."

Miss Ruth sniffed, then her eyes lit up. "You're right about Grandpa John. He was the best."

"In the early days, Da often called Denver the Rev because he preached so much. Ma thought he was preaching to himself."

"I hope he convinced himself of the truth."

They shared the silence as each reached back into their memories. Finally, Sean snickered and said, "Whatever happened to that nasty Thomas?"

"According to Aunt Ellie, he followed an English girl across Europe until her father bought him off. The word around town was he found another European heiress and perfected the art of the ardent suitor worried fathers paid to have disappear."

"Miserable excuse for a man."

"It's just too sad," she said.

"Don't waste your pity on him. He was not a real man."

"Sean, what about Braxton? I haven't thought about him in half a century."

"All that God-talk from Ma finally got to him. He put his detective skills on the case to prove that she was a fool to believe there was a God. Braxton investigated. Ma prayed. Incredible!"

"No one had more integrity than Braxton. Tell me what happened."

"He married a good Christian widow with six kids and pastors a little church in the Ozarks."

Miss Ruth laughed until the tears flowed down her cheeks. She slapped her knee. Much as she tried, Miss Ruth could not picture the Pinkerton man as a pastor, or in the Ozarks, with six kids. "Braxton? God does have a sense of humor."

Sean rubbed his aching leg. He reached for his bowl of lemon drops. "You came to Alaska to find your father. Now that you have, will you stay in the states or come back?"

She threw a pillow at him, which he deftly caught and threw back. "Don't you ever think such a thing. My children are scattered throughout Alaska. Everyone I love is here—you, most of all."

TWENTY-SIX

SAM, 1962

Sam hurried across the street to the Pioneer's Home. Nurse Maddie, nearing retirement age, stood behind the reception desk. Sam made a mental note to interview her about Sean Connor, but not today. "Where's Alice?"

"And good afternoon to you too, Mr. Sam Mitchell."

"Sorry. Didn't mean to be rude. I need to see Alice."

"She just finished her rounds and is in the dining room, I think."

Sam hurried down the hall, waving an envelope. "Alice, I found another letter about Sean. I knew there had to be more. It was misfiled. Actually, it was under Sadsack's blanket." Sam sat down, red-cheeked and out of breath.

"Coffee, Sam?" Alice poured a cup at his nod.

"Before I read it, I want to warn you."

"That sounds serious," she smiled over the rim of her china cup.

"It is. Remember the trial of Anna Marie Wall in Juneau?"

"I read what you wrote in the paper, but you didn't want to talk about it at the time."

Sam felt a wave of heat roll across his face. What kind of hard-nosed reporter was he when a story made him want to weep or throw furniture across the room. He buried his angst and said, "Little Anna Marie helped her sister care for Connor." He pulled a handkerchief out of his back pocket. "Poor kid."

Alice laid her hand on his arm. "I'm sorry, Sam."

"I don't think anyone in this town was unaffected by her murder. I'm sure the trial brought many of those feelings back to the surface."

"What does the letter say?"

Sam stared out the window. "She was a great kid. She used to sell newspapers during the Depression. I remember she conned Dad into giving her the papers, and she kept all the money." Sam appeared lost in thought.

"Read the letter, Sam," Alice said gently.

TWENTY-SEVEN

Dear Kamalei,

Although the news of the war remains grim, I am grateful you and your family are safe. Please keep me informed. I know our letters go through the censors, and so much is blacked out, but tell me what you can.

I have my tickets to Seattle on the Star of Alaska and train tickets to Dallas.

Sean is angry that I will not let him accompany me, but he still needs Nurse Maddie to oversee his rehabilitation exercises. Our Firy and Anna Marie will cook and clean for him while I am gone...

—MISS RUTH'S LETTERS 1942

Miss Ruth opened the gate and walked up the wooden sidewalk to the white clapboard house on Biorka Street. She straightened her collar and put a smile on her face. Popeye's bark announced her arrival before she could knock on the door.

"Do I have to, Miss Ruth?" Sixteen-year-old Firy Wall bit her bottom lip and whined, "It's just that with school and cooking and cleaning..." her voice drifted away when she saw Miss Ruth's face.

"Masha does all the cooking, and Elizaveta could help more, right? You can take Anna Marie with you." Miss Ruth put her arm around the miserable girl. "Someday, you will be a wife and in charge of all the cooking and cleaning. This will be good practice."

"I'd rather work in the yard or garden, paint the fence, anything but cook."

Miss Ruth laughed. "It's only for a few weeks. You'll be fine."

Firy didn't think so, but there was no point in trying to sway Miss Ruth once she had something settled in her mind.

Anna Marie jumped over the low picket gate and ran up the wooden sidewalk. "I'm home."

Miss Ruth hugged her, "I'm glad. I have an important job for you. Our Firy will cook for a dear friend, and I want you to dust and Hoover and visit with him."

Firy's rigid face told Anna Marie everything had been settled and not to Firy's liking. "Who is he? Where does he live? Do I know him? Can Popeye come, too? He's a good dog."

"You might have seen him at the Pioneer's Home. His name is Sean Connor."

"The cranky one-legged man! He just sat in the corner and growled like a big old bear. He never bought my newspapers."

Miss Ruth squeezed Anna Marie's hand. "I met him when he was a little younger than Our Firy and a little older than you—a red-headed boy with a face full of freckles."

"His hair is gone, and he has a face full of wrinkles. Why do you want us to help him?"

"Sean is back in his home now and needs some help. I'm his only family, but I'll be gone for a few weeks."

"You can't be his wife. Everybody knows you're an old maid."

Firy clamped her hand over her little sister's mouth and said, "Sorry, Miss Ruth."

The old maid laughed and tugged on Anna Marie's braid, "He's as dear to me as if he were my brother. He's not really cranky."

"Yes, he is!" Anna Marie pushed her hands into her pockets. "That started when he lost his leg."

"You mean when they held him down in that old mine shaft, and Our Firy's boyfriend cut his leg off?" She made sawing motions.

"How did you know about that?" Firy asked.

Anna Marie put her hands on her hips and stared at her sister. "Puh-lease, this is Sitka; everybody knows everything. Besides, those old men at the Pioneer's Home tell me stuff."

Firy wondered if she should pay those old men a visit. Things happened in Sitka that no seven-year-old should know about, especially since the war had started and all those GIs arrived. Firy mentally rehearsed the lecture she planned to give those old codgers and missed Miss Ruth's last few sentences.

"...so you see, I need your help."

"We can do it, Miss Ruth. Our Firy can cook, and I can dust. That should make him happy." Anna Marie pulled on her braids and said, "Who will give him his bath? Old men get smelly, you know."

Firy's face flamed. She had never been able to teach Anna Marie to think before speaking, but Miss Ruth laughed and said, "Firy's boyfriend, Bumps, said he'd come once a week, more if he can get leave."

"I wish I could go to the United States with you, Miss Ruth. I've never been off the island."

"Me either," Firy said, then muttered under her breath, "Being somewhere else sounds better than taking care of this old man."

Anna Marie turned to her older sister and tugged on her blouse. "You've told me stories about the summer Miss Ruth took you to Port Alexander."

Miss Ruth and Firy smiled at each other over Anna Marie's head as memories of Franella Feddersen and rumors of a Russian princess showed on their faces.

"Port Alexander is on Baranof Island. Our Firy hasn't been anywhere else."

Anna Marie sucked on her bottom lip and complained, "I've never been anywhere but Sitka, and I probably never will." She stuck her hands in her overall pockets and found a piece of bubble gum. Her face brightened, and she grinned. "Never mind. I'm going to ask Mr. Sean what it was like to have his leg sawed off. I bet there was blood everywhere. I asked Bumps, but he wouldn't talk about it."

"It's a serious thing, Anna Marie, tragic. He was unconscious, and when he woke up, his leg was gone. He still hasn't accepted the reality of it," Miss Ruth said.

"Why not? All he has to do is look down and see it's not there."

Firy grabbed her little sister's shoulder and hissed again, "Anna Marie, you can't say things like that."

Miss Ruth pulled several sheets of paper from her pocketbook. "Here's a list of chores and some simple recipes Sean likes. You can pick up stuff at the grocer's as needed, and Sean will settle with him later."

As Miss Ruth left, she wondered how the girls would do. Our Firy would be efficient and silent. Little Anna Marie would say whatever came into her head. If anybody could shake Sean out of his doldrums, it would probably be the freckle-faced little girl.

Sean Connor rolled a cigarette, then pulled the curtain aside when he heard their voices. Here they were again, right on time.

He scowled and grimaced at the phantom pain. When would it stop? When would he feel like himself again? He slapped his thigh and swore at the leg that wasn't there.

"Get the door. These groceries are heavy." Firy did not look at the old man slouched in the overstuffed chair as she carried the groceries through his living room and set them on the kitchen table. As she put them away and prepared the dinner meal, she kept one ear attuned to the conversation in the living room.

"Hey, Mr. Sean, we're here." The little girl perched on the footstool in front of the old man. "It's polite to say hello.".

"I told you before, I can take care of myself."

"Miss Ruth says you can't. So there."

He cursed under his breath and tossed his tobacco pouch toward the table. It fell to the floor. Anna Marie picked it up and patted his leg just above the stump. "Miss Ruth says you're only cranky when the leg that isn't there hurts."

He flinched, and she patted his stump again. "The last time we were here, you made Our Firy cry."

The old man flushed and averted his eyes. "I didn't ask her to come."

"She sniffed a lot and wiped her eyes. That's the same as crying."

Firy came to the doorway, dishtowel in hand. "Anna Marie, stop talking and start dusting."

Cupboard doors slammed, the silverware drawer rattled, and pots banged onto the stove.

"Mr. Sean," Anna Marie tugged on his empty pant leg. "Our Firy made your dinner every night for a long time, and you never said thank you."

He shifted in his chair. "Where's my tobacco pouch?"

"Miss Ruth said you were her best friend, but I don't like you." Anna Marie glared at him.

"She said that? I'm the best?"

"She said you were a brother to her." Anna Marie tugged on the empty pant leg again. "The important part is—I don't like you."

"Anna Marie, come into the kitchen right now."

Before obeying her older sister, Anna Marie stuck her tongue out at Sean Connor. His eyes were on his tobacco pouch, and he didn't see.

Firy got down on her knees and held her sister by the shoulders. "You can't say whatever pops into your head."

The girl stood mute, first on one foot, then the other. She had heard these words too many times, and her eyes glazed over. Firy pulled her little sister close and whispered in her ear. "What would Miss Ruth do if she were you?"

"Our Firy, you are so smart." Anna Marie grinned, ran back to the living room, and sat cross-legged on the stool. She cupped her chin in her hands and stared at the old man but did not speak.

He squirmed, shifted in the well-worn chair, and finally blurted, "I don't like you either."

Anna Marie tilted her head but didn't bat an eye. She reached over and patted the old man's stump again."The trouble with you, Mr. Sean, is that you have never been a grandpa-man."

"Oww! You hurt my leg!"

"But it's not there."

"It hurts anyway. Get me that aspirin bottle." He pointed to the mantle.

Anna Marie handed him the bottle and whispered, "Does it hurt very much?"

"Like he...Like heck," he said.

She poked at the artificial limb leaning against the wall. "Does it make your leg hurt when you wear that thing?"

"What kind of a stupid ..." he saw the concern in her eyes. "Yes," he said softly.

Firy stood in the doorway and motioned her sister over. "Do the dusting, and let's get out of here."

"He's lonely, and his leg hurts."

"He said he didn't like you."

Anna Marie bit her bottom lip, then grinned so big her freckles popped, "Everybody likes me, even Mr. Sean. He just doesn't know it."

Firy tugged on Anna Marie's braid and went back to the kitchen. She added potatoes, carrots, and onions to the browned stew meat, then set the cast-iron pot on the back burner to simmer in a rich, thick gravy. Stew was easy enough and Mr. Connor's favorite.

She tossed the potato peelings onto the compost heap and surveyed the small backyard. There was room enough here for an oil tank. Papa Bill and Mr. Connor must be the only two in Sitka that hadn't converted their old wood cookstoves to oil. Perhaps they were the smart ones with the war's rationing and the high oil prices.

Firy grabbed the ax and attacked the woodpile. She filled the kindling box and thought she'd ask Bumps and a couple of his army buddies to chop some of the bigger logs.

It would be difficult for Mr. Connor to balance himself on his wooden leg and swing the ax. Despite herself, she almost felt sorry for him. Perhaps if her own life weren't so difficult, she might have some pity left over for someone besides herself.

She grabbed the broom and attacked the kitchen floor. The voices in the other room rose and fell. Soon, the broom stilled, and she leaned against the wall near the door to the living room.

"Mr. Sean, Miss Ruth said you're a nice man."

He cracked his knuckles and turned away. Anna Marie scooted the footstool closer. Sean scratched his stump, started to swear, then growled, "I lost a leg. Nothing nice about that."

Anna Marie jumped off the stool, put her hands on her hips, and almost shouted at the old man, "There is a three-legged dog in Indiantown. He's just as fast as the others and nice, too. He's just like all the other dogs, and so are you. Like other people, I mean, except you are not nice." She stamped her foot. "So there!"

Firy put her hands over her eyes and waited for an explosion from Mr. Connor. None came. She risked a peek. The old man's lips twitched, then he frowned and whined, "But you said you didn't like me."

Anna Marie fingered her loose tooth and smiled. "I would if you were my grandpa-man."

He was silent for a moment, then raised his eyebrows and said, "You're a pip, just a pip."

"I don't know what that means."

"It means you are a lot like Miss Ruth. Do you play cribbage?"

"She taught me. I'm not very good."

"I'll not go easy on you. It's a penny a point."

"I don't have any pennies." She turned the pockets of her overalls inside out. A small feather fluttered to the floor, and an empty bubble gum wrapper did as well. A single lemon drop, covered in fuzz and stuck to the pocket fabric, caught Sean Connor's eye.

"Fancy lemon drops, do you?"

Anna Marie nodded, pulled the drop off the material, and put it in her mouth. "Miss Ruth says they do a body good when you need more sunshine in your heart."

He pointed to a glass candy dish on the coffee table. " Spit that one out and help yourself to some unfuzzy ones."

She lifted the lid, popped one in her mouth, and filled her pockets. "We could play for lemon drops."

"Nope. Gotta be pennies."

Firy clenched her jaw and stepped toward them, then backed into the kitchen, smiling, when she heard her little sister say, "A real grandpa-man would give his grand-girls lots of pennies. Especially when they cook and clean for him."

Despite himself, Sean laughed and picked up a wooden bowl filled with copper coins. "Take a handful, a small one."

TWENTY-EIGHT

SAM, 1962

Sam reread the letter that evening and then berated himself for doing so. He pulled a handkerchief from his back pocket and blew his nose. Connor was right; Anna Marie was a pip. What would her life have been had she not lost it so early?

Sam crumpled the handkerchief and stomped to his laundry basket. Say the word, Sam, say it. She didn't lose her life. It was taken from her and brutally. Murdered. He paced and swore.

Who would she have become? What talents would she have developed? What gifts would she have brought to the world?

Agitated, Sam grabbed his jacket and headed to Totem Park. The thick forest of Western Hemlock and Sitka Spruce dominated the woods. Their great height formed a canopy that diffused the sun's light on clear days and the moisture when it rained. Several kinds of moss, as stubborn as barnacles, attached themselves to the tree trunks. Their variegated yellow-greens enhanced the ethereal quality of the forest. The bay, parallel to the park, echoed the sound of the tide's ebb and flow.

This timeless, tranquil forest mirrored Eden and made him think of infinity. He hoped Anna Marie was somewhere in that eternal place, somewhere happy.

He wondered if a phone call to Firy Baas in Washington State would be profitable. The Letter to the Editor he had received from her told him nothing, and Sam sensed there was more to her story.

He shoved his hands in his pockets and walked the mile-long loop twice, but it didn't calm him. He left the park and went out of his way to stop at Alice's house.

"Will you walk with me in Totem Park? The drizzle is light, and there is a patch of blue sky to the east.""

"You seem frazzled. I'll get my coat."

They walked under the calm overhanging green. Jagged stumps from fallen trees were covered with thick moss, and raindrops clung to every surface. The trail looped through the park and was as familiar to Sam as his own backyard.

"It's so beautiful here, Sam. I must remember to come again."

His heart said *with me,* but what came out of his mouth was, "I can't get Miss Ruth out of my mind."

"Out of your heart."

"Why do you say that?"

Alice laughed, "Sam Mitchell, Jr., you think you're a hard-bitten journalist, jaded and worldly-wise."

"Thanks for the compliment."

"It wasn't, and you're not. You're a romantic."

"How can you say that?"

"You have spent over a year finding everyone who had a story about Miss Ruth. You've combed state records, church archives, and all of Alaska's newspapers. No crumb was too small for you to collect. You've poured over Kamalei's letters, reading them multiple times."

"That makes me a good investigative reporter, not a romantic."

"You need to ask yourself why you're obsessed with a woman who was old enough to be your grandmother. Think about it seriously."

"She lived through so much. I just want to see the times through her eyes."

"It's more than that, Sam."

A narrow path through the bushes led to the rocky beach. They sat on a large driftwood log and stared across the bay. A whale breached. Eagles soared. Ravens argued, and Sam confessed he didn't have an answer.

He reached for her hand and blinked into her shimmering eyes. "You think you know, don't you?"

"Oh, I know." She pulled a bag of lemon drops out of her pocket and gave him one.

"How did you know about the lemon drops?"

She popped one into her mouth with a grin, "No one can have a conversation with you without learning something about Miss Ruth. I loved her little lemon drop ministry. I have a standing order at the grocery store."

Sam laughed, "Alice, I just lo...that is... tell me what you think you know."

"I'll tell you part of it, and you can figure out the rest."

"Tell me everything."

She squeezed his hand. "I think you pursue the image of the cynical reporter, although it's not your nature. It keeps you safe and uninvolved. Emotionally, I mean."

Sam picked up a handful of rocks, stood at the water's edge, and threw them into the water, watching them skip and bounce across the surface. This conversation was headed in a direction he didn't like.

Alice watched him for a moment, then stood by his side. "That's why Miss Ruth appeals. You're right; she lived through interesting times and important events. You're a history buff, and that appeals, but I think you're jealous of how she connected with people. She cared deeply for everyone she met, especially the children."

"Hmmm." Sam shoved his hands into his pockets. He didn't want to hear the word jealous and wondered if it hit the mark. "That still doesn't tell me what angle the book should have."

"Throw away your notes and your spreadsheets Sam. Look at how she impacted people emotionally and spiritually. If you do, you'll connect with Miss Ruth profoundly—as deep as those who knew her."

Sam continued to stare across the water.

"Admit it, Sam. You're half in love with her already." Alice picked up a handful of rocks.

He watched this cheechako as she skipped rocks into the calm water. She barely came to his shoulder. Her hair glinted in Sitka's late evening sun, and he wanted to touch its warm softness. Almost without thinking, he raised his hand, then turned away and murmured, "No, not her."

A few days later, Alice, on her way to collect the mail for the Pioneer's Home, met Sam as he came out of the post office. "I'd like to continue our conversation from the other day."

He shifted his mail, threw his cigar in the gutter, and said, "As long as you don't tell me I'm in love with Miss Ruth."

She laughed, "You're drawn to how she loved people."

"I don't know why she fascinates me. She's Alaska."

"Her love was supernatural, mystical."

"She was interesting and lived through interesting times, that's all."

Alice felt like stamping her foot; instead, she bit the inside of her cheek. "I've done my own investigating, Sam."

Sam winked, and his eyes retained a twinkle. "I don't want to offend you, but you don't have the skills or the resources."

"Being a nurse gives me a lot of skill. I have a trained scientific mind. I'm analytical and hope I have a compassionate heart."

He took her arm and motioned her to the bench near the seawall in Totem Square. "You have a good mind and a tender heart. I wasn't implying otherwise."

Alice settled on the bench and breathed deeply in the salty air. "I love this little patch of green between the water and downtown." Gulls called to one another as she turned and faced Sam. "You want to know where Miss Ruth went, what she did, the people she talked to, and how she influenced them. I'm going in a different direction."

"What other direction is there?"

"I'm on the verge of discovering something. I can feel it."

"Not very analytical or scientific."

"The heart has its own way of thinking. We know Miss Ruth connected with people, even the rascals, down-and-outers, and ne'er-do-wells. I think her love and concern for others came from God."

Sam frowned, and Alice tugged on his arm. "Hear me out, Sam. She was involved with various churches and missions. I've visited as many as I could."

"They all say something different, and each one thinks they are in the right."

"I'm trying to find universal themes, common principles, whatever allowed Miss Ruth to be a part of them."

Sam rubbed his cheek, gazed at the top of the totem, and said, "You may be on to something. Miss Ruth had a deep character that drew people to her. It's possible it was supernatural or spiritual."

Alice grinned at him and her eyes danced, "Do I detect a new respect for me, Sam Mitchell?"

"Alice Blakely, I have the greatest respect for you. In fact, I...I... keep going to those churches, and let me know what you find out."

"I will." She tapped her watch. "I'm late for work" Halfway across the street, Alice turned and called to him with a smile and a wink. "You could always come with me. Do a little spiritual investigating on your own."

Nurse Maddie put her hand over the receiver and said, "Phone for you."

Alice shrugged out of her coat, and before she could say hello, a tinny voice came through the receiver, "Did you see the look on his face?"

"Margaret Mary, is that you?"

"Of course, it's me. Answer the question."

Alice twirled the phone cord between her fingers and turned her back to Nurse Maddie, who leaned toward her while stacking papers and fiddling with her pencil.

"I don't know what you're talking about," Alice forced a sternness into her voice.

"I was two steps behind you and Sam, but you were so absorbed in each other you didn't notice me. I even followed you to the Square, sat on the seawall, and listened."

"I can't believe you did that."

"I saw the love on Sam's face, and whenever he stutters, it means he's struggling with his emotions. This is good. This is really good."

"Don't you say anything to him," Alice hissed into the phone.

"I'm just going to push him a little."

"Don't you dare! I can wait a little longer." Alice bit her lip, knowing she didn't want to wait.

"Honey, you aren't getting any younger."

TWENTY-NINE

Dear Kamalei,

After nearly ten years at the school and my constant conflicts with her, the Reverend Mrs. Monroe has given up trying to transform me into her image. Lending me to the Lutherans, Methodists, and others only lasted so long.

According to her, I couldn't perform my duties adequately in the kitchen or the laundry. Her acute lack of qualified teachers forced her to put me back into the classroom.

Now she has banished me to an isolated community north of Kodiak Island. My task is to civilize and Americanize both the Aleut and the Alutiig-Russian children. Can you imagine...

—MISS RUTH'S LETTERS 1901

Miss Ruth answered the knock on the storage room door and greeted the Reverend Mr. Monroe, who tugged at his starched white collar. He looked askance at the small cot in the corner of the room. "I'm so sorry you've been put here. Such a shame."

"I'm fine."

"Not fine. Not fine at all." His Adam's apple bobbed with every syllable, and his sallow face frowned. "I'm afraid you've been assigned to a primitive village on a remote island. The schoolhouse burned several years ago, and the teacher was reassigned."

"Oh, dear."

"There have been no classes since then. Usually, older, more experienced teachers are sent to such remote areas. But my wife thought, she thought—" He pulled at his collar again.

Miss Ruth could imagine what his wife thought. "It's okay, Reverend Mr.—"

"Please, just Mr., I don't feel too reverent." He balanced on one foot and then the other, clearly uncomfortable.

"I'd invite you in, but there is no place to sit except the bed."

He took two steps back, noticed the hallway appeared empty, and whispered, "Quite all right. No need." He wiped his red face with a large white handkerchief.

"Why have you come, uh, Mr. Monroe?"

"Sabotage. She wants you to fail. No supplies, you see." He licked his lips and glanced at the empty hallway again.

Miss Ruth's ire rose, but she smoothed her features and calmed her voice, "Is there a place for me to live, a school?"

"An empty building once used to store furs. Set aside for the school."

"And my living quarters?"

"A room partitioned for you, most unsuitable. What to do?"

Miss Ruth frowned but promised herself she would make do, "Thank you for telling me, Mr. Monroe. I will try to find some books or pencils, something."

He blinked several times and pulled a paper from his pocket. "Address of the government commissioner for the Kodiak region. List of supplies the school is entitled to."

"I will write him tonight and post this before I leave Sitka. How long before I can expect them to arrive?"

"Two months, maybe longer, if he sends them at all." He swallowed, and his Adam's apple bobbed again.

"But what will I do in the meantime?"

The Reverend Mr. Monroe leaned toward Miss Ruth and whispered, "Confiscated a few supplies, a dozen books, old magazines, food, and personals for you. Signed my wife's name. Already on the steamship. A grave sin."

"That was very brave, and I don't think it was a sin. I think you were righting a wrong."

"To be sure. To be sure." He wiped his face one more time, frowned in her direction, and then brightened his face. He looked past her to the shelves and cupboards in the storeroom. "Take whatever you want from here."

Miss Ruth thought she heard him mutter *if you dare* as he hurried away. He turned at the end of the hallway and gave her a long stare. "God bless."

The fully stocked storeroom looked like a mercantile. She poked around the shelves and found enough supplies for the year and extras for fun activities and celebrating Christmas.

She found three steamer trunks in the corner under an old canvas. She pulled the largest to the center of the room and filled it. Then for good measure, she packed another with additional materials, everything she thought she might need. She laughed aloud and danced around the trunks. *I dare, Mr. Monroe. Oh, I dare.*

That evening Miss Ruth left the school grounds for her favorite trail in Totem Park. In 1890, the same year she had arrived in Alaska, President Harrison had declared the site a national park. To the people of Sitka, it was where the Russians and Tlingits had battled so many years ago.

The first star appeared in the darkening but cloudless sky. Miss Ruth felt the rumblings of war within her. She wasn't sure where the battle lines would be drawn, but drawn they would be.

She almost wished she could be like many other teachers and staff, stern and unyielding when the Reverend Mrs. Monroe was in sight, quietly comforting and encouraging the students when she was not. This was a battle tactic Miss Ruth could not employ. It confused and upset the children.

The edges of the trail to the beach were jammed with blueberry, salmonberry, and devil's club bushes. A lone totem stood vigil, and a single fishing boat was moored in Jamestown Bay.

She sat on a log near the mouth of Indian River. Behind her, towering Western Hemlock and Red Alder spread their canopies and crowded out the once abundant Sitka Spruce.

Miss Ruth clenched her jaw and rubbed her palms on her thighs. She took several deep breaths and tried to calm herself. It had been a challenging decade.

Her decade-long conflict with school authorities and frustration over strict rules and policies she had no power to change had taken their toll. She spent most of her days glancing over her shoulder, wondering if she would be reprimanded again for being kind to the children.

The moonlight reflected off the water— serene, peaceful. Miss Ruth was not. Her decade in Alaska had given her little time and less opportunity to inquire after her father. The failure settled heavily in her heart next to her classroom frustrations.

Above her, stars like gemstones glittered in a navy sky. A faint clapping raised her head; she stood and circled herself searching for the origin of the sound. The sky undulated with translucent purple streaks laced with seven shades of green. The colored light reached down, swaddled the Tlingit's pole, and wrapped itself around the white man's boat.

It encased Miss Ruth, centered between the totem and the boat. She turned around again, eyes wide, breathing hard. This meant something, but what?

In awe, Miss Ruth stood immobile at the water's edge of this Alaskan forest. She watched the aurora until it gradually faded. The night sky— vast, unending, and beautiful. Her future—arduous, challenging, and unknown.

Rachel Ruth Merritt raised her hands to the One who created it all. Her battle plans fell away, and a wave of peace as inspiring as the Aurora Borealis flooded her soul. She would love God and do the right thing no matter how difficult. She would keep her eyes on the night sky wherever she was sent and whatever she was sent to do.

She returned to her little cot in the storeroom and slept.

The weather from Sitka to Kodiak cooperated, and the steamship made the over five-hundred-mile trip in record time. Miss Ruth, bundled in her long wool coat, leaned over the rail and wished she had worn the clothes the Tlingit elder had given her so many years ago.

She viewed the choppy, gray waves and thought about the Reverend Mrs. Monroe's last lecture delivered with a voice as frigid as these waters:

"Miss Ruth, I have tried these past ten years to guide you, and you have thwarted me. Even lending you to those cold-hearted Lutherans did not change you. Indeed, you disappeared for weeks after they returned. God alone knows what you were up to during that time." She shook her head and shuddered. "My letters to the Reverend Jackson have not been answered as I would have liked."

Hands folded in her lap, Miss Ruth asked, "What answer were you expecting?"

"To have you terminated, of course. I have made no secret about my opinion of you." The older woman had shuffled the papers on her desk and observed Miss Ruth over her spectacles. "I must say you seem rather unconcerned about your future."

Miss Ruth curled her toes inside her cowboy boots and used all of her strength not to respond in anger or frustration. She swallowed twice and kept her voice low. "I imagine you will inform me of your plans for me."

The Reverend Mrs. Monroe stood and leaned over her desk. Spittle gathered at the corners of her mouth, and her eyes narrowed. "I want you out of my sight! You have been disrespectful, obstinate, arrogant, and stubborn. Everything I abhor in the younger generation. Since I cannot fire you, I have another solution. You are going to a remote village across the Gulf. You will agree that my perspective is correct once you see how primitive and savage these people are."

Miss Ruth held tight to the ship's rail and remembered how she did not give in to her anger as she struggled to remain calm in front of the Reverend Mrs. Monroe. The peace she received on the night of the aurora again infused her soul.

She rubbed her gloved hands over her face and glanced at the shoreline of Kodiak Island. The first stop on her journey to the small villages on Afognak.

Miss Ruth's things had been deposited on the beach. She leaned against the steamer trunk and waited, but the escort from Afognak did not arrive. After a time, the Lutheran pastor, Mr. Nystrom, was informed that Afognak's new teacher was stranded on the beach. He and his wife hurried to her.

"How long have you been here, my dear?" Mrs. Nystrom's face was encased in a fur hood and could barely be seen. The sealskin parka and fur mukluks made the petite woman appear as broad as she was tall.

"Long enough that my teeth are chattering and my toes are frozen."

"You must come home with us. The inter-island steamer to Afognak is not due for two weeks."

"I was to be met and taken to Afognak straight away. Classes are to start in a few days."

The minister laughed, then hailed several men to come and help. They carried her luggage to the parsonage, tipped their caps, and left.

Mrs. Nystrom, not at all wide once her furs had been removed, settled Miss Ruth in the parlor close to the wood-burning stove. The pastor's wife explained how things worked in this part of Alaska. "My dear, your classes will start when you are ready, not before, and the school year will end when you say it does."

"I have instructions and schedules from the Reverend Mrs. Monroe, a list of government policies and standards. She said the District Commissioner will oversee and police me."

"Fortunately for you, the District Commissioner does not often visit. I teach at the school here in Kodiak, and I have not seen him for the last five years."

Miss Ruth's grin nearly split her face, and Mrs. Nystrom raised her eyebrows.

"But my instructions, my lists?" Miss Ruth tried to sound concerned and failed.

"You might as well tear them up. Your classes will be interrupted, and the school forced to close by storms, blizzards, sickness, Russian holidays, fish camp, clamming, hunting, and a host of cultural conflicts."

"I didn't see any Russian holidays listed for school closure."

"My dear Miss Ruth," Mrs. Nystrom handed Miss Ruth a cup of tea. "This part of Alaska is more Russian than American. My advice is to make friends with the Orthodox priest. It will make your life much easier."

"I will do that, although surely, he has no authority over the school."

The Swedish woman's titter was tinged with frustration, "The Yupiks and Aleuts have no concept of democracy or how the United States functions. It means little to them that we bought Alaska. The Tsar is the highest authority for most villagers, and the priest is his representative."

"But surely—"

"You will see a picture of the Tsar in nearly every home. In fact, almost everyone thinks the Tsar is in charge of America. I can tell you all I have learned about avoiding the District Commissioner and how to deal with the culture, although I teach at the white school. The best thing you can do is make friends with the priest."

❧

Two weeks later, Miss Ruth and her belongings were again deposited on a beach. This time, it seemed the whole village came to meet the steamship. The boys and men carried her belongings and escorted her to the empty fur storage shed.

It took several days for her to scrub and organize the schoolroom. For now, the children would have to sit on the floor. There were no desks or benches. She commissioned someone local to build them and a large desk for her and a storage cupboard.

The abandoned fur shed lacked a source of heat. Miss Ruth purchased two wood stoves, one for the school and one for her small quarters. She sent all the invoices and bills to the District Commissioner and hoped he would pay them and not visit.

The storekeeper arranged for the stoves' installation and had several cords of seasoned spruce delivered and stacked outside her door. He would replenish the supply as needed.

Oliver Virtanen, the Finnish manager of the fish cannery, brought his two sons to meet her. Even if there had been a school here for white students, his children would not be allowed to attend since their mother was a Yupik.

After seeing that she had no furniture, he sent a bed, two chairs, and a small table. He also dropped off a dozen wooden crates used to pack the cans of fish.

Grateful she had packed a small toolkit she found in the storeroom, Miss Ruth nailed the crates to the wall to use as shelves. She pulled a small bear rug from the steamer trunk and placed it in front of the wood stove. She felt cozy and at home once the stove had warmed the room.

Miss Ruth determined the smell of uncured furs and her spartan living quarters would not lessen her desire to have a meaningful impact in this isolated and unknown village. The children here were as important in God's eyes as children anywhere. She put her tools away, smoothed her apron, and made a list of remaining tasks to accomplish before she could open the school.

She spent the next few days visiting and encouraging each family to enroll their children. Miss Ruth remembered Mrs. Nystrom's advice and sought out the Orthodox priest.

The middle-aged man clad in priestly garb invited her to tea.

"May I have a list of Russian holidays when the children will not be in school?"

"What?"

"And can you teach me about them so we can celebrate them in class?"

"What?"

"And are there any special foods the children favor at holiday time? Perhaps the mothers could show me how to make those special treats."

"What?"

"Are there any other traditions, Alutiig, Yupik, or Russian, that I should know about?" She handed him a list of words several pages long, "Can you translate this list into Russian and whatever language the others speak?"

The priest's wife poured tea into a delicate china cup and offered Miss Ruth an assortment of tea cakes.

"This is a beautiful cup and saucer." Miss Ruth held it high before taking a sip. "And your home is lovely, especially your crocheted tablecloth and curtains."

"The porcelain tea set is from Russia. Over half of my dinnerware did not survive the trip, but all the teacups arrived intact." Her dark eyes sparkled. "I've crocheted everything you see. Every woman in the village crochets and knits." She smiled often, although she did not participate in the conversation again.

Everywhere Miss Ruth looked, she saw white crocheted antimacassars spread over every chair's arm and settee's back. Several crocheted pillows covered the velvet settee, and the priest's wife wore a crocheted shawl.

After taking several tea cakes and thanking his wife, the priest smiled slightly and said, "Miss Ruth, surely you are aware you cannot teach our traditions or culture.

"Cannot?"

"Not allowed to." He smiled, and she knew he understood her. "Nor are you allowed to use our words. Only English is spoken in the schools, although many of your students will be trilingual, English, Russian, and their respective Native languages. But in the classroom, only American ways are tolerated. After all, we are savages and must be civilized."

Miss Ruth's face flamed, "I realize that is the official policy, Father, but it's not mine. I find great difficulty in being official." She smoothed her skirt and fingered the packet of lemon drops in her pocket.

He chuckled and reached for another teacake, "Although you may be good for my village and its children, I am afraid you will not last long." His bushy eyebrows merged as he drew them together.

Miss Ruth studied the man across the elegant tea table. He was of mixed heritage, and seemed to be sympathetic. She smiled at him and said, "Perhaps I can do some good while here. The island is fairly isolated. I may be here longer than you think."

"We will hope so. When the Russians came, they were cruel and mistreated us, but they intermarried in time, and there was no shame in having mixed blood. I myself am a Creole. My mother was Yupik, and my father, a Russian. I was educated in San Francisco, studied for the priesthood, and ordained in St. Petersburg."

"You are a long way from St. Petersburg." Miss Ruth lifted her head and responded, "And I'm far from the officials in Washington, DC."

"But not so far from the Reverend Mrs. Monroe. I'm afraid she has the ear of the district's Educational Commissioner."

"I will pray she doesn't hear anything about my activities on poor little Afognak."

"Just so." He stood and held out his hand.

"Thank you, Father. Are we allies?"

"Yes, allies!"

THIRTY

Dear Kamalei,

I wonder if the Reverend Mrs. Monroe was right...no, I refuse to even entertain the thought.

Two weeks ago, Captain Walker delivered freight to Kodiak, and while some minor repairs were made to The Aloha, he came to Afognak. I miss him dreadfully now that he is gone. He visited my classroom every day and delighted my students with sea-faring tales. I traced his travels on my large wall map, but I don't think the children understood how big the world really is. How could they...

—MISS RUTH'S LETTERS 1903

The Dora's deep-throated whistle thrilled Miss Ruth, and like the rest of the villagers, she bundled up, braved the cold rain, and hurried to the beach. The malevolent weather had kept the intrepid little steamer away for nearly four weeks.

The still wicked wind and waves forced the ship to anchor offshore. The United States mail, many crates and boxes of freight, and a single passenger were lowered into the steamer's lifeboats.

Members of the Dora's crew, clad in bright yellow sou'westers and oilskin slickers, pulled for shore. One rowboat flipped, flinging the mail and freight into the breakers. The two oarsmen clung to the boat as it crashed through the waves pounding the shore.

Unmindful of the freezing water, the villagers ran into the surf, rescuing the mail sack and as much freight as possible. They helped the drenched and sputtering oarsmen to the shore. The storekeeper pulled several blankets off his shelves and draped them around the men.

The Russian priest and the Aleut chief conferred with Miss Ruth. At her nod, they directed the villagers to take everything to the school.

She heard her name above the biting wind and turned. "Captain Walker!' she screamed and threw herself into his arms for the longest hug she had ever given anyone.

Others on the beach stared at this breach of convention and good manners, then shrugged and returned to the business at hand, except for the saloon keeper who slithered closer.

Captain Walker held her hands against his chest and searched her eyes. He beamed and said, "You know how I feel about you?"

She froze for a moment as she saw the love on his face. "Y-yes, I believe I do."

"And?"

She pulled away and stared at the crashing surf. Its sound roared in her ears, or perhaps it was her heart. She bit her lip as her bruised heart cried out for her to love him, to follow him wherever he sailed. She felt his presence behind her. Not a day went by that she didn't think of him.

Small brown faces crowded into her mind, white ones, too. They needed her, and in a way, she didn't understand; she needed them. How could she toss aside her calling from God?

He deserved an answer. What could she say that wouldn't hurt him? Or her? She licked her lips and tasted salt. Was it from her tears or the sea's spray? Miss Ruth convinced herself the wetness on her face was spray from the sea. She forced herself to smile, linked her arm through his, and led him toward the schoolhouse. She kept her eyes focused on the building and prayed for Bozhe to steady her voice. "You pulled Grandpa and me out of the Pacific Ocean and taught me how to properly scale the ratlines all the way to the Crow's Nest. You gave us a place to live and brought me to Alaska." She fingered the chain around her neck. "You even gave me the Pearl of Great Price, which I continually wear. Of all the people on this earth, you are the dearest to me. A true, loyal friend."

He had also kept his focus straight ahead. When she finished speaking, his shoulders bowed, then he took a deep breath and exhaled in a long slow sigh.

Arm in arm, they entered the chaos of the schoolroom. Children poked through the soggy contents of the split-open boxes. Villagers eyed the mail spread across tables and desks as the storekeeper sorted and swore when the ink blurred the addresses.

The saloon-keeper, a Swede from Minnesota, leaned over the storekeeper's shoulder and snarled, "Miss Ruth is not as pure as she wants everyone to believe."

Captain Walker fisted his hands and stepped toward the small blond man, but Miss Ruth restrained him. "Don't pay any attention to Mr. Eklund. He's lost a lot of regular customers since my arrival."

Captain Walker quirked an eyebrow.

"I have organized after-school activities and clubs of all kinds; cooking and preserving food, working in our school garden, sewing, quilting, Bible clubs, and a chess club. We have regular dinners, socials, school programs, and holiday celebrations for the whole family. I even persuaded several of the fathers to teach wood-carving and carpentry. There has been less time for drinking."

"And, of course, this Eklund blames you for that."

Miss Ruth hung her head and blushed. Captain Walker asked, "What did you do?"

She blushed again, "You will think me foolish, and perhaps I was. Several Aleut boys showed me where Mr. Eklund had hidden his still. One night, several weeks ago, I couldn't sleep..." She shrugged her shoulders.

"You destroyed it."

"Yes, and I'm glad I did, although he is now my enemy."

Captain Walker rubbed his hands over his eyes. "Are you in any danger?"

"I don't think so. He just complains and speaks negatively about me."

"I'll have a word with him."

She shook her head. "Don't bother. He is all bluster. Let me introduce you to the priest. His house is the only one on the island with an extra bedroom."

The Captain indicated his pack. "I came prepared with a tent, but I will gladly accept the priest's hospitality."

"He was educated in Russia and is well-read. You will enjoy his company. His wife is shy but an accomplished musician. She plays the organ and has a lovely singing voice."

Captain Walker searched the crowded schoolroom. "You said there were two distinct groups, Russian and Aleuts; I can't tell one from the other, especially with the children."

Miss Ruth laughed, "Good, that means I'm succeeding. The Russians, who are actually a Russian-Aleut mix, are better off financially. They have better housing, more food, and nicer clothes. The Aleuts are still living at a subsistence level. Everyone here thinks those who have some Russian also have a higher social standing. That attitude has filtered down to the children."

"Everyone seems friendly."

Miss Ruth hesitated and raised rueful eyes to the Captain. "I sometimes wonder if the Reverend Mrs. Monroe was right about civilizing the indigenous people."

"Surely, you don't mean that?"

"I despise her means and methods, nothing should be forced, but I must admit those in Russian Town have a better life than those in Aleut Town."

"How so?"

"When the Russians inter-married, they taught their wives gardening and preserving food. They have more access to food in winter, and their diet is varied; consequently, they are healthier and less hungry than the Aleuts. The clay-clad wood-burning Russian-style stoves keep their houses much warmer, and the banya keeps them cleaner, again leading to better health."

"What's a banya?"

"A Russian steam bath." Miss Ruth chuckled, "When a Lutheran Ladies Missionary Circle sent a barrelful of clothes for the Native children, I wouldn't hand them out until they had visited the banya. Now they go weekly and take their families."

"You have been busy."

"I noticed that the children felt better about themselves since getting clothes as nice as the Russian children's. This past winter, they only had dried fish to eat and little enough. They were listless and dull. I gave them breakfast every morning. They soon perked up and learned just as well as my Russian students."

"You are making a difference."

"I hope so; all the parents on Afognak are proud of their children and anxious for them to learn."

He took her hands in his and rubbed his thumb over her knuckles. "Are you happy, Miss Rachel Ruth Merritt?" he whispered.

Mr. Eklund saw the intimate gesture. "I'll get her, I will," he mumbled.

She turned and spread her arms wide as if to hug all the children in the room. "Come and sing for Captain Walker. If you ask him nicely, I believe he will tell us about his adventures sailing on the beautiful clipper ship, The China Doll."

Captain Walker laughed and said, "I will tell you how your teacher, who was barely out of the schoolroom, climbed the main mast of that clipper ship and was aloft one hundred and seventy feet above the ocean."

At the opposite end of the schoolroom, Mr. Eklund nudged the shopkeeper. "I tell you, something is up between those two."

The shopkeeper, who was also the postmaster, paid no attention and continued to sort the soggy letters, still cursing when the ink ran.

"I have a mind to write the District Commissioner and lodge a complaint. A woman of loose morals shouldn't be allowed to teach our children." Mr. Eklund kept his voice low.

"You don't have any kids, and you don't know anything about her morals."

Mr. Eklund spat his tobacco juice into the corner, where it dribbled down the wall. "As half-owner of the saloon, you should want to get rid of her as much as I do. We're losing money, and it's her fault."

"All I did was stake you." He shook his head. "It's money I'll never see again. You're just a lousy businessman."

"It's her fault, I tell you, and I'm going to have her removed," Eklund growled.

"I want no part of it. My kids love her."

THIRTY-ONE

Dear Kamalei,

The Boy of Thirteen Summers has returned to me. His life has been filled with pain and loss, and I believe it will continue. He is strong and stoic but without direction. I do not know how long he will stay in Afognak, but I hope his sojourn here will benefit him...

—MISS RUTH'S LETTER'S 1904

Miss Ruth stoked the fire in the woodstove and added several logs. She saw the villagers stream past her window and heard that plucky little steamship, the Dora, Afoknak's link to the outside world. It was the week's highlight when the Dora whistled, a signal for everyone to gather on the beach and help unload the skiffs.

The sturdy but diminutive ship was past due by two days which meant she was practically on time. Whenever the Dora arrived with the United States mail and other goods ordered, it felt like Christmas. Six more papers to grade, and she'd join the others.

Miss Ruth scurried down the bluff to the shore and saw the villagers carefully avoiding a taller than average Indian. He was not Aleut or Yupik, definitely not from this side of the Gulf. Visitors were not common on this isolated island, and he was from a strange tribe and clan.

He turned, and his strong profile caused her to exclaim, "White Water Otter!" Miss Ruth picked up her skirts and ran. The villagers parted like the Red Sea, and she dashed down the rocky beach.

As she approached him, she slowed to a walk. Social strictures and decorum prohibited her from throwing her arms around him. The villagers would not understand if she hugged a full-grown Indian male.

He had always appeared older, but she knew he was now in his early twenties. "It is so good to see you. I have missed you and thought of you often." She frowned and wrapped her arms around herself. "If you are here, your mother has walked into the forest. I am sorry."

The waves crashed on the beach as they always had. The wind pushed the smell of rotting kelp and seaweed away from them. Ott stood silent. The wind could not take the pain from his eyes.

The villagers hovered, glancing then looking away, straining to hear. They frowned when Ott answered in Haida. They gasped when Miss Ruth responded in kind.

"It has been difficult," He said.

"Come to the schoolhouse. I will feed you, and we will talk."

"There are things I cannot say."

"Those are the very things you must speak."

He sat at her desk in front of the large window. A continuous stream of villagers passed by, their attention fixed on him. Miss Ruth set a tray of sandwiches and stewed fruit in front of him.

"Our shaman said my Spirit Animal had become white and called other white men to our land." He choked on his last bite and looked out the window. "This does not seem to be a prosperous place. I hoped to find work."

"Most of the work is at the fish cannery; I will introduce you to the manager."

"I have not lived well. Four white men camped near us. They could not find gold, so they traded their hooch for our furs."

"Even you, Ott?"

He turned his face away and nodded almost imperceptively.

"Is that the reason you left?"

Another nod.

"They enticed our women with trickery. The entire village fell under the spell of their evil drink." He picked up the last sandwich but did not eat it. "I went into the woods to trap, but the animals are not what they once were. They had gone deeper into the forest. Even so, the hunger for the drink consumed me. I went into Haines and fed that hunger. I am shamed." He still refused to look at her. "I awoke one morning face down in the mud. That is when I knew I must come to you. I worked on a steamship from Haines to Sitka, and when you were not there, I worked my way across the Gulf."

"I am so glad you are here."

"The hunger for the drink still consumes me." His eyes beseeched her. "I am afraid I will shame myself again."

Miss Ruth raged at the unscrupulous men who gave alcohol to her dear boy. Like many Natives, he seemed to have little tolerance for it. "You are fighting the drink's evil hold on you, and each day you do not give in makes you stronger."

"I do not know what to do with my life. To you whites, I am nothing but an Indian. To my people, I think too much in white ways."

"God will show you the way to go, but now we must find you a place to stay."

For the first time since they entered the schoolhouse, Ott smiled, "Do you have a woodshed?"

Her eyes lit up, and for a moment, he was her Boy of Thirteen Summers.

❧

"Mr. Virtanen, I appreciate you giving Ott a chance. I know the fishing season has started, and you are fully staffed."

"If he's as dependable as you say, I'll need him; someone is always sick or drunk. There will be plenty of work for him. Dirty, cold, wet work."

"He is quite intelligent. I will tutor him when the fishing season is over, and I think he can be matriculated next year."

"Education doesn't seem to do the Natives much good, not the ones I know."

"Your children are half-native and excellent students."

Mr. Virtanen puffed out his chest and said, "They are my children, after all."

Miss Ruth was unsure if the man had insinuated his children were good students because they were half-white or his. She let the comment go.

A few months later, the schoolhouse became her parlor once more, and she served Mr. Virtanen coffee and cookies at her desk in front of the windows in full view of everyone.

How grateful she was for those windows. A single schoolteacher was not allowed male visitors, and since her living quarters were a partitioned part of the building, it was tricky. She shook her head and focused on her visitor. "How is Ott doing?"

"Something must be done about him."

"Is he in trouble?"

The fish cannery manager shook his head. "I explain things once, and he's got it. I show him how something works; he studies it and often makes suggestions for immediate improvement or greater efficiency."

"Then what's the problem?"

"The others in the cannery's dormitory gamble, especially after payday. They also drink too much. I'm not sure, but I think he's had a drink a time or two."

Miss Ruth put her hand to her face, "I hope not."

"I often pull him off the line and have him work with me, easier jobs, sometimes putting him in charge, which has caused some jealousy."

"What do you want to do?"

"Short term, I want him to move in with my family. We have the room."

"It will be good for him to be part of a family and long term?"

"That boy needs to go to University. He's concerned about how the big canneries are overfishing and destroying spawning grounds. Some of the smaller canneries have been put out of business."

"You sound bitter."

"I am. Sometimes there is barely enough fish left for the Natives. You've seen how they struggle during the winter. The big companies take all the fish, and it's all legal. Ott and I have had many discussions about Native rights and conservation. He knows nothing will change unless the laws change. Fishing must be regulated, protected from greed and corruption."

"What are you saying?"

"He wants to study fisheries, business, and law, and I think he can do it."

"It's a long and difficult road for an orphaned Haida from Alaska. He will suffer because of his color, culture, and poverty. There's also the cost. And the time, he could be gone for years."

"We've talked about all of that. Hopefully, he'll trap on north Afognak this winter and cache enough furs for his first year's expenses. He'll come back to Afognak every summer. As long as I'm the manager, he'll have a job.""

"I appreciate you're taking an interest in him, Mr. Virtanen, and I will do whatever I can to help."

"The longer I've worked with him, the more I've depended on him. It will be hard to see him go, but for Alaska's sake, he must."

Saturday night and the beer flowed in Eklund's saloon. Cards were drawn, tempers flared, and a fight or two proceeded to entertain the onlookers.

"Did you hear that Haida moved into the boss's house?" The head fish slimer asked.

"Boss is always pulling him off the line, giving him the easy jobs." The retort operator barked.

"Won't gamble, won't drink. Thinks he's better than the rest of us." The box builder shot back.

The saloon owner, Mr. Eklund, passed around a bottle of whiskey. "I think maybe you fellows ought to teach him a lesson."

The more the alcohol flowered, the braver the men became, and soon they were eager to do Eklund's bidding.

Six against one, Ott never had a chance. Bruised and bloodied, he crawled to Miss Ruth's. She heard his feeble knock and low moan. The foul smell of alcohol rose from his battered body. She pulled him inside. "Ott, what happened."

"I don't know. They came out of nowhere. Two of them held me. The others beat and kicked me. They poured hooch down my throat. I am sorry."

"There is nothing for you to be sorry about." She put a pot of water on the stove to heat, removed his alcohol-soaked shirt and pants, and helped him into her bed. She washed the blood from his face and stitched a gash in his shoulder. Fortunately, he had passed out.

Miss Ruth pulled out her washboard and tub, scrubbed his clothes, and hung them near the woodstove. She sat up the rest of the night watching over the Boy of Thirteen Summers.

Mr. Eklund orchestrated the fight from the shadows. "She took that drunk Indian into her house in the middle of the night. She's an immoral woman, not the kind we want in our village."

"I'd say that's exactly the kind we want," the retort operator said. The others slapped him on the back and agreed.

"I'm going to write the District Commissioner and get her fired. You are all witnesses." Mr. Eklund rubbed his palms together. His plan was working better than he had planned.

"Aint it enough we beat him and poured your hooch down his gullet?"

"All over him, you mean."

"I don't mind teaching that Native a lesson, but I ain't going after a woman."

"Come on, fellows," Eklund wheedled, "Free drinks to whoever signs my letter as a witness."

THIRTY-TWO

Dear Kamalei,

I have been recalled to Sitka. My five years of teaching on little Afognak were wonderful, but the District Commissioner received complaints about my moral character and classroom activities. I have been advised to change my ways...

—MISS RUTH'S LETTERS 1906

Subsequent letters from the District Commissioner and the Reverend Mrs. Monroe were ignored, then answered with detailed explanations. They were not well received, and the accusations against Miss Ruth were forwarded to the Reverend Jackson.

The emphatic letter from him couldn't be dismissed so easily. Apparently, the incessant communication and complaints from the Reverend Mrs. Monroe had worn him down.

So, with a heavy heart and several little 'going away' gatherings, Miss Ruth said goodbye to her students and their families.

Once the steamship arrived in Sitka, Miss Ruth paid a dock-hand to take the borrowed steamer trunks and luggage to the boarding school. She watched him load her luggage onto his wagon and wondered if she would remain in Sitka.

Would she be assigned to another school, put back in the kitchen or laundry? Perhaps her services would no longer be required.

She shook her head, put on a brave face, and greeted several townspeople as she slowly walked through Sitka.

❧

"I am sorry you could not adhere to our policies, Miss Ruth. I cannot afford to lose you."

Miss Ruth stiffened her spine, cleared her throat, and said, "I am a good teacher."

"I do not question your abilities, merely your methods. You do not adhere to the plans laid out for you."

"Surely you agree; those plans must be adapted to fit each school, day, and student."

"In an ideal world, that might be possible, perhaps beneficial, but this is not an ideal world. You have been accused of theft, misappropriation of school funds, and a low moral character."

"I have written extensive explanations explaining each accusation. I am sorry you do not believe me."

He sighed and said, "What I believe is immaterial. Your good name has been sullied, and your morals questioned, which does not reflect well on this agency. We must have no hint of impropriety or scandal."

"I resent my morals being questioned, but I can guess who the complainant is and why he made those accusations. I assure you they have no basis in fact." She sat stiffly and rigidly and faced the man who held her fate.

The Reverend Jackson held a letter aloft. "Most of Mr. Eklund's letters are easy to disregard, but this one is signed by several witnesses."

"Again, I have given you the facts, the truth."

"I have received letters from the Orthodox priest on Afognak and several parents. All defend you and hold you in high regard. I tend to give them more credibility than the man making accusations."

Miss Ruth folded her hands in her lap and remained silent.

"The rumors and gossip that erupted did not reflect well on the school. However, that matter aside, we must have uniformity across the district, and the government policies do that. It makes the schools more efficient, easier to manage." He removed his spectacles, wiped them with his handkerchief, and replaced them.

Miss Ruth focused on school policies. There was no point in trying to defend her character any further. "I'm sorry your policies are so severe and extreme."

"I am bound to follow every rule from the government. It's the law."

"Rules, regulations, policies, procedures; you give them the force of law to the detriment of the children." Miss Ruth sighed. She was one small piece of a large bureaucratic machine and had no power or influence over those who wielded that machine. She put on her gloves and prepared to leave.

Reverend Jackson stood and held out his hand. "I am afraid there is nothing I can do to enable you to keep your job. I must avoid all appearances of evil. Nevertheless, I wish you well in your future endeavors."

She paused at the door and said, "There is one more thing, sir."

He looked up from the ledger he had just opened.

"What can you tell me about an old sourdough named Denver Dan?"

"I don't recall the name."

"It would have been around the late 1880s, perhaps a little earlier."

His brow furrowed, and he shrugged his shoulders.

"He traveled with you for a time. Helped with your dictionary."

"Ah, yes, the wordsmith. He was only with me for a few months. Interesting fellow." Reverend Jackson leaned back in his chair and focused on the ceiling as if the past was written there. "We had many philosophical and theological debates. Well-educated man, but not anchored, a lost soul, really. We argued over Greek and Hebrew words of the Scriptures and their meanings. We also discussed the nuances of Tlingit and Tsimshian definitions of everyday words. He left my team to do a deeper exploration of those indigenous languages." He studied her over his spectacles. "That was almost twenty years ago. Why do you ask?"

"I heard about him. As you said, an interesting fellow." She fiddled with the buttons on her coat and tightened the scarf around her neck.

He turned back to his ledger. "If there is nothing else, I wish you well, Miss Ruth."

The steamship had arrived that morning, the interview with Reverend Jackson had taken place before noon, and by early afternoon Miss Ruth had picked up her well-worn valise, a large suitcase, and her small satchel of books, and left the school grounds.

Misty drizzle and a chilly breeze so typical of Sitka this time of year accompanied her on her trek into town. Where exactly she was going and what she was to do was a question she could not answer. Her limited funds would pay for a few days at the hotel. Then what?

She had come to Alaska to find the man who had conceived her. She had failed. She had learned the art of teaching in Hawaii. It was not appreciated here in Alaska, another failure. Did she have any other talents or skills to earn her way? She didn't think so. What was to become of her? These questions pulled at her soul, and she pushed the thoughts away.

Her suitcase pulled on her shoulder muscles, and she felt the strain across her upper back. She set her luggage down, stretched, and rubbed the back of her neck.

The spire of St. Peters-by-the-Sea Church rose behind her. Across the road, the sound of Crescent Bay's ebbing tide soothed her. The pungent smell of the bull kelp was as familiar as the aroma of her morning coffee. She hummed a favorite hymn and hoped she could believe the words:

"Be not dismayed whate're betide God will take care of you. Beneath His wings of love abide. God will take care of you. God will take care of you, through every day, o'er all the way. He will take care of you. God will take care of you."

"Lady! Lady! Help!" Four-year-old Mary Beth Houghton ran from St. Peter's parsonage behind the church. She stumbled, fell, and skinned her knee. Seeing the blood, the little girl screamed, hiccupped, and screamed again.

Miss Ruth dabbed at the knee, and soon her white handkerchief was blotched with blood and dirt. Mary Beth hiccupped again, grabbed Miss Ruth's skirt, and pulled her toward the parsonage.

"Mama! Mama! I got someone." The little girl ran to her mother, who struggled to control the boy writhing on the floor. The woman stared wild-eyed and unblinking at Miss Ruth.

Miss Ruth rushed to the distraught woman. "Hold his legs so he can't kick, but use the least amount of strength possible to restrain him." Miss Ruth cradled the boy's head in her lap and held his arms across his chest. Several minutes later, she rolled him onto his side and rubbed his back. Slowly the convulsions lessened, and his shaking ceased.

"How long has he had these convulsive fits?"

"Since he was six, almost a year now. The doctor treated him with borax, which worked for a time." Mrs. Houghton pulled a handkerchief from her apron pocket and wiped her face.

"But no longer?"

"He says we must go to Seattle for more modern treatment for this, this...epilepsy."

"And your husband?" Miss Ruth asked as little Mary Beth crawled into her lap.

"He's at a mission station up north and won't return for three more months. I don't know what to do." Mrs. Houghton held her son.

"You will take him to Seattle, of course."

"Not without my husband," she raised her face to Miss Ruth and moaned, "besides, we don't have the funds."

"Did the doctor say you could wait three months?"

Mrs. Houghton shook her head.

"I will make the travel arrangements for you. Do not worry about the funds."

The young mother's face lost all color. "I've never traveled without my husband. I don't think I could."

"For the sake of your son, you must."

"But the funds?"

"There is a steamship, The Aloha, bound for Seattle in three days. I know the captain well. You will be under his protection. Do you have anyone in Seattle?"

"My husband's aunt in Ballard."

"Captain Walker will escort you to her and explain the situation."

"I haven't heard from my husband for several months. The mail service is almost non-existent. How can I leave without him knowing?"

"You will write to him, and I will find someone heading north. If any letters arrive from him, I will send them to Ballard."

"But I..."

Miss Ruth laid her hand on the woman's shoulder, "Don't let your fear cost you your son."

"Yes, Miss Ruth." The young mother wiped her eyes and lifted them to Miss Ruth. "For my son."

"You know who I am?"

"Everyone does."

"But I've been gone from Sitka for years."

"You are memorable. Mrs. Hansen speaks well of you. In fact, that gives me an idea. Could you stay and take over for me like you did when she had her baby?

"Of course."

"Just the Sunday School and the children's choir, for the white children, of course?"

Miss Ruth nodded and pulled Mary Beth's thumb away from the little girl's mouth, who then crawled to her mother and put her thumb back in its favorite place.

"During the week, I teach sewing and housekeeping to Tlingit girls and tell them Bible stories."

"I can do that, too."

"I clean the church, keep the wood box filled, cook for the priest from Wrangell when he comes to preach. It's only every six or eight weeks, and he stays at the hotel when my husband isn't here."

Miss Ruth got to her feet and said, "We'll make a list. I will do everything that needs doing until you return."

"I may never come back." Mrs. Houghton hugged her children and looked at Miss Ruth with steely eyes. "I've decided to insist my husband take a church in the United States."

Miss Ruth held the hurting woman. "Then I will stay until your Bishop sends another. Now let's get these worn-out children down for a nap. You can set the kettle to boil, and I will retrieve my luggage from the side of the road."

"Are you sure I can do this, Miss Ruth?"

"Your husband would want you to do what's best for his son, and I will send you regular reports. You are a strong woman, and Captain Walker will help you."

Over several cups of tea and many tears, Mrs. Houghton said, "You are the answer to a prayer I was too distraught to pray."

Miss Ruth smiled over the rim of her teacup and whispered, "And you are the answer to mine."

THIRTY-THREE

SAM 1962

"Chuck, do you have any relatives on Afognak?"

The Tlingit teenager laughed, "Boss, that's like me asking if you have any relatives in Indiana? Being Native doesn't mean I'm related to all other natives in Alaska."

Sam blew cigar smoke toward the ceiling, "I'm not that insensitive. I thought your aunt was from there."

"Sorry, Boss. One of my mom's cousins married a gal from Afognak, but they live on the Kenai now. I don't really know them. Why so interested?"

"Miss Ruth, of course. She taught on Afognak for several years. Apparently, our Miss Ruth had a little trouble obeying all the government rules. She was recalled to Sitka and fired. I just wanted some local input."

"What rules?"

"Mainly ones about eradicating Native culture and customs. She broke those consistently."

"I think I like her." Chuck shuffled through some of the letters. "I'd like to do a report on her for my Alaska history class, but we have to choose a Native."

Sam set several letters in front of Chuck. "White Water Otter or Otto Virtanen as he was known. That's who you should write about. Do a good job, and I'll run it as a feature."

"Who is he? What did he do?"

"His early life is relatively typical, sent to a boarding school here in Sitka, but he ran away and right into Miss Ruth. You'll find that part in her letters. After graduating from UW with several degrees, he returned to Alaska. Caused a bit of a stir in the legislature. Back in the 20s and 30s, he proposed fishing reforms and conservation. He was mostly unsuccessful."

"Why's that?"

Sam threw a wadded-up piece of paper at the boy. "Do your own investigating. Much of what he predicted has come to pass and could have been prevented if his policies had been implemented."

"And he knew Miss Ruth?"

"They paddled a canoe from here to Haines. In winter!"

Chuck whistled and picked up the letters. "White Water Otter it is."

THIRTY-FOUR

Dear Kamalei,

Jack and Sean Connor are on a steamship bound for the Kenai Peninsula, almost five hundred miles across the Gulf of Alaska and north of Afognak Island. There is a possibility they have discovered my father's whereabouts deep in the wilderness. I pray they find him, and I hope they do not. My emotions are conflicting and confusing; I cannot sort them out...

—MISS RUTH'S LETTERS 1906

Miss Ruth hugged Mrs. Houghton and her children, knowing Captain Walker would deliver them to the aunt in Ballard. The Aloha backed away from the dock, and the Captain sounded the ship's horn; two short blasts and one long; his particular signal to Miss Ruth.

Unmindful of the drizzle, she waved back. When the ship slipped out of sight around the tip of Japonski Island, she crossed the street to the post office. A letter from Maureen. Joy! She pushed it deep into her coat pocket, where it would remain dry. She turned her collar up and her hat down. The old mariner's hat had been oiled over the years and was watertight and pliable.

As it often did, Sitka's drizzle had turned into a downpour with a thick cloud cover darkening the sky. Lacy wisps of those clouds swirled around Mt. Verstovia like a shawl. Its crooked peak rose above them, similar to an old woman's tilted head.

She clutched her coat tighter as she passed Crescent Bay. The water glistened like black diamonds as heavy raindrops bounced off its surface. She breathed in the salty sea air, raised her head, and reminded herself that the sun still shone above the cloud cover.

Miss Ruth admired the stonework and gothic lines of the little church as she climbed its steps and entered the foyer. She let the sanctuary door close softly behind her and stood for a moment at the back of the room. The patina on the pews shimmered as the sun broke through the clouds and streamed through the frosted stained-glass windows. Sparkling shades of plum and amber filled her eyes with delight.

She sank into the nearest pew and let the peaceful presence of this sacred place envelope her. That peace evaporated as she read Maureen's letter. She let it fall from her hands, stumbled to the front of the church, and knelt before the altar. The uncarpeted stairs rubbed against her legs, but she was unaware.

Her thoughts were of Jack and Sean and what they would find in the Kenai. Are the rumors they heard about a white man living with the Yupiks and studying their language true? The information was several months old, but Jack had felt it worth investigating.

Maureen phrased her warning delicately but advised Miss Ruth to not get her hopes up. They must pray for a good outcome and God's leading as Jack and Sean try to locate this village.

Her father was alive! Her hope surged, and she prayed he would be thrilled to know he had a child. At the same time, she vowed to not forgive the man who had abandoned her before she was born.

She longed for his embrace. She wanted to lean against him

and listen to his heartbeat and have him hear hers. She wanted him to say he loved her and thought about her daily.

Just as quickly as that picture filled her heart, so did another. She saw herself pounding his chest and sobbing. He stood stoic as she poured out all her little girl feelings of loneliness and confusion. The bitterness of knowing he had deliberately left.

Why didn't you want me? Why didn't you want me? Her tears watered the altar, and she lay on the sanctuary floor, silent and exhausted. *Oh, God. I don't know what I want or how to feel. I can't even pray.*

Drained, after alternating between anticipation and apprehension; joy and rage, Miss Ruth felt nothing. Her mouth was dry, her chest hurt, and she had a vile headache. She gathered her things and left the little church.

The rectory or See House, its Gothic Revival architecture matched that of the church, would be her home for the near future. She made a pot of tea and a piece of toast. She found a packet of white willow powder and took some for her headache. When the powder alleviated her throbbing head, she thoroughly inspected the See House.

Mrs. Houghton had told her to make herself at home and use any bedroom she wanted. Two of the upstairs bedrooms had views of Crescent Bay and Sitka Sound. The others faced Harbor Mountain and Mt. Verstovia. She saw a narrow staircase leading to the attic when she opened the last door.

Its gabled alcoves were used for storage. One small room contained a narrow iron bed and a small chest of drawers. She moved the boxes stacked on the bed and next to the window to another room.

She rubbed the dirty window with her handkerchief. The view of Sitka Sound was worth the climb to this small attic retreat. Miss Ruth chose it for her living quarters.

She made the small room as cozy as possible with her books, the small trinkets from the children of Afognak, and the Hawaiian gifts from Iolana's family. She found a blue-flowered water pitcher and basin with a matching chamber pot in one of the storage nooks. There was also a small mirror that she placed on her dresser.

She surveyed the room with a sense of satisfaction. Perhaps, she might be allowed to stay if a new cleric with a large family was assigned to the church. She could work as a teacher, housekeeper, cook, or even a nanny if the children were young.

She reviewed the list she had made with Mrs. Houghton and vowed she would do her best for the children, both white and brown. There was such a discrepancy in how the two groups were treated. Miss Ruth noticed that Mrs. Houghton, while ignorant of native culture and customs, loved the children and had no malice toward them.

Nevertheless, Miss Ruth hoped to be an agent of change here in Sitka. She planned to bring the separate classes and clubs together, although she was unsure what one woman with no influence could do in the wild and primarily lawless District of Alaska.

She wondered if the teacher assigned to Afognak in her place would undo everything she had accomplished. Miss Ruth had wanted to change so much, but a powerful bureaucratic system replete with foolish government policies had stood in her way.

The government couldn't stop her from loving those precious children and doing her best for them.

THIRTY-FIVE

Dear Kamalei,

I find myself embroiled in a love affair between a young United States Marine and the daughter of the Lieutenant Governor of Alaska. I have been asked to convince the father to consent to the marriage. I'm uneasy and am not entirely sure this is a good idea...

—MISS RUTH'S LETTERS 1906

"We'll run away."

"Phillie, be reasonable." The tall, freckle-faced Marine pleaded with the young woman.

"I have a little money saved, and we can find a fisherman to get us off this blasted island."

"Nobody in Southeast Alaska will marry us without your father's permission." He took her hand, "Philomena, I love you, but I want you to have your father's blessing. You'll regret it if we don't. We are going to see Miss Ruth; she will help us."

"Why would she? She doesn't know us."

"It's what she does. At least, that's what I've heard. Haven't you seen her around town, the lady dressed in black from head to toe? She's always on her way somewhere to help someone with something."

"I heard she teaches Sunday School and to the Indians, no less. I don't need some do-gooder spouting religious nonsense to me."

"I hardly think she'd do that, Phillie. Besides, the stories I've heard about her adventures would amaze you."

"No need to talk about that, young man."

The young couple spun around, and just a few steps behind them on the wooden sidewalk Miss Ruth stood in her ankle-length black dress and coat.

Philomena ignored Miss Ruth and pulled on the young man's arm. "We'll go where nobody knows us and pretend we're married."

"Sometimes, Phillie, you sound as young as you are, but I love you anyway." He raised her hand to his lips.

He extended his hand to Miss Ruth. "Second Lieutenant Malcolm Burke, ma'am. We were just on our way to see you."

"And you are the Lieutenant Governor's daughter, Philomena Taylor?" Miss Ruth handed each of them a lemon drop and asked, "What can I do for you?"

"We want to be married." The Marine officer stood tall and directed his gaze into Miss Ruth's eyes.

"Nothing. There's absolutely nothing you can do. We can take care of ourselves." Philomena grabbed Malcolm's arm and tried to pull him along.

He stood, unmovable, and told the woman he loved, "I'll not run away with you, Phillie, and I'll not marry you without your father's blessing." He turned to Miss Ruth, "I want to do things honorably. But I'm out of ideas, and Phillie is..."

"Go ahead and say it. Headstrong. Stubborn. Contrary." The fashionably dressed young woman tilted her chin, her eyes flashed, and she sounded proud of these traits.

"Adorable. Pretty. Funny." Second Lieutenant Burke gazed into her upturned face.

Miss Ruth saw that Philomena was much too pretty for her own good. Petite, dark-haired, violet eyes.

"I'm not funny, and I get so annoyed with your honorable intentions, but I love you anyway." Philomena kissed his chin, then laughed when his face turned almost as red as his hair.

"What were Mr. Taylor's objections?" Miss Ruth ignored the girl and spoke to the Marine.

"I've tried to make appointments several times. His secretary says he's too busy preparing for the government's final move to Juneau."

"That is a massive undertaking that's been going on for months," Miss Ruth said.

"I hope Alaska will become more law-abiding when it becomes an official territory," the Lieutenant said.

"When do you think that will happen?" Miss Ruth asked.

"Not for some years yet. Perhaps, one day, it will become a state."

Miss Ruth saw the irritation on Philomena's face as the conversation turned away from her. The childish young woman tossed her head, tugged on Malcolm's sleeve again, and exclaimed, "Never! Alaska is too far away from civilization."

"The world is changing, Phillie. We have underwater telegraph cables that connect us to some of the islands and Seattle. We are getting more steamship routes every year. The world is not only changing; it's getting smaller."

"I don't care about the world or Alaska. I care about us."

"So, to answer my question, you don't know what his objections are?" Once again, Miss Ruth ignored Philomena and addressed Malcolm.

"No, ma'am, but I can guess. I have no family, no money, and no social position. I do plan to make the military my career." Malcolm put his arm around Philomena's shoulder. "At least her father has allowed us to see each other. But I want to meet him and get his official permission to court her properly."

Philomena let out the breath she had been holding, hung her head, and murmured, "I have to tell you, when he found out I had a man friend, he threatened to ship me back to my grandmother's." She pushed out her lower lip.

"Phillie!"

She turned to him, "I know I told you he gave us permission, but he didn't. In fact, I promised him I wouldn't see you again."

"We must stop meeting until I speak with him."

"No, Malcolm, I couldn't bear it." Teardrops clung to the edge of her lashes.

"Hmmm." Miss Ruth felt every one of her thirty-six years. *Was I ever that young, that self-absorbed?* Fortunately, Malcolm seemed like a mature young Marine and hopefully would be a steadying influence on the woman he loved.

Miss Ruth tapped her finger on her chin, took a step closer, and said, "I can see you are a very determined young woman."

Stubborn anger flashed in the young girl's eyes, and she tossed her head. "No matter what Father says, I'm not going back to my grandmother's! I'm not going to Juneau either!"

"I will help you, but you must promise to do exactly what I say even if you don't understand my reasons. You must learn a little restraint and diplomacy," Miss Ruth gave Philomena another lemon drop, but the girl dropped it in the bushes when Miss Ruth wasn't looking.

Miss Ruth handed her a handkerchief as she saw Philomena's tears threaten to spill again. Philomena pulled at the linen cloth, then leaned against the wooden fence surrounding the Russian Bishop's house. "I don't know what you could do."

"Phillie, Please."

She turned to her young man. "I won't make any more promises to my father that I can't keep. That's a good thing, isn't it, Malcolm?"

"Maybe you didn't want to keep them," he said softly.

"I want to marry you now. That's all I know."

Miss Ruth walked away. She had almost reached the end of the street before Philomena called, "I'll try to take your advice."

Miss Ruth turned, but she did not walk toward them. "Trying is not good enough, my dear. Is your young man worth waiting for? Could you show a little restraint for him?"

"I'd do anything for him, but I will not wait."

"Will you obey every command from Miss Ruth?" Malcolm squeezed Philomena's hand and bowed to Miss Ruth.

"Malcolm, no!" Philomena's eyes watered.

He turned to Miss Ruth and said, "She will.'

Philomena bit her lip and averted her eyes. Miss Ruth smiled at the Marine but wondered about the girl.

"Miss Ruth, come inside and bring your friends. I have just received a new brick of good Chinese tea," Father Kvasnikoff called from his open window.

They sat in the Bishop's reception room under a painting of Tsar Nicholas the First, even though the Second now ruled Russia.

The Bishop had his housekeeper break off pieces of the solid tea brick, wrapped it in paraffin paper, and presented one to Miss Ruth and Miss Taylor. The other he dropped into the large samovar. Soon the fragrance of the Chinese oolong permeated the room.

Father Kvasnikoff asked general questions of the three until Miss Ruth signaled with her eyes and a nod toward the young couple. Then the priest directed more personal inquiries to the Marine and the pretty young woman, whose young love shone from their eyes.

"Alaska is destined for great things, and I want to be a part of it, even if I'm stationed elsewhere. After retiring from the military, I'll return to Alaska," Malcolm told Father Kvasnikoff.

"What about our future?" Philomena asked before the Father could respond.

"I see our future entwined with Alaska's."

Philomena leaned toward him, resting her hand on his heart, "I can't see it, Malcolm." She paused, pouted, and said, "I don't know why you're enthralled with this miserable place. You need to think about me when you think about the future."

Miss Ruth set her teacup on the linen tablecloth, leaned against the back of the velvet settee, and watched the interplay between the young couple. Philomena had a lot of maturing to do. Miss Ruth closed her eyes. After several minutes of silent prayer with no indication of how to proceed, she reached deep into her reticule and shared her bag of lemon drops with everyone.

Mr. Taylor, the Lieutenant Governor, finished dictating to his secretary, who gathered his papers, and hissed at Miss Ruth, who stood in the open doorway, "I told you repeatedly he has no time for you."

"Nonsense, Thornwood, I always have time for a lady. Sit down. Miss Ruth, is it?"

Miss Ruth saw his frown and heard the impatience behind the polite words. "I'll try to be brief, Your Honor."

"Mr. Taylor will do. Phillie said you were coming to see me, but I'm extremely busy. Silly girl. I'm sending her back to my mother's. Blasted governess, traveling companion, really—since Phillie is out of the schoolroom. Anyway, the blasted woman up and quit after seeing a bear in Totem Park," Mr. Taylor muttered, almost to himself, as he pushed papers and files around the large mahogany desk.

"Are you confident Philomena will stay with her grandmother? She seems as determined and as stubborn as..."

"As her father?"

"You have a reputation in Alaska, sir, as a man who gets things done and gets them done his way. Your daughter is a lot like you."

He slumped in his chair, opened his cigar box, and raised his eyebrows. Miss Ruth nodded, and he lit the cigar. "I had hoped she'd be my hostess. A lot of business takes place at social gatherings. What a disaster."

Having met the young woman, Miss Ruth could imagine the mishaps that must have taken place.

"The girl had too much time on her hands. Bored. Took long walks on the beach and in the park. Alone. She must have met this ne'er do well somewhere along the way."

Miss Ruth folded her hands in her lap and let her face soften as the governor rambled on. She had learned that most people had a need to fill the silence. It seemed as if he had forgotten she was there.

Finally, he shook his head and said, "I was in the military, posted out west when my wife died. After the funeral, I took two-year-old Philomena to my mother's, and when Phillie was old enough, I sent her to boarding school."

"So, you don't really know her." Miss Ruth kept her voice soft and non-judgmental.

"I confess I don't know my daughter at all. Nothing to be done about it, I'm afraid."

"Tell me about your wife."

There was pain around his eyes. He drew in the fragrant tobacco and fiddled with his pocket watch. "We were too young. Her parents disapproved." He opened the watch and showed Miss Ruth his wife's photograph. "Her parents disowned her. I regretted that."

"Will you do the same to your daughter if she marries without your consent?"

He stubbed out his cigar and growled, "It's not the same thing. Phillie is too young, immature."

"As you were."

"I don't want her to make the same mistakes I did."

"Your marriage was a mistake?"

"Of course not! Really, Miss Ruth. I've taken Phillie in hand. She will be on the next steamship heading south."

"With no travel companion? What's to stop her from heading right back to Sitka?"

Mr. Taylor stroked his mustache, opened the cigar box then slammed it shut. "I know nothing about this man."

"Second Lieutenant Malcolm Burke."

"He's a Marine? An officer?"

"He's going to make it his career. He tried for months to get an appointment to see you."

"Thornwood!" Mr. Taylor bellowed.

Thornwood poked his head around the open door, "He's been here every Friday for months but never gave a reason for wanting to meet. I assumed you were too busy to see a lowly Second Lieutenant."

"Find him and bring him to me."

"But sir?"

"Immediately. And Thornwood, don't assume."

"Yes, sir."

Mr. Taylor reached for another cigar, "I'll not go easy on him."

"I don't expect you to."

"And I'm not saying I'll give them my blessing."

Miss Ruth folded her hands in her lap and smiled, "It might be better if you don't," and wondered what Philomena would do if her father denied her permission to marry.

His shoulders slumped, and he frowned. "My daughter is as pretty as her mother but as headstrong and impulsive as me. It's not a good combination." His eyes brightened. "Perhaps, this Marine will be the making of her."

Every morning at precisely six o'clock, Miss Ruth marched into Philomena's bedroom, threw back the covers, and opened the drapes. And every morning, the young woman groaned and shoved her head under the pillow.

"The Bible says a married woman gets up early and sees to the needs of her household." Miss Ruth pulled the pillow away.

"I told you no God-talk or Bible commands. I'm not married yet and haven't seen Malcolm for ages. He's probably forgotten all about me." Philomena wailed, but it was muffled as she pulled the covers over her head.

"You know he's busy training his unit. And you know how much he loves you. Get dressed. You have much to learn."

"I know enough," her muffled voice came from under the covers.

"When you marry Malcolm, you will live in a small cabin or house. No servants. You do not know how to cook. You can't kill a chicken or gut a fish. Today's lesson is shopping."

"I love to shop. I'm an expert." Philomena sat up in bed, and her eyes sparkled.

"We are going to shop for food. How to get the best quality for the least amount of money. How to make your housekeeping money last until the next payday, how to budget."

The girl's eyes dulled, and her voice lost enthusiasm, "That sounds so boring. I can play the piano, arrange flowers, do needlepoint, and even sketch a little. That should count for something. And now that Father has decided he needs my assistance every afternoon, I'm learning the tedious business of government which has nothing to do with being a good wife."

Miss Ruth laughed, "At least you two are getting to know each other."

"He said it was your idea. I don't mean to complain." She wrung her hands, and a tear clung to her lower lashes. "Truly, I don't. Malcolm says complaining makes a person ugly, and I want to be beautiful for him."

"What else do you want, Phillie?"

The young woman sat at her dressing table and picked up her hairbrush. "I want to marry Malcolm. Be happy. And I don't want to gut a fish or clean a chicken."

Miss Ruth raised an eyebrow.

"I want Father to give me his blessing now. I want a huge wedding with a beautiful dress. I want to dance all night with my Malcolm."

Miss Ruth frowned at the girl.

"Oh, I suppose I want to learn all those things you are so determined to teach me." She threw her hairbrush among the bottles and lotions on her dressing table.

Miss Ruth laughed and said, "Today, you must learn to do a lot with a little, and the sooner you show me some expertise, the sooner I tell your father you're ready for marriage."

Philomena grabbed the hairbrush again, her eyebrows drew down, and she growled at the older woman. "Tell Father I'm ready now."

THIRTY-SIX
SAM, 1962

Romance was in the air, and Miss Ruth was in the middle of it. Did the lowly Second Lieutenant and his girl marry? She sounded self-centered. Why couldn't this Malcolm Burke see that? Did love blind you to what a person was really like? How could one be sure?

Sam ran his hand over his face. He needed a shave. He felt slightly ill at ease and didn't know why. Probably all this romance. He stared at himself in the mirror as he lathered his face.

This Philomena would have to make a considerable adjustment if she became a military wife. Of course, Miss Ruth would be there to help. Why wasn't she here to help him?

Sam nicked himself and raised startled eyes to his reflection. He wiped away the blood and lather. Why wasn't Miss Ruth here to help him? What kind of a question was that? Help with what?

He made a note to check Alaska's military records to trace Second Lieutenant Malcolm Burke's career, and he'd search through the letters to see if Miss Ruth wrote about them again.

Sam splashed his face with Aqua Velva and winced when it stung his nick. He looked in the mirror again and said, "Sammy boy, this is one letter you will not share with Alice."

THIRTY-SEVEN

Dear Kamalei,

It disturbs me that I have totally misjudged someone's character. I tried to be helpful and kind, but it blinded me to what was happening. A young man was heartbroken, and a young woman went on her selfish way unscathed.

Sometimes people are not what they seem. What could I have done differently...

—MISS RUTH'S LETTERS 1906

"Miss Ruth, the United States Navy is coming to Sitka in a few weeks." Philomena Taylor twirled around the four-poster bed. "There will be dinners, receptions, and a grand ball, and I'm in charge."

"Your Father approved?"

"Why wouldn't he?"

Miss Ruth quirked one eyebrow and sat on the bench in front of the girl's bedroom window. The view from Castle Hill, as it was called, overlooked Sitka and the surrounding islands.

Philomena chewed on her lower lip, "He said it was my final chance to prove myself capable and responsible, especially after the last time. He was mean to remind me. Help me."

"I've never been to a formal reception or a fancy ball, much less organized one. I'm not sure I'd know what to do."

The girl eyed Miss Ruth's outdated clothes and frowned, "I can see you aren't the type for a formal ball, not unless you had a fairy godmother."

"Hardly," Miss Ruth muttered and ignored the girl's rudeness. "And what are you in charge of?"

"Preparing the menu, procuring the food, choosing the linen and china, arranging the flowers, the music, the décor. It will be difficult since much has already been sent to the governor's mansion in Juneau. I will also need to instruct the servants and organize the Naval Officers' introductions. Everything."

"But Phillie..."

"Don't worry. I've been to several balls. I know what they should look like." She managed a perfect pirouette, and her skirt fanned out. She curtsied to the bedpost. "It will be glorious, the most elaborate and grandest ball Sitka has ever seen. Imagine all those Naval Officers in their immaculate dress uniforms. More impressive than the Marines, don't you think?"

"What about a certain Second Lieutenant?"

"Malcolm will understand. After all, I'm doing this for my father. I'm going to dance all night."

Philomena rifled through her closet, throwing dress after dress onto her bed. "The trouble is I have nothing to wear." She threw herself across the dresses and rolled into a ball. "I'll be ugly, and no one will want to dance with me."

"Phillie, I see four or five lovely gowns. Get up; you're crushing them."

"They're old, out of season, awful. What am I going to do?"

"Let's make separate lists for the reception, the dinner, and the ball. You will need to ask Thornwood what china and stemware have already been sent to Juneau and what linens are available. Have you thought about a menu at all?"

"Thornwood! That's the answer."

"I thought your father put you in charge. You can't shirk your responsibilities by giving them to Mr. Thornwood."

"Mrs. Thornwood, the old biddy—I heard she brought her own seamstress to Sitka and several trunks full of fabric. Sh—She might have something wonderful." Philomena's lower lip jutted forward in an unbecoming pout.

"You don't sound too sure about her."

"She had me for tea when I first arrived. Tried to tell me what was appropriate for the Lieutenant Governor's daughter. She felt it her duty to explain how things worked at the mansion. Proper decorum and civility. Ugh! She's just a glorified secretary's wife. I didn't need to listen to her."

"Surely, you didn't tell her." Miss Ruth saw the answer on the girl's face. "Oh, Phillie!"

"She'll probably hold it against me and not help with a new dress."

"Perhaps if you send her a note, ask her to tea, then explain how sorry you are."

The cunning that crept into Philomena's eyes troubled Miss Ruth. She rubbed her shaking hands together and hoped she was mistaken about what she saw.

"I'll say father gave me all this responsibility, and it crushed me; I was naïve and thought I could do everything myself." Philomena crossed to her dressing table. She fiddled with the bottles and jars, then picked up her hairbrush. She gazed at her reflection and said, "I'll tell her how difficult my life has been without a mother. I don't have to mean any of it. I just have to say it."

Miss Ruth grabbed her by the shoulders. "Do you hear yourself? Aren't you the least bit repentant?" She gentled her voice, "What does your heart say?"

Philomena set her jaw and spoke through clenched teeth, "My heart says what it always says—do what you need to get what you want."

"What about treating people kindly and honestly? What about striving to be a good person?"

The girl stomped to the bed and stuffed her gowns into the wardrobe. "I am a good person, and I don't appreciate you insinuating otherwise. You can't talk to me like this. I'll have Father fire you."

"He didn't hire me. I'm helping you as a kindness."

"What?" Philomena stared out the window, her eyebrows furrowed, and she asked, "What do you get out of it?"

Miss Ruth's heart blanched. The girl was genuinely puzzled. "The knowledge that I can be of service to people gives me a sense of well-being and purpose. It satisfies me as I see people grow and find their way through their problems. It's a blessing."

Miss Ruth put her arm around the confused girl. "I'm sorry, Phillie. I can't force you to become a better..." Miss Ruth led the girl to the dressing table's stool, and picked up a hairbrush.

"As I recall, Malcolm insisted you help me." Philomena lay her head amid the bottles, lotions, hair ribbons, and powders. Muffled sounds came from the girl, then she turned her head and lifted her eyes to the older woman. "I do need you, Miss Ruth. Will you be my fairy godmother and help me plan the ball."

Despite her misgivings, Miss Ruth rejected the sticky sweet odor of the girl's voice and the cunning look in her eye. "I will assist you with the logistics of the reception and the ball. I want no part of your blatant hypocrisy and manipulation toward Mrs. Thornwood."

Philomena's eyes narrowed and pierced Miss Ruth, who braced herself. The girl turned away. "Really, Miss Ruth, that rude tone is extremely unbecoming."

❧

Miss Ruth carried a notebook in her handbag whenever she was with Philomena. She never knew when the girl might remember something vital about receptions, dinner parties, and balls. Miss Ruth added to those lists.

The closer the Navy's arrival, the more Miss Ruth felt like she was drowning. "You must simply organize these lists, Phillie, and begin implementing them. They are not at all cohesive. I'm afraid you are heading for a disaster."

"They are your lists, fairy godmother." The girl kissed her cheek. "I'm late for a dress fitting. Mrs. Thornwood thinks we are the best of friends and does whatever I ask. I'm getting a whole new wardrobe."

Miss Ruth couldn't put the girl's lack of responsibility out of her mind but continued with the lists. What did the cook have available? What could be purchased locally? How many townspeople would be needed as temporary hires since most of the Governor's staff and servants were already in Juneau? What about flowers? There were no florists in Sitka, and the wildflower season was over.

Miss Ruth rubbed her forehead and the back of her neck. Philomena had repeatedly refused to do anything. Miss Ruth tore up all the lists and made an appointment to see Philomena's father.

❧

"Not to worry, Miss Ruth, it's all a ruse."

"I don't understand."

"I wanted to give her one more chance to succeed."

"She will not listen to my instructions or take my advice."

"You're saying my daughter has not made even a rudimentary attempt to prepare for the festivities."

"She has had several fittings for her new ballgown."

Mr. Taylor snorted and mumbled, "Having the girl in my office the past few weeks, I have seen how vain and self-centered she is. Irresponsible."

Miss Ruth opened her mouth, but no words came.

Mr. Taylor laughed, but Miss Ruth heard the pain behind it. The Lieutenant Governor shuffled the papers on his desk and said, "I've come to realize she will not change. My daughter's only hope is to marry a wealthy man who wants her for a showpiece."

"But sir..."

"If she has social events to attend, a vast wardrobe, and a competent staff to run the household, she will be fine."

Miss Ruth tightened her lips but refrained from giving her opinion. "About our present predicament, the Navy's arrival? All the scheduled events?"

He chuckled, "Thornwood has been taking care of me for years. It's all under control."

"And Second Lieutenant Burke?" An image of the besotted young Marine came into Miss Ruth's mind.

"My daughter is who she is, much as it pains me, but our young Marine is honorable. She has the power to hurt him badly." Mr.

Taylor snorted, "If only he could see her as she is."

"Let me think about that." Miss Ruth shook her head and fingered her lemon drops. "Nothing comes to mind."

The Lieutenant Governor leaned back in his ornate chair and clasped his hands. "No need. I think I have something that will open his eyes."

Miss Ruth raised her eyebrows.

"It will be painful, but he will survive."

Seabirds huddled in the rafters of Sitka's fish canneries. Gulls shivered deep in whatever shelter they could find. The sun's warmth could not penetrate the low-hanging clouds thick over Sitka Sound.

Cozy under a thick fur blanket in her father's recently imported Model T Ford automobile, Philomena Taylor chatted on the two-block ride to the docks.

"I don't see why I couldn't have accompanied you yesterday. I've always wanted to be piped aboard a ship."

"Do you even know what that means, my dear?" Her father patted her hand.

"I wanted the sailors to see me and wonder who I was, especially the officers."

"You're my daughter. Everyone knows who you are." He parked next to the dock, in front of the sea wall. "How are your plans coming? Do you need any help?"

"Everything is fine." She waved her hand dismissively. "Thank you for my new wardrobe. I do wish Mrs. Thornwood's seamstress worked a little faster. She must finish my ballgown in time." Philomena chewed on her fingertip, then realized she wore white doeskin gloves and quickly folded her hands in her lap.

"You're certain everything is ready?"

Philomena nodded. Surely, Miss Ruth had everything under control? She joined her father on the dock and watched a skiff as it was lowered from the Navy's ship. She tracked its progress as it streamed across the channel, a trip of a few minutes.

The dismal gray day could not dim the luster of those Navy uniforms, medals on their chests, swords dangling at their sides. So distinguished, impressive.

Philomena's heart quickened, and her cheeks gained a rosy glow when her father pointed out Captain Donald Moore. He commanded so much more authority and respect than a mere Second Lieutenant.

Her smile faded a bit as she watched the men disembark. The Captain was perhaps a few years older than she would have liked, but he was tall and pleasing to the eye.

Introductions were made, and the appreciative but cautious gleam in the Captain's eye told Philomena that her age would be an issue. She tossed her head and smiled. She could make him forget she had only recently left the schoolroom.

"Captain Moore, I'm afraid duty calls. My daughter will be your guide. The rain is holding off, so perhaps, a walk through the town?"

"Delighted." Captain Moore bowed toward Philomena.

"After that, perhaps a drive over what few roads we have. My automobile is available, and a carriage and driver are waiting in my stable." He pointed to a small building at the base of Castle Hill.

"I would relish getting behind the wheel of an automobile

again." Captain Moore turned toward Philomena and asked. "That is if you would trust me, Miss Taylor?"

Philomena linked her arm through his, "I have a picnic basket in the back seat. But first, our walk?"

The sailors waited for his command. "You have shore leave for the next eight hours, men. Behave yourselves."

"Aye, aye, Sir." They bolted for the few amenities Sitka had to offer.

The loud pounding on the front door was heard throughout the See House; it woke the baby and broke the Bishop's concentration. He thrust his sermon notes aside and answered the door.

"Where is she?" The Lieutenant Governor's daughter shrieked as she pushed past him.

"Baking bread," he followed her as she stormed to the kitchen.

"Not her! Miss Ruth!" The young woman's shrill voice had not decreased, and the baby still howled.

"Attend to the baby, husband." The woman's floured hands continued to calmly knead the dough. "Miss Ruth is in the church."

Philomena marched across the yard and into the sanctuary. "How dare you!"

Miss Ruth finished wiping the window sill and laid the dustcloth on her cleaning supplies. "What is it, Phillie dear?"

Philomena snapped, "The cook, the butler, the musicians. They've all come to me for instructions."

Miss Ruth remained still and did not speak.

Philomena's voice rose an octave and echoed through the sanctuary, "Nothing has been done."

"But, I thought you were in charge."

"You know I expected you to do everything."

"That was a mistake, dear. Let's not raise our voices in God's house."

"I'll raise my voice anywhere I want. You've ruined everything! I thought you were my friend."

Miss Ruth led the girl to the front steps of the church. "What are you going to do?"

The girl sank to the steps and put her face in her hands. "It's too late to do anything. The reception is tonight, the formal dinner party tomorrow night, and the ball two evenings later."

Miss Ruth, appalled at the girl's utter lack of responsibility, sat next to her. "Think. What can you do?"

"I'll have to tell Father." She lifted a blotchy red face to Miss Ruth, "He'll blame me, even though it's all your fault."

Miss Ruth's eyes settled on Philomena with pity. She knew the girl was only two years old when her mother died, and she had rarely seen her father during her childhood years. According to Mr. Taylor, his vain, self-centered mother had raised Philomena in her own image. *What kind of person would I be without Grandpa John's and Aunt Ellie's godly influence?*

"Philomena, look at me and tell me the truth. Do you care what your father thinks of you?"

A lift of her shoulder and a spark in her eye told Miss Ruth the girl was ready with an explosive answer. Miss Ruth put a finger to her lips and whispered. "Think for a moment."

Philomena wiped her eyes and stared across the street at the open waters of Crescent Bay. "I think I do."

"Why?"

"I never had a chance to know him. I think I might like to." Another long silence and sweat appeared on Philomena's upper lip as if the effort to find the answer was too difficult. "Grandmother always found fault. I could never do enough or come close to her high standard. I was not good enough."

Miss Ruth put her arm around the girl. "It's going to be all right."

"It's not going to be all right. I've just proved to my father that grandmother was right."

"So everyone came to you for instructions, and you had none?"

Philomena's face crumpled.

"It was all a ruse, dear one. The invitations were sent two weeks ago. Cook is even now preparing the delicacies for tonight's reception. The servants are attending to their duties. The same is true for the dinner and the ball."

Philomena choked, then jumped to her feet. "How could you be so cruel? You let me worry and fret, and all the time, you had everything under control." Her hands fisted, and a vein throbbed in her temple. "You tricked me, you mean, evil woman." She ran to the street, then turned and yelled, "You are no longer welcome at the governor's mansion or anywhere else I am."

Miss Ruth did not tell the girl that her father was the one who expected her to fail and had made all the arrangements.

Second Lieutenant Malcolm Burke raced up the steps to Castle Hill. He had tried to arrange meetings with Philomena for a month without success. Last week he had even come to the mansion but had been told she was not receiving.

A message was delivered to the barracks today. She wanted to see him. His heart pounded when he saw her standing near the edge of the hill near the flagpole. She stared across to Japonski Island and the Navy vessel docked there.

Cheeks ruddy and slightly chafed, hair unbound and blown about by the wind, a small smile on her face; this was his Philomena.

"I've missed you, Phillie." He reached for her hands, but she thrust them into her pockets.

"I've been busy. As my father's hostess, I have so many responsibilities." She never took her eyes off the vessel.

"I've been trying to see you since the night of the ball."

"Don't be tiresome, Malcolm. I said I've been busy."

He winced at her harsh tone, then forgave her as he always did. He stepped nearer, and she turned her back to him.

"Not too busy to flirt and dance with a Navy Captain all night." He couldn't control the bitterness in his voice, which angered him.

"Don't be childish, Malcolm; I had certain obligations."

"You seem to enjoy them a little too much. As an engaged woman—"

"Are you accusing me of something?" She faced him now, and he saw the selfishness in her eyes.

"I was part of the color guard that opened the ball." He cleared his throat. "After we presented the flag and your father welcomed everyone, we retired the colors and were stationed around the perimeter of that immense ballroom. I watched you."

Her face flooded with color. She turned her collar up against the wind and moved away. "Perhaps we should sit on the veranda," she shivered.

"Admit it, Phillie; you did not act with proper decorum."

She thrust her hand in front of his face, fingers spread. "Do you see a ring?"

Malcolm blanched and took a step back. He tried to gentle his voice as he reminded her, "You know I send a portion of my wages to help my family. I am saving for a ring, but it will take more time. We talked about this."

"Mrs. Thornwood said it's not a proper engagement without a ring. She said a man in love puts his woman above everything. She said the greater the love, the bigger the ring."

"But Phillie..."

"My name is Philomena. Captain Moore said Phillie sounds like a young horse, not a beautiful full-grown woman."

"But Phillie, Philomena, we love each other."

At last, she faced him and put her palm on his cheek. "You are a sweet boy, dear Malcolm, and I will always care for you."

He stiffened, his face flushed, and words failed him.

She bit the end of her finger and looked at him from under her lashes. "I think what I felt for you is what any young schoolgirl would feel for a man in uniform. But, I'm not a schoolgirl anymore."

"You're certainly acting like one."

"I've decided to accompany my father when Captain Donald Moore transports the remaining staff to Juneau next week."

"It's not your father you're eager to accompany; it's that Captain, that middle-aged Captain. I thought you were young, but you are also stupid and foolish." With each word, Malcolm's voice increased in intensity, if not volume. He caught himself and finished the sentence through clenched teeth.

She raised her hand as if to slap him.

"I wouldn't," he whispered.

She examined his face, then dabbed her eyes with an embroidered handkerchief. "Dear Malcolm. Let's not part enemies. I can't help it if I've outgrown you."

He left her on the veranda, still watching Captain Moore's ship.

He stomped away and wondered if Captain Moore knew Philomena had set her mind on him.

THIRTY-EIGHT

SAM, 1962

It was a three-cigar letter, and the faster Sam read, the more furiously he puffed, causing the cigars to overheat. The smoky-sweet aroma of his favorite stogies no longer permeated the room. Instead, an acrid scent filled the hazy cloud circling his head, and a bitter taste filled his mouth.

Sam opened the windows, disgusted with himself. Cigars were meant to be savored slowly, and he had squandered three of his most expensive. He stuffed the long letter back into its envelope. This was Philomena's fault.

"I hope Malcolm found someone else, someone like Alice." He put his humidor out of reach as penance for ruining his smokes. "Sadsack? Wake up and tell me why I compare every woman to Alice and why they're all lacking?"

The cat licked his paw twice and then jumped onto the side table next to a pile of Miss Ruth's letters. He looked at Sam and blinked.

"You're right, Sad. Miss Ruth is in a category all by herself." He pulled on his jacket and hat. He opened the door and threw these words over his shoulder. "Alice comes close, you lousy cat, extremely close."

THIRTY-NINE

Dear Kamalei,

The priest from Wrangell will be in Sitka for four weeks. He is newly married and brought his wife. To give them privacy, I have taken the opportunity to visit the Connors in Juneau.

Did you know there have been rumors for the past few years that Wyatt Earp passed through Juneau on his way to Nome? I never met him, but I did encounter his wife, Josephine. She has touched my heart...

—MISS RUTH'S LETTERS 1907

Miss Ruth's cowboy boots played the wooden sidewalks of Juneau like Ragtime Hattie's piano pounding. Its syncopated rhythm danced out the door of the Red Dog Saloon and slapped passersby in the face. Many a toe-tapping foot changed direction and entered the drinking emporium.

Miss Ruth tapped her toe against the door jam. Covered from neck to ankles in a long black skirt and jacket, she and Ragtime Hattie couldn't have been more different.

The orange-haired, nearly sixty-year-old piano player was short, stout, and overly rouged. She wore a halter made of silver dollars, long white gloves, and bright red petticoats over an even redder chemise. Ankle bracelets and a toe ring adorned her bare feet.

Hattie didn't hear Miss Ruth enter. The bartender caught Hattie's eye and jerked his head in Miss Ruth's direction. Hattie's ragtime version of "When the Roll is Called Up Yonder" reverberated throughout the saloon. Patrons of the Red Dog stopped mid-drink and mid-bet as the two women embraced.

Most of the sourdoughs and old-timers hailed Miss Ruth with a raised glass and a loud hello. The cheechakos wanted to know if this woman in black was some kind of nun? Where did she come from? What was she doing in the saloon? Their comments were ignored. It wouldn't take the newcomers long to learn in Alaska; you didn't ask.

Ragtime Hattie guided Miss Ruth to a private dining room and served tea. Miss Ruth pulled off her doeskin gloves and reached for the sugar bowl, "Hattie, it's good to see you again, but your message sounded desperate."

Hattie lit a long, thin cheroot and blew the wispy, gray smoke toward the ceiling, "Do you remember several years back when that lawman and gambler, Wyatt Earp, was here in the Red Dog?"

"I heard rumors the judge politely invited him to make his way elsewhere," Miss Ruth answered.

"It was about the time gold was found in Nome. There was a mad rush out of town," Hattie put her elbows on the table and stared at Miss Ruth.

Miss Ruth patted the older woman's hand, "Hattie dear, what has that to do with me?"

"I want you to fix her."

"Fix? Who?"

"Josie, Wyatt's wife."

Miss Ruth shook her head and filled her teacup, "What do you mean, fix?"

"You fixed a lot of folks around here with your God-talk and your do-good ways. I seen it."

"Thank you for the confidence. But if there is any fixing to be done, the Lord will do it." Hattie's lips quivered, and a single tear hovered on her blackened eyelashes.

"I'll be in Juneau for a while. When does Mrs. Earp want to meet?" Miss Ruth asked.

Ragtime Hattie stubbed out her cheroot in a teacup and hid her hands in her lap.

"Hattie?"

A shake of her head was Hattie's only answer.

"She doesn't know about me, does she?"

"You are the most peaceable person I know, and poor Miss Josie, she needs that."

"If she's agreeable, I'll meet with her. But I can't make her talk to me."

"I thought maybe you could preach at her or something."

Miss Ruth laughed, "It doesn't work that way."

"I heard you preach in this very saloon not too many years ago."

"As I recall, it nearly tore the place apart, and I only did it because the Lord insisted."

Hattie swiped at her rebellious tears and held out her hand, "How about you meet Miss Josie and do what your God tells you."

"Deal." Miss Ruth shook her hand. "I'll make a reservation at the hotel's dining room."

The dark misty weather was not unusual for this time of year. Miss Ruth studied the petite woman walking beside Hattie. The wooden sidewalks protected their skirts; the muddy streets did not.

Josie's face, gray as the day, her steps heavy as the fog, appeared as miserable as the weather. Hattie held Josie's arm, pulled her along, and talked incessantly. Josie, eyes down, barely nodded now and again.

Miss Ruth offered her hand to the younger woman. "Good afternoon, Mrs. Earp. I'm pleased to meet you."

"Josie, don't stab me with that glare. You and Miss Ruth are my favorite people in all of Alaska. It's only right that you should meet, especially since you said you're never coming back once you're in the States," Hattie's voice quivered.

"I'm always ready to make a new friend," Miss Ruth said.

The three women pulled their skirts above their boots and crossed the muddy street.

"As long as you don't preach," Josie muttered under her breath, then her face flamed.

Miss Ruth leaned over and whispered in Josie's ear, "A friend would never do that."

Josie lifted her head and saw the twinkle in Miss Ruth's eyes but shuddered when she heard Miss Ruth add, "At least, not too often."

They settled at a table in the corner of the room. "Who would have thought to have this lovely linen and china shipped north while the miners beg for tools, winter clothing, and foodstuffs?" Miss Ruth reached for a neutral topic of conversation as the three women placed their napkins on their laps.

"Wyatt says there's always a market for the finer things."

Ragtime Hattie laughed, "So that's why Wyatt had all that finery and frippery shipped to his saloon in Nome."

Josie placed her hand on Hattie's, "You could make a fortune at our saloon in Nome. Please reconsider our offer."

"This is as far north as I go," Hattie said, "six months of darkness ain't for me, besides money ain't everything."

"I also hate the darkness, so Wyatt and I usually go south for the winter. But Nome is where we need to be to mine the miners."

"Mine the miners?" Miss Ruth raised her eyebrows.

"Wyatt says it's easier to make money from drunken miners than dig it out of the ground ourselves."

"Is the money so very important to you?" Miss Ruth poured another round of tea and signaled the waiter to refill the pot.

Josie's eyebrows shot up, "It's everything!"

"What about family? Friends? Health?"

"Wyatt says with enough money we can buy all of that."

"Don't you want more?" Miss Ruth refused to let Josie look away, "Isn't life more than money?"

Josie knocked over her teacup as she reached for the sugar bowl. The stain spread across the white linen, "You sound like my parents—poor, religious Jews—always pushing goodness and God at me. I left when I was fifteen; I seen and done things no God should allow."

"He can forgive you all of that," Miss Ruth whispered.

"I ain't asking. Nobody's going to take care of you in this world. Only money can do that."

"Josie, God loves you."

Josie Earp stood and threw her napkin on the table, "If He did, He wouldn't have let my babies die before they was even born. Good day, Miss Ruth." Josie turned to the older woman, "Hattie, my boat leaves for Seattle in two days. Best you don't contact me."

She left unaware of the tears in Hattie's eyes and the wound in her heart. "I was only trying to help. She will never forgive me." Hattie sobbed.

Miss Ruth stroked Hattie's orange-dyed hair, "Forgive you for loving her?"

"She hurts so much. I want her to have what you have."

"You must pray for her."

Hattie mopped her eyes with the hotel's napkin, "Now, Miss Ruth, you know I leave the praying to you."

"You promised me you would talk to God."

Hattie sighed and hung her head. Miss Ruth kissed her cheek, dabbed at her own eyes, and raised a hurting heart to heaven.

FORTY

Dear Kam,

The Klondike Rush has been over for nearly a decade, but it has changed Alaska forever, as have the big strike in Nome and the smaller ones in the interior. Juneau and Skagway, especially, have been inundated with every kind of evil. Saloons, whorehouses, gambling dens, and the like are everywhere. The women and children suffered the most in these lawless, uncivilized towns...

—*MISS RUTH'S LETTERS 1909*

He gazed at his sister with old eyes as he shared his food. She had the same dirty blonde hair and sallow skin, and they were about the same size, although he was two years older.

Mama worked nights and tried to bring them food every morning, "This is for you. I had something at work," she'd say.

When Mama wasn't aware, he gave half of his portion to four-year-old Ada. She always snatched it and held out her hands for more.

Their shack was neither wind nor rainproof, and the thin blankets were often damp. When it was not raining, Mama built a fire outside the door from scraps of lumber she found in the alley. But it had been raining for two weeks, the unheated shack was damp, and they could not get warm.

Mama had been in bed for a long time, maybe days. Usually, she would come home, feed them, and hang her fancy dress on the peg above the mat they called the bed. She'd tell them stories about when she was a little girl and then sleep.

Yesterday and today, there was no story and no food. Ada had fussed and cried herself into exhaustion. Now she clutched her stomach and lay next to Mama, "I'm hungry. I'm cold. My belly hurts. Why doesn't Mama wake up?"

His hunger and Ada's whining drove him out the door, "Stay with Mama."

"Don't go, Sidney."

"I'll be back soon."

He grabbed the water bucket and hoped to find someone willing to share. He knew there was a creek outside of Juneau because he'd been there with Mama. He wasn't sure if he could find it by himself. The bucket bumped against his leg with every step.

The businesses along the waterfront often provided scraps from their garbage bins, but he had to fend off the wharf rats who believed they had exclusive rights to the docks and alleys. His grip on the bucket tightened, and he feared he and Ada would be hungry again today. He stumbled and leaned against the building on the corner.

He looked up and picked out the letters above the door and sounded out the name—the Red Dog Saloon. That's where Mama worked. The place was nearly empty. There was a man behind the bar counting bottles and polishing glasses. Sidney could see the back of the man's bald head in the mirror behind him and a picture of a naked lady. He turned his eyes away; somehow, he knew Mama would disapprove.

He glanced around the room and saw the orange-haired lady Mama knew. He squeezed his eyes tight, trying to remember her name. She rifled through and sorted a pile of papers, sometimes stopping to write on them. Once, she leaned a paper against the piano and pounded on the keys.

"How's that, Clyde?"

"Music to my tin ears."

A deliveryman knocked over the boy, "Out of my way, boy." The man had a keg under each arm. "Where do you want these, Clyde?"

"In the storeroom, same as always, and use the back door."

"I ain't going all the way around back," he gestured to the open front door, "and you better get rid of that brat. He nearly tripped me. You don't want to pay for spilled beer."

Clyde frowned toward the door. The boy shrank back.

"Hattie," the bartender said as he lit a cheroot and flicked the ash toward the door.

Hattie gathered her papers, tucked them into the piano bench, then moved toward the door, "What do you want, boy?"

He stared at her three chins. Even as he held out his bucket, his stomach growled.

"You hungry?"

He nodded and clutched his belly. His hunger pangs were more intense than yesterday's.

"Make a couple of sandwiches," she yelled to Clyde.

"You feed one brat, and they'll soon be swarming the place like wharf rats."

The boy shuddered and dropped his head. Ragtime Hattie reached out to pat it but grabbed the bucket instead. "Clyde!" she hollered.

"All right." He grabbed a knife and a loaf of bread, "Dang fool woman."

She filled the bucket from the water barrel in the back room and picked up the sandwiches. The boy's eyes never left her, and he breathed easier when she stood before him holding the bucket and the sandwiches.

"What's your name?"

Instead of answering, he cupped his hands and plunged them into the bucket. He brought them to his mouth and repeatedly slurped, never taking his eyes off the food.

Hattie said, "Let's get you washed up so you can eat."

Hungry as he was, he shook his head and grabbed her hand. She freed her hand, dashed into the saloon, yanked her shawl off the top of the piano, and told Clyde she'd be back later.

Clyde slammed a shot glass onto the bar, "Dang fool woman."

Ragtime Hattie offered the boy a sandwich and asked again, "What's your name?"

With a full mouth, he mumbled, "Sidney." He chewed slowly and, after another small bite, put the rest of the sandwich in his pocket.

He pulled her down the alley, past more saloons and dance halls, around the corner, and up a slight hill. Wedged between a boat repair shop and a herring packing plant was what could only be described as a hovel. Made of discarded packing crates with rags and moss for chinking, it was unstable and fragile enough that a good wind could blow it over.

Sidney pushed her toward the door. She had to bend over to find it. The makeshift doorway was barely visible and no taller than the boy.

"It's okay, little man," she said. But it wasn't. Ragtime Hattie groaned as she stooped and entered. Dank, musty air greeted her. The smell of decay and disease made her wince, and she breathed through her mouth.

She looked around the tiny room. Broken boards formed a floor, but dirt and mud seeped through. A woman lay huddled under a thin blanket, ashen and still.

"That's Mama," Sidney said as he picked up his Mama's dancing shoes and threw them one after the other toward a giant rat in the corner. It bared its teeth and hissed but did not move. Sidney raced toward it, shouting and kicking until the rat fled.

"Don't cry, Ada. The rat's gone."

Ada scrambled to the end of the mat. Sidney tried to pick her up. He was six and three quarters after all. But she was fussy, so he settled her by Mama's feet and fished the sandwich out of his pocket, "I brought food."

This was the new dance hall girl, Ruby Rose, hired a few weeks ago. She had not appeared at the saloon for the past few days. Hattie dropped to her knees and felt for a pulse. Thready, but there. Feverish eyes glittered in the gloom.

Ada whined for more food, so Hattie broke a small corner off the remaining sandwich. Ada reached for the larger portion. "No, this is for Sidney."

Ada ignored Hattie's instructions to eat it slowly. Hattie turned toward the boy, "I'm watching you, Sidney, see that you eat it all."

Sidney nodded and turned away. He didn't want to see Ada watch.

Hattie dipped the end of her shawl in the bucket. After wringing it, she wiped the woman's face, "Why didn't you send word you were sick? I didn't even know you had kids. We would've helped you, Ruby."

"Afraid I'd lose my job," Ruby whispered, "Take care of my babies."

Ragtime Hattie could pound any tune on the piano, and she could break up a bar fight. She could knock back a shot of whiskey, smoke a cheroot, and deal five-card stud. What she could not do was children. But she took them home and had Clyde deal with Ruby's body.

The boy, too old for his years, followed her constantly with his eyes. If she was honest with herself, she'd admit it got on her nerves. The little girl sat still for hours, cradling her rag doll.

Hattie rubbed her eyes and tried to push her wild hair back into its bun. She pulled her feet out of the bucket she was soaking them in. Sidney handed her a towel and turned away. He didn't see her try to smile.

Why was this so hard? Last week, she talked two miners out of killing each other, threw a card shark out of the saloon, and arm-wrestled Clyde for a month's wages. Kids were a different breed altogether, not easy to understand.

Hattie's bright orange hair frizzled, and she smoked too many cheroots. She struggled into her fancy dress and called the kids. "Time to go to the Red Dog."

"Boss says you can't bring them brats in here no more."

"I don't know what else to do. You got any ideas?"

Clyde polished his already gleaming bar, "Can't say that I have."

"I can't leave them in the street."

"All I know is, boss says you can't bring them here no more."

Hattie leaned over the bar, "You think he'll fire me?"

Clyde laughed, "You and I both know you could work at any joint on the waterfront. It would be the busiest place in town."

Hattie grinned, nodded, and headed to her private parlor with her silent little charges, confident the boss would do nothing.

Clyde reached under the bar, "Almost forgot, Captain Walker left a message for you."

Hattie grabbed it and read quickly, "Hallelujah." Her face brightened, and she waved the paper in Clyde's direction. "Captain Walker says he's bringing Miss Ruth on his next run, four days from now. She'll be staying with those hoity-toity mine owners, the Connors, but she wants to visit me first."

"You going to dump those brats on her?" Clyde smirked.

Hattie winced, knowing the children heard, but yes, that's precisely what she would do.

Clyde leaned over the bar and whispered to Sidney, whose eyes darted between the two adults, "Don't worry, boy, Miss Ruth is," he searched for the right word as the piano player glared at him, "much softer than Ragtime Hattie."

Sidney gave a slight nod and hoped it was true.

FORTY-ONE

Dear Kamalei,

I've written to you often about the Connors. They are my best friends in Alaska, just as you and your family were in Hawaii, Ohana—family. I recently visited them in Juneau and delivered two little orphans into their care.

And wonder of wonders, Jack will build me a house in Sitka! What do I need with a house? I told him a small cabin that he could rent out until I'm too old to work would be just fine...

—MISS RUTH'S LETTERS 1909

Ragtime Hattie leaned toward the mirror and frowned at the dark serge dress she had worn to Alaska nearly two decades ago. It was a little snug, but it was all she had beside her fancy saloon dresses. She fiddled with the buttons and swore as one popped off.

"It will just take a moment to sew it back on," Miss Ruth reached into her reticule for needle and thread. The large drawstring bag was packed for whatever mishaps might occur.

"I know you said Mrs. Connor was a regular person like me, but that can't be."

"Why's that?"

"I'm a drinking, swearing, gambling, sinning kind of woman."

Hattie lowered her eyes and turned away from Miss Ruth, "A soiled dove even in my younger years."

"Do you know what I see when I look at you?" Miss Ruth asked.

Hattie dropped her head and mumbled something about not wanting to know. She pulled on her hair and then grabbed a brush. Her heart would crack to have Miss Ruth describe her.

Miss Ruth took the brush and stood behind the distraught woman. "I see someone who has staked miners down on their luck, who's paid passage home for men who failed in the goldfields and had no way to get back to their families. I see a woman who protected the girls at the saloon from being abused. You are a lady I admire and respect."

Ragtime Hattie wiped her nose with her sleeve and said, "But Miss Ruth, I've done awful things."

"You are a sinner, Hattie, and so am I."

"Not you, Miss Ruth."

"The only difference between us is I've accepted the Lord's mercy. I long for the day when you do the same."

Hattie's face flushed as she remembered some of her wanton ways. She pushed those images away and mumbled, "All I can think about is meeting Mrs. Connor, one of the few married white women in Alaska. Respectable. A real lady."

"Don't put Maureen on a pedestal of virtue and respectability. She's not perfect."

Hattie tugged on Miss Ruth's sleeve. "I don't need to go with you. I'm sure Mr. and Mrs. Connor have taken good care of Sidney and Ada these past few weeks."

"Maureen has invited us to visit, Hattie. It would be rude to refuse."

"I can't sit in a fancy parlor and make small talk. I don't know any of the mannerly rules," she shuddered. "I can see you are trying to shame me into going."

"It would be embarrassing for me to explain that you didn't care enough to come for a simple visit," Miss Ruth said.

Hattie reached for a cheroot. She needed its soothing aroma to relax her tangled nerves. She sighed and pulled her shawl around her slumped shoulders. She scowled at Miss Ruth and said, "You don't play fair, young woman."

"I've never been on this road." Ragtime Hattie couldn't keep her eyes from the forest's beauty. The road was nothing more than a deeply rutted track cutting through the woods. Sunny days had dried the mud, and the wagon lurched along without getting stuck.

"There's nothing out here besides the Connors' place," Miss Ruth said, "but there used to be a lot of placer mines in these hills. They were abandoned when news of the strike came out of the Yukon."

An icy stream flowed parallel to the track. The unattended sluices, dredges, open pits, and abandoned equipment did not mar the landscape. Underbrush and young saplings had encroached and almost covered the abandoned equipment.

Ragtime Hattie saw beyond the evidence of man's sojourn in the forest to the woods itself. Green Ash, Red Alder, and Mountain Hemlock. Of course, Hattie didn't know the names of the trees, only that they were thick, lush, and lovely.

Every shade of green filled her vision and overwhelmed her.

She lifted her eyes to the painfully blue sky, a rare occurrence in normally rain-soaked Juneau. Hattie breathed deeply, pulling the color and cleanness of the countryside into her lungs.

Miss Ruth turned into the Connors' drive, and Hattie's stomach clenched. The unsullied woods on either side of the dirt road leading to the house seemed to mock the taint and decay she lived with at the Red Dog.

She put her hand on Miss Ruth's arm, "Please, stop! I can't do this."

"Whoa." Miss Ruth pulled on the reins and turned to face the older woman. "We'll wait until you're ready."

"It's lovely out here, unspoiled, pure, just like Miss Maureen."

"No one is pure in God's eyes, Hattie. Not until He makes them pure. He can do that for you."

Hattie sniffed, then wiped her nose with her handkerchief. "I know you love me, Miss Ruth, vile as I am. God knows why." Hattie wiped her eyes.

"God loves you, and Maureen will too."

Hattie raised her face to the treetops, "I hear birdsong; it must be what peace sounds like."

Miss Ruth sat in silence as Hattie absorbed some of that calmness. Finally, she turned to Miss Ruth, smiled slightly, and shrugged.

"Giddyap," Miss Ruth flicked the reins.

The log house, it could not be labeled a cabin, sat atop a knoll, facing a small cove. Jack Connor had cleared the area around it, planted a large garden, and built several outbuildings. Blueberry bushes ringed the perimeter.

"Window boxes?" Hattie exclaimed.

"Maureen is determined to have her flowers. She even has a

lemon tree growing inside the house. It has an honored spot next to the woodstove."

"She must favor lemon in her tea like a proper English lady."

Miss Ruth laughed.

"Is that funny?"

"You'll see."

"Please, Miss Ruth. I'm so nervous. I can't take any more suspense. Have some sympathy for this old woman."

"Maureen makes lemon drops. She will probably send you home with a bag full."

Hattie's head jerked; she shaded her eyes and gasped as she caught sight of Maureen Connor coming around the corner of the porch. "That can't be!"

Miss Ruth helped Hattie from the wagon and replied, "I'm afraid it is."

"But she..." Hattie's picture of a genteel lady broke from her mind like an iceberg from a glacier in spring. She stood staring with her mouth open.

Maureen met them on the front steps. "Forgive my attire, Hattie. May I call you that? I was chopping wood all morning and time got away from me. I ran to the porch as soon as Sean saw you turn into the drive."

Hattie stared at Maureen's miner's boots and Levis. Maureen also wore a man's flannel shirt. She had removed her Irish cable knit sweater and tied it around her waist. "I'm not exactly dressed for a tea party, am I?"

"No, Mrs. Connor. I mean, you look very nice," Hattie said.

Miss Ruth laughed, "Don't let her fool you, Hattie. This is how she dresses most days."

Miss Ruth and Maureen made small talk as the three women entered the massive log home. The burnished Red Cedar reflected sunlight streaming through a wall of windows, where Hattie stood and stared at the islands and seabirds beyond. It appeared as if they could come right inside.

Maureen stood with her back to the windows. "I know it's odd, and Jack thought it couldn't be done. He had the glass shipped from New England. So much of it broke on the way we had to re-order twice. But isn't it wonderful?" She turned and stared out the window, hugging herself.

Hattie had never seen anything like it and started to say so. She was interrupted by squeals and screams as Sidney and Ada ran through the room, followed by a good-looking man who turned out to be Maureen's son.

Hattie jumped when she heard Maureen bellow, "Sean! Manners!"

"I'm over thirty, Ma. You can't be correcting my manners."

Maureen laughed, "Just the lack thereof, me boy-o."

Sean rolled his eyes and marched the two little ones outside the door. They quietly reentered the room.

"Good day Miss Ragtime," Sidney said with a bit of a bow.

Ada pulled her thumb from her mouth and tried to make a little curtsy. She plopped to the floor. Her face scrunched, but Miss Ruth scooped her up and kissed her cheek.

"Ragtime Hattie?" Sean asked and extended his hand.

Face flaming and unable to meet his eyes, Hattie nodded and shook his hand.

"I'm going to ask her, Ma."

A slight shake of her head, "It wouldn't be polite, son."

Disappointment tried to settle on Sean's features and failed. He winked at Miss Ruth and stooped to whisper in Sidney's ear. Since coming to live with the Connors, Sidney had worshiped Sean, who had worked hard not to let the little boy become a willing slave. However, this was too important, "Go on, Sidney."

Maureen took a step forward to stop him. Instead, she whispered to Miss Ruth, "That boy is so much like me. He almost always finds a way."

Miss Ruth laughed, "I'd hardly call him a boy."

Sidney took Miss Hattie's hand, led her to the piano, and pushed her onto the bench, "I can play. Miss Maureen teached me." Sidney plunked out the first line of "Jesus Love Me" with one finger.

Hattie smiled and said, "Very nice." She started to rise. Sidney looked at Sean, who nodded. The little boy grabbed the dark serge dress and pulled, "Play it ragtime."

Hattie's eyes darted to each person in the room. She gulped and looked toward Maureen. Even if she was dressed in men's clothes, Maureen was still a respectable lady, and this was no barroom.

Maureen clapped her hands and leaned on the piano. "Please."

"Oh no, Miss Maureen, it ain't respectable."

"Says who?"

"All the people who don't go to the saloons, I guess."

"Everybody in Juneau goes to the saloons."

"You don't, Miss Maureen." Hattie's chin quivered, and tears threatened.

"Just Maureen. Please play it for Sidney."

"For me too," Ada called from Miss Ruth's lap. Sean added his pleas as well. Ragtime Hattie took a deep breath, swallowed past the lump in her throat, and played "Jesus Loves Me" in ragtime.

Sean and Maureen clapped the loudest and longest, "It's such happy music, Ma."

"Yes, me boy-oh, it is." She nodded toward the little ones, and Sean ushered them out of the room. He lifted the plate of cookies as they went.

Maureen sat next to Hattie and played Beethoven's "Ode to Joy" from his Ninth Symphony. Hattie, frozen, dared not breathe.

"What can you do with that, Hattie?" Maureen asked.

"Nothing. It's perfect."

"Can you teach Maureen to play it in ragtime?" Miss Ruth called from across the room.

"I've had lessons for years, Hattie, and I'm good." Maureen took Hattie's hands in her own.

Hattie nodded but kept her eyes on Maureen's hands.

"But you are brilliant, innovative, and creative. You must be my teacher, Hattie."

"All I do, Miss Maureen, is pound on the piano."

"Then Hattie dear, you must teach me to pound."

Hattie gestured to Miss Ruth. Get me out of this, her eyes pleaded.

Miss Ruth smiled and said, "I think it would be a great kindness if you would teach Maureen, either here or at the Red Dog."

"We can't have the likes of her at the Red Dog," Hattie almost shrieked.

Maureen put her hands on her hips, "Are you saying I'm not good enough for the establishment?" Maureen's Irish brogue was thick, and her eyes twinkled, but Hattie didn't notice.

She flushed and covered her face with her hands. Maureen pulled them away and smiled into Hattie's eyes, holding her gaze. "I worked my way across the West working in hotels and saloons, mostly cleaning or washing dishes. I had to earn my daily bread as a dance hall girl for a short time. I praise God that someone like you protected me and kept me from falling. I've been told you've done the same for others." Maureen kissed Hattie's cheek, "I love you for that, dear Hattie."

The orange-haired, cheroot-smoking piano player took a deep breath and, with tears falling, pounded the piano in what was indeed an ode to joy.

Several hours later, Jack and the others came inquiring about their supper. Jack saw the women still in the throes of their music and conversation. He herded everyone back the way they came and said, "Come on, kids, we'll have a cookout."

"Good idea Pa. Beans. Bacon. Biscuits." Sean yelled, "Like real cowboys." He caught Miss Ruth's glance and winked, then took Ada and Sidney by the hand, "I'll tell you about the time I spent on a real ranch in the American West."

"With real cowboys?" Sidney yelled.

"Yes, and a real cowgirl who could almost outshoot and out-rope me."

"Whoa, that can't be." Sidney's voice broke. "Say it's not true, Sean."

Sean pointed to Miss Ruth, "That's the cowgirl."

The little boy laughed aloud, "Stop funnin' me, Sean."

Maureen looked at the delicate gold watch pinned to her sweater, "You must forgive me, Hattie, and stay to eat. I've made you play all afternoon with not so much as a cookie or a cup of tea."

"I must get back to the Red Dog."

Fiery red locks touched wild orange hair as Maureen embraced the older woman. "We're going to be great friends. You'll teach me ragtime, and I'll teach you," Maureen shook her head, "I don't know what, but something."

Miss Maureen was as great a force as Miss Ruth. Hattie swallowed and accepted the inevitable, then leaned over and whispered in Maureen's ear. The Irish woman squeezed Hattie's arm, "If that's what you want."

❧

"By this time next year, I expect to be an expert in ragtime," Maureen said the following day as she cleared the dinner table.

"That's not your primary objective, is it, Miss Maureen?" Miss Ruth exaggerated the name.

Maureen's eyes sparkled, "Ragtime Hattie wants me to teach her genteel manners so she can be accepted anywhere."

"I recognized a longing in her."

"You and I both know it's not a longing for polite society."

"Whenever I try to talk to her about eternal things, she goes silent."

"Words don't matter to a lot of people. It's how you live. Hattie's watching you."

"I'm glad you're here for her, Maureen. It's not often I'm in Juneau."

"I plan to start a little Bible study for the girls at the dance hall."

"Hattie will never go for that."

Maureen threw her head back and laughed, "It's going to be her idea, and we're going to help those that want to leave that life."

Miss Ruth hugged this Irish woman from whom she had learned so much, "I believe you."

Ada and Sidney rushed in; the little girl presented some bedraggled wildflowers to the two women, "These are for you, Mama Ruth, and you too, Mama Maureen."

Sidney dug in his pockets and let out a howl. The salmonberries he had picked were squished, and the juice leaked down his pant leg. Maureen snatched a saucer from the tea table, and the little boy emptied his pockets, sniffing the whole time. "Ah, me boy-o salmonberries make the best jelly. You saved me a lot of work by squishing them already."

The boy's face brightened, and he wiped his berry-stained hand on his pants. She looked over the boy's head at her husband leaning against the doorframe. "Really, Jack? You couldn't have taken a bucket?" He shrugged and clapped his hands. "Time for baths and bed." The response was groans and moans. "Hurry now, and there'll be time for an extra story."

Tears in her eyes, Maureen turned to Miss Ruth, "Thank you for bringing those sweet babies to us. They've made us young again."

"I couldn't think of anyone better."

"I wonder you didn't keep them for yourself, start a boarding school or orphanage."

Miss Ruth felt a pang near her heart, then shook her head. "They need a real family."

"Speaking of family, still no news of your father?"

"To tell you the truth, I haven't thought about him since Jack returned from his unsuccessful trip to the Kenai."

"I'm glad to hear it."

Miss Ruth raised startled eyes to Maureen's. "What do you mean?"

Maureen crossed the room and knelt beside the rose velvet chair. She took Miss Ruth's hand in her own. "Your father was a broken man in search of himself. In many ways, it consumed him, and he had little left to give a child."

Miss Ruth nodded. "I came to Alaska to find the man who fathered me, but I have realized my Dad, my Papa, is buried in Hawaii. Robert Merritt may have conceived me, but Grandpa John was the best father any girl could have."

"Hmmmn." Maureen handed Miss Ruth a dainty cotton hanky and a freshly made bag of lemon drops.

"I sometimes wonder what I'm doing in this vast land." Miss Ruth shrugged her shoulders and lowered her eyes.

"You let your dream fade so your destiny could shine."

Miss Ruth sat up straight. "Grandpa said something similar right before he died."

"What do you think he meant?"

"I thought finding my father was both dream and destiny."

"Your grandfather wanted the matter about your father resolved, but he knew your destiny was something grander."

The younger woman laughed, "I've never done anything grand."

"John told me once that even as a young girl, you wanted to live a big life and be significant."

"That sounds prideful."

"I don't think you wanted to be notorious or famous. You wanted to be useful, and you have been."

"How can you say that? I haven't accomplished anything."

"Lean back and close your eyes. Let the images of everyone you hold in your heart appear before you."

They sat in silence for several minutes. Miss Ruth leaned against the soft cushions and pondered the older woman's words. Little brown faces and some tall ones mingled with blonde and ruddy Scandinavian ones. Could Maureen be right?

Tears formed in Miss Ruth's eyes, and she reached for her handkerchief. "Oh, Maureen, I am most blessed."

"You are and will continue to be Alaska's Mama."

Miss Ruth gave a great sigh of contentment. "I hope you are right, but tell me, what's next for Sean?"

"He finally graduated from the University of Washington with degrees in business and mine engineering."

"It took him a while."

"As you know, he kept taking time off to prospect or visit a certain teacher in several isolated communities, and I'm glad he did."

Miss Ruth laughed, "I was grateful for those visits, but it put me in an awkward position. A handsome young man visiting a single female teacher in the wilds of Alaska! Fortunately, each village had a Russian church, and Sean stayed with the priests. We were never alone."

Maureen looked through the window. Sean, shirt off, and muscles bulging, swung the ax expertly. The stack of kindling multiplied as the pile of logs declined. She turned to Miss Ruth, "I shouldn't say this, but he was always in love with you."

Miss Ruth sat up straight and put her coffee cup down with a thud, "I never knew."

"He didn't want you to and finally fell for a girl at the University."

"Where is she? When can I meet her?"

"Despite rumors around the campus, Sean convinced her he was not wealthy. She had heard he was the son of a successful mine owner, but when she thought there was no mine..." Maureen sighed and reached for the coffee pot.

"Poor Sean. You don't think he'd consider me again? After all, I'm half a decade older than he is and officially a spinster."

Maureen laughed, "Enough about Sean. He will find his way. Here are the plans for your house in Sitka."

"Really, Maureen, I travel so much and don't need a house. My room at the See House fits my needs."

"Jack thinks you do."

"Small cabin, maybe."

"You'll have to convince Jack of that. You know how he is when he gets an idea."

"You know how I am when I get one."

FORTY-TWO

SAM, 1962

Agrefena's French crullers remained in the bag with an unopened thermos of the Cafe's coffee. The haze from half a dozen cigars wafted through the room and swirled around Sam's head.

It nearly choked Alice as she entered the newspaper office. "Quick, Sam! Open a window." She waved a hand in front of her face.

"It's cold out."

"The cigar smoke's burning my eyes; besides, it's way too stuffy in here."

"Oh, sorry." Sam opened the window, picked up several letters, read them aloud, and remarked, "Don't you love Ragtime Hattie? Pure Alaska," Sam laughed out loud.

"Yes, but..."

"Can't you picture her in those red crinolines? I don't even know what they are."

"A type of underskirt."

"I'm not sure what those are, either. Never mind. Red on the bottom, silver dollars on top, and bright orange hair. She must have been a sight." Sam shook his head in delighted disbelief.

"But Sam..."

"I can imagine the scene in the Red Dog Saloon, sourdoughs drinking and gambling, boasting or moaning depending on the outcome of their time in the goldfields, dance hall girls flouncing, Hattie banging on the piano. Just like a Western movie."

"But Sam..."

"I've heard the legend of Wyatt Earp in Juneau, but to know Miss Ruth actually met his wife—unbelievable! And Sean's parents take in the two little orphans. Good people. Odd, Connor never mentioned the kids." Sam grabbed a pen and scribbled a note for Chuck to search the letters for Sidney and Ada.

"Sam, you're missing the point."

Sam choked back his rambling enthusiasm and poured coffee for both of them. He drank half the cup and said, "What point are you talking about?"

Alice leaned over the desk with a dreamy, unfocused expression on her face. "Maureen said Sean was in love with Miss Ruth. IN LOVE!"

Sam shook his head and reached for a cruller. "He never mentioned it."

"Why didn't he tell her?" Alice whispered.

"Maybe he knew she loved Captain Walker." Sam pulled another cruller out of the bag and offered it to Alice. She shook her head.

"Did she? I don't think she would let anybody know."

"What would her life have been like if she had shared her feelings with the Captain," Sam wondered.

"Many people's lives would have been very different. Still, marriage and family are the norm for most people."Alice looked at him over the rim of her cup. Keeping her eyes fixed on his, she lowered it to the desk, put her coat on slowly, wrapped her scarf around her neck, and picked up her hat and gloves while her eyes remained locked on Sam's.

She fished a cruller out of the bag, grabbed her purse, and backed toward the door, her eyes still glued to his. "Think about that, Sam Mitchell."

FORTY-THREE

Dear Kamalei,

This is the most difficult letter I have ever written. A dear friend of mine has lost all but one family member, and there is no guarantee that the lone survivor will ever be returned to him. I have felt a bitterness erupt in me that I didn't know I still carried.

My heart is in pieces, and I do not know if it will ever come together again. Perhaps, if I write it all out, it will help me accept what I cannot change...

—MISS RUTH'S LETTERS 1912

"Sean, you remembered my birthday! Now that I'm in my forties, I don't expect you to come all the way from Juneau for a piece of cake. Have you heard from the folks? I'm so glad they adopted those poor little orphans, Sidney and Ada. When will they return from Europe? It's been so long, and I'm eager to hear about their adventures. Come in, Come in." Miss Ruth hugged Sean and pulled him into the parlor of the See House. "Would you like some coffee?"

Wordlessly, he shook his head and sank into the brown leather sofa in front of the window. She noticed his ashen face, sat beside him, and said, "What is it?"

"I couldn't send a telegram. I had to come myself."

Telegrams only meant one thing. Miss Ruth could not breathe. "Who?"

"All of them," his voice cracked, and he put his face in his hands, "or as good as."

"What do you mean?"

"Ada is alive."

"What happened?"

"The Titanic."

Miss Ruth wheezed, put her hand over her heart, and felt its heavy beat. "I had no idea they were passengers."

She cradled him as if he were a small child, and they wept together. When he wiped his eyes, she said, "Sean, that ship went down over a month ago. Why didn't you...."

"I'll take that coffee now."

He followed her into the kitchen. She peppered him with questions that he didn't answer. "Forgive me, Sean. If I stop talking, I'm afraid I'll scream."

He opened his arms, and she went into them. Now he was the comforter. "We're both orphans now, Ruthie."

"We will always have each other, little brother."

"If only I was your brother."

She pulled away and held his eyes. "In every way that matters, we are family. You live in my heart."

She poured the coffee into large stoneware mugs and handed one to Sean. He nodded his thanks and said, "Is there somewhere private we can talk?"

"The Bishop is upstairs in his office. His wife should return from her errands soon. Although the Bishop will not approve our taking the coffee, we can go to the church."

He set his mug on the table. "I needed something stronger anyway."

The lemon oil used to polish the pews sent a citrusy aroma wafting through the sanctuary, giving it a freshness that belied the damp weather—its opaque grayness filtered through the stained-glass windows.

Miss Ruth and Sean sat in the last pew near the free-standing stone baptismal font. She turned to face him, and he leaned against her. Silent. Mournful. She wanted to weep and howl but remained as quiet as he.

After a time, he braced himself and said, "I received a telegram from Molly Brown, who insisted I meet her in Seattle; she didn't say why. They're calling her unsinkable, you know."

"Go on."

"I had no idea my folks were even on the Titanic. They weren't due to leave England for another week." He stretched his legs out, slid down until his head rested on the back of the pew, and nearly broke down again. "Molly had friends whose plans changed at the last minute. She bought their tickets for the folks. Da thought it would be exciting for Sidney and Ada to sail on the great unsinkable ship."

The bitterness in his voice was not lost on Miss Ruth, who said, "Poor woman. I hope she doesn't blame herself. God was sovereign even over that."

"I stayed in Seattle for three days. Molly wanted to tell me everything personally. We had to hide from newspaper reporters. They followed her everywhere."

"But Sean, what about the lists in those newspapers of those who perished?"

"There were no Connors registered, just the names of Molly's friends."

Miss Ruth imagined how grief-stricken the ticket holder's family were and relieved they were when they learned their loved ones were alive. She squeezed his hand. "Tell me as much or as little as you like, dear one."

He spoke with passive hopelessness. "Molly was nearby when Da helped Ma and the kids into the lifeboat. As he helped Molly into the boat, Ma fought her way out. Molly grabbed her arm and screamed over the chaos, 'What do you think you're doing?'

"Ma pleaded with her, 'Let go of me, Molly, my place is beside Jack. Take Sidney and Ada to Sean, give him my love, and tell him he has my heart.'

"The children, not yet teenagers. How horrifying it must have been for them." Miss Ruth pressed her handkerchief to her lips.

"Sidney hollered, 'I'm ten, nearly a man! Didn't you hear me cuss? I'm the one who should stay with Da.' Molly grabbed him and set him down in the bow. She kept Ada beside her while people pushed and maneuvered and tried to shove them aside."

Miss Ruth squeezed her eyes shut. "I don't know what to say. My heart hurts." She passed her small bag of ever-present lemon drops back and forth, one hand to the other. Sean grabbed it and hurled it away. It snagged the edge of the altar, tore, and lemon drops clattered across the front of the church.

He inhaled loudly, held it a moment, then said in a thin voice, "I'll get them."

Miss Ruth laid a hand on his arm. "I'll deal with them later. Lemon drops won't help us now."

He jerked his arm away and snapped, "I said I'd get them." He folded the ripped bag into a cone. His voice became more strident as he picked up each lemon drop. "How could she be so stupid! Selfish!"

He crawled under the front pew and picked up half a dozen pieces of the candy. "How could she leave me? Why didn't she want me?" He let the cone of recovered lemon drops fall to the floor, cradled his head on the pew, and cried like a child.

Miss Ruth watched him in silence, frozen in place. Many years ago, Grandpa John had told her that anger, often caused by deep pain or hurt, was energy and must often be released.

The pain in his words pierced her soul and revived feelings from her past. She wiped her teary face and knelt beside him. "She didn't leave you, Sean. She went to be with her husband." *Not like my father, who left my mother and me.* "She didn't want him to die alone in the cold North Atlantic. She was brave." *Not a coward like my father, who abandoned my mother during her difficult labor.*

"I still need her."

"No... no, you don't. Maureen and Jack raised you well and gave you the tools you need to live a good life." *Not like my father, who gave me nothing.*

"Maybe need is the wrong word" His face crumpled. "I want my Ma and Da. Sidney and Ada, too."

"I know. I know." *At least you have had them for the past thirty-some years. I never knew my mother or my father.* Miss Ruth clamped her lips shut and trembled with the effort to keep her resentment at bay.

She thought she had accepted the circumstances of her life, yet this deep disappointment returned. She sent a plea to heaven as her emotions threatened to overcome her.

Sean's voice penetrated her thoughts, forcing her to focus on him. "Molly described the scene, and I felt like I was there. Horrible. The sea was rough, the water icy. People died from hypothermia. Basically, they froze to death in the water. I can't bear to think of them." He took a moment to regain control of himself.

"The stars and lights from the doomed ship brightened the night. People screamed and fought to get into the remaining lifeboats. When there were no more, they jumped in the water and begged to be pulled into the boats. They were pushed away by the oarsmen and beaten away by the passengers.

"Ada cried and screamed. She was in her nightclothes and had no shoes. Molly opened her fur coat and wrapped Ada close to her body; tried to keep her warm and, more importantly, keep her from seeing the chaos."

"Those poor babies." Miss Ruth put her fist to her mouth.

"Sidney sat in the bow immobile, eyes darting across the ship. As the Titanic upended itself, he spotted the folks. 'I'm coming! I'll get you!' He jumped overboard and swam toward the sinking ship. Molly screamed, 'Sidney! Quick! Row toward the boy! That way! Hurry!'

"It didn't matter how Molly screamed and pleaded; the oarsmen wouldn't go after the boy. They had to get away from the ship or risk being sucked into the vortex."

"Poor Ada, what will she do without Sidney? He practically raised her before their mother died, and I brought them to your folks."

"What good did it do?"

"Sean! They had several wonderful years with your parents, a real family. Love. And Ada is alive."

"She might as well be dead."

Miss Ruth moaned and leaned against him. Sean had given this report in a low monotone and continued with the same leaden voice. "Apparently, Ada has some kind of psychosis. She is completely out of her head. Molly had her admitted to an asylum, the best in New York. Molly plans to send her to a good boarding school if the girl ever recovers, but the doctors say there is little chance. Ada's in a decent place, and Molly's plan is the only solution, although I can't bear to imagine her there."

"I'll pray for her and the doctors and nurses who care for her."

"We're just arguing over who is going to pay."

"From what you and Maureen have told me over the years, Molly Brown is just as stubborn as you. You will probably end up splitting the expenses."

Sean tried to chuckle, but it sounded more like a sob. As he lapsed into silence, she held his hand and said, "I'd like to pray."

"That's fine, Ruthie. I can't."

After a week at the Sitka Hotel, Sean said, "I'm going home tomorrow."

"What are your plans?"

"The mine is almost played out. I'll sell it to my Chinese employees. They are the hardest workers I've ever had. They have ways of scraping up every particle of gold from the ground."

"Then what?"

"There's a sweet parcel of land on Sawmill Creek Road. I thought I'd build a small house here in Sitka, sell the folks' place in Juneau."

Miss Ruth took his hand. "It will be wonderful to have you close. You're still a young man. You won't be content to do nothing, even if you can afford it."

"I can't think beyond selling the house and moving here. I feel old."

"Once this intense period of grief passes, and I know from personal experience it will, your energy will return."

"I've had offers in the past from several mining companies to do research and discovery in the interior. I'll do something when the time is right. Right now, it doesn't appeal."

"In time it will, me boy-o."

"You sound like Ma," his voice cracked, and she saw his eyes fill with pain, "I don't have a gravesite for them. No place to honor them, to visit."

"We'll plant a tree in your backyard. One for each of them."

His face brightened, "I'll bring cuttings and seedlings from Juneau, Ma's favorites."

"I have something to ask you."

"You know I would do anything for you."

"Bring me your mother's lemon tree."

His eyes filled, "Ah, Ruthie."

"I promise you, little brother, someday we will tell stories about your parents and laugh. We'll let the lemon drops melt in our mouths and remember the good things." She took his hand and kissed it. "I promise."

FORTY-FOUR

SAM, 1962

"Here are the Letters to the Editor." Chuck, the biracial teenager Sam had hired six months ago, hefted a large cardboard box onto the work table. "Sarah and I made a spreadsheet and cross-referenced the letters by date, subject matter, and name."

"Boss?"

Sam handed the letter he had just read to the boy. While Chuck read it, he opened a new box of cigars but didn't have the energy to light up. Like Sean, Sam imagined himself on the deck of the Titanic. When Chuck handed the letter back, Sam said, "Where is Sarah? She hasn't been here for a while."

"She auditioned for the school play and is always rehearsing. I hardly see her anymore,"

"She chose acting over journalism?"

"Women!" Chuck's disgust was evident on his face. "A guy just can't figure them out."

Sam laughed and put another sheet into his typewriter, "You got that right."

"But you have Miss Ruth figured out, don't you? All those letters the Hawaiian dude brought."

"Dude? If you want to be a professional journalist, no slang."

"It's the newest word, Boss. I heard it on television." He unfolded the spreadsheet in front of Sam. "I sure would like to read the letters from that fine, elderly gentleman from the South Pacific," Chuck exaggerated every syllable.

Sam's face brightened, and he said, "That's a good idea. You could give me a cultural perspective."

"Sure, Boss. You know I love Alaska history."

"Here, no cultural perspective needed on this one."

"Dude, the Titanic." Chuck held the letter close to his chest, then reread it."

Sam closed his eyes and saw himself in the church with Connor and Miss Ruth. He remembered how lost he felt when both his parents were no longer living and he had become an adult orphan. A wave of grief rose in him, and he pushed it back.

Sam rubbed the back of his neck and told the teenager. "Miss Ruth's letters have a way of making everything real."

Chuck shook his head. "It seems like something from my history book. What do you think Miss Blakely will say?"

Sam glanced at Sean Connor's wooden leg leaning against the file cabinet. "All the people in the letters exist for her, and these were Sean's family. She'll be extremely sad."

Chuck poured himself a cup of coffee, black, with no sugar.

Sam rubbed his own burning stomach. "Are you sure your mother lets you drink that sludge? It will eventually rot your guts."

Chuck guzzled his drink and poured another cup. "It's because Miss Blakely is female. Sarah gets all weepy over books, movies, lost dogs, and all kinds of nonsense."

"Women," Sam said.

"Yeah. I can't imagine this Maureen choosing to die alongside her husband."

"It's hard to know what a person would do in that situation."

"What about the little girl, Boss? Do you think she ever left the asylum, came to Alaska to be with Connor?"

"I've made a note to search for her name in other letters." Sam turned away from the emotion of the story, "How's that spreadsheet coming? You did a good job on the Letters to the Editor."

"Slowly, fifty years of letters, thousands, and you want locations besides names, dates, and subject matter. I do have other things in my life, you know."

"Like Sarah?"

Chuck lifted his eyes to the editor. "I must admit I liked her better before she started acting. She wears a little make-up now and has her hair all done up. She looks good, and the other guys are starting to notice. I don't like it."

"The question is, does Sarah like it." Sam enjoyed the irritation on Chuck's face. "Afraid of a little competition?"

"Don't sound so smug, Boss. From what Sarah says, it could happen to you."

Sam shuffled some papers on his desk, poured himself a cup of coffee he knew he shouldn't drink, and said, "What do you mean?"

"The men at the Café think drastic measures are called for since you haven't asked Alice out. They are conducting interviews to find her a fellow, someone to make you jealous."

Sam clenched his jaw and his fists. "I'll kill them!" He realized he had said the words aloud when he saw Chuck's startled reaction. He was glad the boy ignored the remark.

"I'm going to tell you something, Boss because I know you'll keep it to yourself. I'm thinking about asking Sarah out." He held a three-by-five card, "Everything I want to say is on a scrap of paper.

I've practiced, too."

"Brilliant."

"It was Margaret Mary who wrote everything down for me. I'm sure she'd do the same for you."

FORTY-FIVE

SAM, 1962

Dear Kamalei,

I spilled coffee down the front of my blouse. My floor is littered with crumpled sheets of stationery. My fountain pen leaked, and my hands are ink-stained. I've smeared many of the words of this letter with my tears.

It doesn't matter. The paper cannot contain my thoughts, and the pen cannot write my feelings.

The Aloha's arrival in Sitka was overdue by nearly a week, and rumors of her demise spread quickly. I closed my ears to them and prayed, how I prayed.

Two days ago, one of the dock managers received a telegram from a freight company in Kodiak. The Aloha had capsized just south of Kodiak Island. A fishing boat that nearly went down in the same storm rescued one passenger, a Russian Orthodox priest.

Oh, Kamalei! My Captain is gone! Our dear, dear Captain Harlan Walker has perished! My hands shake as I write the words.

Scripture tells us that we do not grieve like those with no hope; I know and believe that the Captain is with our Lord, but I am consumed with grief. I ache with it; my heart is bruised and in pieces. I do not know if I shall recover.

I shall put my pen down, walk through Totem park, and think of my dear Captain. He has walked into the forest, as the Tlingits say when death comes to one...

...I walked until I wore myself out, then I sat on the beach and stared at the waters of Sitka Sound. But all I could see was The Aloha sinking. Did he suffer? Was he afraid? Did he think of me in his last

moments? How many people were on board? What about their loved ones? And the priest? Could I find him? Talk to him? Did he see my Captain perish?

On my way back to the See House, I deliberately turned my mind away from such thoughts. They will destroy me.

It's been several days, dear Kamalei, since I began this letter. Today I stiffen my heart and write about practical things. It's the only way I can get through the day.

As you know, Captain Walker had no family, and I do not know if he left a will. Perhaps your mother can find out since she took care of his house while he was at sea.

If he did not leave instructions, could you maintain it as a guest house? Your family, indeed the entire village, was special to him, and I am sure he would have embraced the idea.

I remember when Grandpa John and I journeyed to Hawaii on the Captain's ship and then stayed in his house. It meant so much to us, but those memories are painful.

I will send more details as I learn them.

—MISS RUTH'S LETTERS 1919

Sam tossed his cigar into the large glass ashtray where it smoldered, and he reread the letter. Then he read it aloud to Chuck. Sam remembered how Miss Ruth's grandfather, John Merritt, had recorded their unexpected journey to Hawaii on Captain Walker's clipper ship, The China Doll.*

"I know she was in love with him. Why couldn't she see it?" Sam muttered, "That's right, she admitted it to herself but turned away from it. Why would she do that?"

**Book Two: About Miss Ruth*

"What's that, Boss?" Chuck laid the advertising copy he just proofed on Sam's desk. "These are ready."

Sam pushed the copy aside. "I want you to research maritime records for the name of that priest and where he lives. I want to interview him."

"You mean if he still lives."

"The Aloha sank forty-three years ago. Even if the priest was middle-aged, he should still be alive."

"What do you want to ask him?"

"What was the storm like? How did he feel as the lone survivor? What was his opinion of Captain Walker? Did he know Miss Ruth? Had he heard of her?"

Chuck took notes as Sam spoke. "Seems like you want to know everything about everything."

"Curiosity, that's the stock and trade of every newsman," Sam said.

"But Boss, not everything is news."

"But we won't know what is and isn't news until we know everything."

Chuck scratched his head, "You journalists go down so many rabbit trails. Seems like a waste of time."

"You've said that before, and I told you that the best stories are often at the end of those trails." Sam propped his feet on his desk, clasped his hands behind his head, and said, "You're too young to know where the stories are. But you'll learn. Now get me those maritime records."

FORTY-SIX

Dear Kamalei,

I hate funerals, and I've attended many during my forty-six years in Alaska. The land is rugged and beautiful but unforgiving. There is a scarcity of doctors and adequate medical care. Today, I will attend the home funeral of my dear Anna. Soon I will write about her tragic life. Today all I can think about are her children...

—MISS RUTH'S LETTERS 1936

Miss Ruth turned the frayed edge of her long black skirt and quickly hemmed it. How many times had she done that to the sturdy fabric? The skirt had grown shorter over the years and now reached the tops of her cowboy boots. It was still unfashionable and easily recognized on Sitka's sidewalks.

She would look her best by making these minor repairs and pressing her jacket and skirt. It was a way of honoring her friend. She was determined to do all she could to help Anna's children. Life was not easy in the best of times, and this was not the best of times.

Miss Ruth walked the three blocks to Bill Wall's white house on Biorka Street, praying all the way. It took her twice as long as usual, but the prayers were important. She opened the gate and then quickly caught an errant baseball. Ten-year-old Henry and all the neighborhood boys played ball in the front yard. "Take your game to the vacant lot down the street," she said as she gave them the ball.

Henry, eyes red-rimmed, pleaded with Miss Ruth. "I wish...I wish..." He gave her a fierce hug, picked up his mitt, and ran after the boys. Miss Ruth sniffed and wiped her eyes, then sent an extra prayer heavenward for poor Henry.

Mourners spilled out of the house and gathered on the steps and wooden sidewalk. They were primarily men who reached into their back pockets for a little something to add to their coffee. Miss Ruth responded to their greetings with a nod but did not stop.

Organized chaos reigned inside the crowded house. Along with plates of cookies and tea cakes, platters of sliced meat and fish rested on every available surface. The samovar steamed with hot tea, and friends and neighbors refilled their cups. Masha weaved in and out among the crowd offering coffee and juice.

Miss Ruth found an empty chair in the corner of the kitchen. She smiled at Bill, who sat at the kitchen table and held Anna's hand. Although everyone averted their eyes, her body lay on the table for all to see.

Miss Ruth motioned for Masha and asked where the girls were. Anna Marie was taking a nap despite the noise. Elizaveta had locked herself in her room.

"And Our Firy?"

Masha motioned toward the table, and Miss Ruth saw Firy crouched under it. The girl wrapped her arms around her knees and rested her chin on them. The people's conversations didn't seem to register with the grieving girl. She remained unfocused and unmoving until Father Alexi left.

Firy pushed back the tablecloth and stuck her tongue out at the priest's back.

Miss Ruth crooked her finger at the girl, who threw her hands over her mouth, mortified she had been caught.

The two sat on a log in the backyard. The pine coffin leaning against the back porch gave silent witness to their grief. Miss Ruth eventually coaxed eight-year-old Firy onto her lap. Soon Firy's stiff body began to relax, and she leaned against Miss Ruth, the Sunday School teacher who was old enough to be her grandmother.

"Tell me more about your Mama?"

"Mama flew away to heaven, but she came back. Why can't she come back now?"

Miss Ruth rested her chin on the top of Firy's head. "When did your Mama fly away?"

"I was little. Down by the lily pads."

Miss Ruth was silent as her mind filed through all of Sitka's events over the last few years. "You were about four years old, I think."

"Mama flew away to heaven, and I was scared, so she came back."

Miss Ruth's heart cracked, and all the love Anna had for the girl they called 'Our Firy" rushed in. "I remember," Miss Ruth kept her voice soft and soothing, "There was a noise in the sky we had never heard before, a buzzing from a flying machine. The noise became louder the closer it came. By the time the aviator landed on Swan Lake, it seemed like the whole town had come to meet him. He was Russian and was flying around the world. Your sweet Mama spoke Russian and acted as his interpreter. As a thank you, he gave her an airplane ride."

"I thought she was going to heaven. I didn't want her to go without me."

"It was just an airplane ride."

"I wanted to go to heaven with her."

"Someday," Miss Ruth whispered.

"She won't come back this time, will she?"

FORTY-SEVEN

Dear Kamalei,

I've heard Our Firy has just been pretending to attend school. She has spent all her school hours sitting by her mother's grave. I have to do something...

—MISS RUTH'S LETTERS 1936

Miss Ruth's morning routine now included a daily visit to Bill Wall's house. She helped Masha make breakfast and saw that Henry, Elizaveeta, and Firy were out the door in time for school. Masha wanted to stay home and care for Anna Marie.

"You are not going to quit school. You will be the first in your family to graduate from high school. Don't give up your dream because life is hard."

They seemed to have the same conversation every morning. After pushing Masha out the door, Miss Ruth did the breakfast dishes and tried to get Bill to eat. Most days, he sat in his chair and stared out the window. On days Miss Ruth had pressing church business or chores, she bundled Anna Marie into the buggy and wheeled her over the unpaved roads to Ollyanna's house.

"I'm afraid Our Firy has not gone to school for several weeks," Ollyanna said, "Her teacher couldn't get any response from Bill, so she called me. I don't know what to do."

"Let me think about it." Miss Ruth held out her cup for more tea.

❧

Miss Ruth met Firy at the end of Baranof Street. "The school is the other way, dear."

Firy ducked her head and kept walking. Miss Ruth fell in step beside her. Firy increased her pace, but Miss Ruth matched her step for step.

"It's a nice day for a walk." Miss Ruth waited for a response. None came. "I wonder if you're heading to Totem Park. You have spent most of your days at the Russian Cemetery the last three weeks. Why not today?"

Firy ran past the Sheldon Jackson School and into the park, unaware of the totems she always feared. The one-mile loop was bordered by salmonberry and devil's club bushes, moss-covered stumps, and rotting logs. Today a misty fog softened the forest.

Miss Ruth followed at a walk. She hoped Firy would tire herself and be willing to talk, or at least listen.

She found the girl sitting on a log where the Indian River empties into Jamestown Bay. Firy's tear-stained face showed evidence of her grief. Miss Ruth wondered if the girl could verbalize her suffering or share her pain.

Miss Ruth settled herself on the log, folded her hands in her lap, but did not speak. Five minutes turned into ten. Ten into fifteen.

Finally, Firy turned and said, "Aren't you going to tell me I'm stupid for going to see Mama every day."

"No."

"Are you going to tell me I must go to school?"

"No."

Firy stared at the bull kelp floating in with the tide. Miss Ruth followed her gaze and saw several otters floating on their backs with their babies resting on their stomachs. She lifted her eyes to the horizon. Shore, sea, and sky; creation's trinity.

A smooth little hand crept into the older wrinkled one and gripped it tightly. Miss Ruth rested her chin on Firy's head nestled against her. "Our Firy, I have a plan."

"Papa Bill won't give his permission."

"Sometimes we will have a lot of work to do, but sometimes we will go and see your mama. We can plant forget-me-nots on her grave."

"But Papa Bill..."

"You leave Papa Bill to me."

"But my teacher..."

"That may be a problem. I will teach you what I can, but Our Firy, whatever choice we make, there are always consequences. You might have to repeat third grade."

Firy shrugged.

"If you go back to school now and make up the work for the time you skipped, you will probably pass."

Firy shook her head no.

"You can spend your days with me. It's okay to repeat third grade. Stick with me, and you will learn all kinds of things."

"Like what?"

"Now, that would be telling." Miss Ruth stood, brushed her long skirt, and held out her hand. "Happy things, sad things, forever things. We might even have an adventure or two."

FORTY-EIGHT

Dear Kamalei,

I promised to write and tell you about Our Firy's mother, Anna Oskolkoff. Life has not been kind to either of them.

It's difficult to understand why some seem born to tragedy and some to triumph. Some seem to rise above dire circumstances, and others fall into even grimmer situations. Of course, we all make decisions that tend to lead us in one direction or another. Other people's choices undoubtedly affect our lives as well, poor little Anna, I met her in 1924...

—MISS RUTH'S LETTERS 1936

Father Alexi sent a message to the rectory requesting Miss Ruth's presence at his house. When she arrived, he introduced her to a young Native girl, Anna Oskolkoff, sitting in the purple velvet chair with her hands folded over a pregnant stomach. Her oval face with high cheekbones, high forehead, and straight nose spoke of her Russian Ancestry. Dark doe eyes, black hair, and cocoa-colored skin showed her Native blood.

The Tlingit housekeeper served tea in the upstairs reception room under the portrait of the Tsar. Miss Ruth had heard rumors that Father Alexi had escaped from the Bolsheviks several years ago, but like everyone else in Alaska, she would not ask. During her time on Afognak, she learned how the Tsar and Tsarina continued to be held in high esteem, especially after their tragic demise.

The young Native girl sat unmoving and silent. Her eyes, darting from the portrait to the Father to Miss Ruth and back again, told the older woman the girl was uncomfortable.

The housekeeper served tiny cakes and cookies on Royal Doulton porcelain. The girl's eyes widened; she appeared hungry but did not eat.

Miss Ruth smiled at her, and the girl looked away. "Father, perhaps the child is not used to such a formal tea and would be more comfortable in the kitchen."

Father Alexi nodded and spoke to the girl in Russian. She almost smiled and followed after the housekeeper. "What to do is the question. I cannot offer her refuge here."

"What about the baby's father."

He shook his head. "I believe he was white, and she was unwilling, although she will not speak about it. There will be no help from him".

"You sound like you know who he is."

Father Alexi reached for the sugar bowl. "I'm afraid he is untouchable."

Miss Ruth's heart constricted. "Indiantown?"

"My housekeeper said the girl is a Yupik from the Kenai. She is far from home and will not return to her village in shame. I thought perhaps you..."

"Another new cleric and his family arrived at the See House two days ago. I am afraid there is no room. My small bed-chamber is in the attic."

Father Alexi frowned. “She is not the only poor child who has been abused this way. The tribes care for their own, but she has no one.”

“It sounds like she has you.”

“All I can offer is my pity and my prayers,” Father Alexi sighed and pulled on his beard.

Miss Ruth viewed him over the rim of her teacup. “There is always a solution, Father. We just have to find it.”

“She is afraid and bitter, although she appears calm. The priest in Ninilchik sent her to the boarding school here. She becomes agitated when I mention her returning.”

“Perfectly understandable.” Miss Ruth’s heart ached, and her mind raced.

“She seems bright enough, speaks Yupik and Russian, a little English. She understands more than she speaks. I’m sure the Salvation Army Orphanage would take the child once it’s born.”

Again, an arrow pierced Miss Ruth’s heart. “You would force her to give up her baby?”

Father Alexi stared through the double-paned windows; the gray sky reflected his mood. “Why would she want to keep a bastard child, especially when she was…well,”

“Raped.” Miss Ruth saw the priest blush. Such subjects were not discussed, especially between a man and a good Christian woman. “She should be allowed to make the choice about her child.”

The priest nodded and refilled their teacups.

There is an answer to every problem, Father.”

“I hoped you would find it, Miss Ruth. I cannot.”

And so, Miss Ruth smuggled the confused and traumatized young Anna Oskolkoff into the attic of the See House.

"Are you an Elder," Anna asked? She sat in a wooden rocker next to the small attic window. "You seem to be an Elder."

"Just a middle-aged lady in my fifties."

"The Father treats you with the respect and authority of an Elder."

"He is too kind."

Miss Ruth, her arms full of blankets, stood in the doorway and said, "I found a cot in the storage room. Help me move it in here."

Miss Ruth informed the Tlingit cook she would take her meals on a tray for the foreseeable future. The Native woman shrugged. Miss Ruth carried her meals to the attic three times a day.

Miss Ruth fasted for two weeks and continued to pray; there had to be a way out of this dilemma. She couldn't hide Anna much longer.

"Someone to see you, Miss Ruth," the cook said.

"Show him to the parlor." Miss Ruth finished folding the towels.

An older man stood in the middle of the parlor, hat in hand. "Miss Ruth? I'm going outside to live with my son and his family."

"Yes?" What had that to do with her?

"Been sending the rent money to Connor's lawyer over in Juneau. He cabled I should tell you I'm leaving."

"Thank you, Mister...?"

"They call me Sleepy Jim. I packed up my things and cleaned the place as best I could. Needs a woman's touch." He twirled his hat in his hands. "I best be going. The steamer's leaving in an hour— almost forgot to stop by."

Miss Ruth remembered her manners. She stretched out her hand. "Thank you, Sleepy Jim. You are the solution to my predicament."

"Huh?"

She laughed and practically pushed him out the door. "Hurry now. Don't miss your boat."

❧

Miss Ruth had never lived in that cabin near Indian River, but it would be perfect for her and Anna.

Anna's pregnancy progressed, and so did her English lessons. She was eager to learn, and Miss Ruth delighted in her new pupil. Each evening there were reading and writing assignments and sewing and cooking classes as well.

As her stomach grew, Anna seemed to think more about the new life within her and less about how it got there. "I am afraid to have the baby, Miss Ruth."

"To keep it, you mean?"

Anna's eyes flashed, and her arms rounded her belly. "Mine!" She took a deep breath and whispered, "My mother died giving birth."

Miss Ruth held this young woman, barely in her teens, "I will do everything I can to help you. The doctor will be here."

"And a medicine woman from Indiantown?"

Miss Ruth frowned as she reached for the flapjacks and turned them onto their plates.

"Please."

Miss Ruth could not deny the fear in those dark eyes. "I will persuade the medicine woman to come."

❧

The medicine woman came, but the doctor refused. The baby boy had flashing black eyes and dark hair. His skin was just a shade lighter than his mother's. The birth was difficult for the young teenager.

"She has lost a lot of blood, Miss Ruth."

"What can I do?"

The medicine woman reached into her bag. "Make a broth of these herbs every hour. Make sure she drinks it for the next ten days, give her meat broth when she can keep it down." The woman cackled, showing her few teeth, "The herb tea tastes terrible. Do not let her spit it out."

Miss Ruth nodded. Poor Anna, her body covered in sweat, her face wan. The herbal tea helped, and Miss Ruth decided she'd ask the Tlingit medicine woman to teach her all about Native medicine.

Anna slept on and off for three days, only waking to nurse the baby and when Miss Ruth forced her to drink the tea. On the fourth day, she sang to her baby, told him stories about her life, and named him Henry, after a trapper who had saved her grandfather's life. The baby grew quickly and delighted them both.

Anna might have been a young teenager, but she was a fierce and protective mother. Miss Ruth could cook and clean, but Anna alone cared for Henry.

The months passed, and Miss Ruth wondered if Anna and the baby would be here forever. She rather liked being a parent to this new young mother. Perhaps, one day Henry would call her grandma. The thought pleased her, and she began to make plans to add another bedroom to the cabin.

Miss Ruth hurried through her daily tasks at the church and rushed home to be with Anna and Henry each evening. One day she brought home a buggy. "You and Henry should take walks every day. The weather is better, and the fresh air would do you both good."

Anna circled the buggy, "This is a wonder. Thank you, Miss Ruth."

Several weeks later, Miss Ruth came home to an empty cabin. All of Anna's things were gone. A note on the kitchen table broke Miss Ruth's heart.

Dear Miss Ruth,

I have met a man. He will care for me

and Henry. We will be a real family.

I will remember your words to love Bozhe

and do what's right.

Anna

Miss Ruth put her head on the table and sobbed. *Oh, Anna, who is this man, and why didn't you bring him home to meet me?* Would he be good to her and little Henry? For how long? Was he going to marry her? Were they still in Sitka? Could she find Anna and force her to return? Anna was too young and trusting despite all that had happened to her. Or perhaps, just not a good judge of character.

FORTY-NINE

SAM, 1963

The door to the newspaper office opened, and Alice hurried in. "That rain is so cold. What a way to start the new year."

Sam laughed, "Tradition. We start every year cold and wet."

She shrugged out of her coat. "I hope the coffee is still hot."

Sam frowned. "I'm afraid all that's left is the Sentinel's day-old sludge."

"You drank all of Agrefena's good coffee, the whole thermos?"

"I saved you a cruller."

"Thanks a lot, Sam." The words were said with a smile and a wink.

Margaret Mary bustled to the windowsill, grabbed the pot, and poured.

Alice held the mug to her nose. "Smells good. You must have made a fresh pot. Somebody around here pays attention. Somebody cares."

"Hmmph." Margaret Mary poured herself a cup and hurried back to her linotype.

Sam blushed. Alice took pity on him and quickly asked, "How did Miss Ruth seem the last time you saw her. You've never said."

Sam brushed his hand over his head and blew out his breath. After a moment of thought, he said, "If I had known that was the last time...maybe that's why I can't let her go."

"What do you mean?"

"Judge Cooper pronounced the sentence, and I had a lot of

questions for her and Firy Baas. They refused to answer. Miss Ruth said she'd be in Sitka in a few weeks, and we could talk then."

"How was her health, her energy? After all, she was in her nineties."

"I know most of the elderly you work with at the Pioneer's Home are none too spry, but Miss Ruth seemed ageless. To me, she looked the same as when I was a kid."

"I just realized I've never seen a picture of her."

"I must have one around here, somewhere." Sam riffled through the papers on his desk.

"Describe her."

"Wrinkled. White hair piled on top. Big feet."

Alice laughed, "Okay, Sam. I'll wait for the photograph. And Firy, what was she like?"

"Kept her head down, didn't speak."

Sam poured himself a cup of coffee and held out the pot. Alice put her hand over her mug.

"Firy was just a kid when her mother died. Miss Ruth must have become a mother figure to her. I vaguely remember that wherever Miss Ruth was, Firy stood there in her shadow," Sam handed her the letter he had just finished.

"Poor Anna, I can't imagine how difficult her life was. And her poor children. It's all so tragic and sad. Did you know them well, Sam?"

Sam scratched his head, "It's a small town, Alice. Everybody knew everybody, at least a little. You know about Anna Marie and her tragic death. Henry, the brother, was on one of my baseball teams even though he was a couple of years younger. Firy was several grades behind me in school. I can't recall the other sister's name."

Alice wiped her eyes again, "Oh, Sam, my heart hurts. These are not just names in letters. They are real people. They loved and lost.

They lived through hard times. Sometimes they made the wrong choice or suffered the consequences of other people's actions. Oh, I hope Anna found some happiness."

"Don't cry, Alice. Most of the people in Miss Ruth's letters are long gone."

"How can you be so heartless."

"I only meant your tears and pity can't help them now. You can read about their lives and admire what they did right. See their mistakes and hope you don't follow their examples."

Alice mopped her eyes with her now soggy handkerchief. "You are right, Sam. I'm just being foolish."

"Foolish is not a word I would use to describe you. You're compassionate and sympathetic. There is a kindness and grace in you. Lovely. You..." Sam coughed.

"Those are wonderful things to say, but I'm not."

"You are! In fact, that is... I'd like to say..." He cleared his throat.

She lifted her shimmering eyes to his. "Yes?"

Sam's face burned. "Drat! I need a cigar."

Alice sighed and gathered her things. "Time for me to go to work. I'll see you next week... maybe."

The lemon drops formed a heart on Miss Ruth's grave. Alice Blakely hurried after the woman who placed them there. "Excuse me, I assume you knew Miss Ruth?"

"Why do you ask?"

Alice pulled a small packet of lemon drops from her pocket. "I'm Alice Blakely."

"Yes, the new nurse at the Pioneer's Home."

Alice lifted her eyebrows, and the other woman laughed, "The locals know who all the cheechakos are as soon as they arrive."

"But I've been here several months." Alice clearly didn't see.

The woman laughed again, "You'll be a cheechako until you've survived several winters. I'm Ollyanna Bunderson. Whenever I visit my sister in the Russian Cemetery, I come here to see Miss Ruth."

Before Alice could offer her condolences, Ollyanna said, "You're helping Sam, right?"

"Whatever do you mean?"

"Everybody knows you two lovebirds are working on a big project about Miss Ruth."

Alice felt herself blush and hoped the other woman could hear the frost in her tone. "I'm sure I don't know what you are talking about. Surely, no one is gossiping about us." Alice often wondered if she would ever adjust to this small town's intrusive ways.

"Let's have coffee at the Café. I know you're partial to Agrefena's French crullers." Ollyanna led the stunned and hapless nurse to the Café.

The two passed the round table in the backroom. It was occupied by Ollyanna's husband, fisherman Ade Bunderson; shoreboat pilot Jake Steiner; retired Chief of Police Stormy Durand; and boatbuilder Ivan Mishkin, who considered himself the only true Russian left in Sitka.

"It's about time you got in touch with Alice; now we can get down to business," Ade called to his wife.

Alice bit the inside of her cheek and shrank into herself. She slipped into a chair with her back to the round table, stared out of the window, and wished she was on one of the boats in the Sound.

Ollyanna patted Alice's arm, "It's okay, honey." She winked at her husband and said, "We aren't here for business. Alice just wants to know some more about Miss Ruth."

Alice blushed and wished she could think of an excuse to leave, but then she would have to pass that table of awful men.

Ade asked his tablemates, "We need to think like Miss Ruth. What would she do to bring these two together?"

"Nothing illegal." Stormy Durand finished his breakfast and patted his ample belly. "Agrefena is such a good cook."

"That's it." Jake slapped his napkin on the table. "All we have to do is sabotage Sam's dinners. Mick, can you help us?"

Mike shook his head and backed away from the table, coffee pot in hand. "Sorry, fellas. I won't go against my Ma. You had better be very careful."

"A few weeks of bad food would bring Sam around," Jake insisted.

"We'll have a party, and Alice can demonstrate her cooking skills—if she has any." Ade's brow furrowed, and he glanced at the table where the two women talked quietly.

Stormy rubbed his mid-section again. "Nothing means more to an old bachelor than his stomach."

Aware that Agrefena was taking an order at a neighboring table, Ade quietly hissed, "Sam's been picking up his dinner here for years. He won't believe Agrefena became a bad cook all of a sudden."

Agrefena slapped Ade with her ticket book. "I am the best cook in Sitka and will be until the day I die. Be careful, or I will take an ax to your table." She stomped to the kitchen.

"She means it," Jake said.

"Quiet! I think," Ivan bellowed. "Yes. Is good. One must die."

Ivan, the oldest member of their group by a decade, had said some strange things over the years. Perhaps, dementia had claimed his mind as numerous aches and pains had claimed his body. No one ventured a comment or question.

Ivan finished his coffee and smoothed his mustache. "Is perfect. I die."

Stormy put his hand on the old man's shoulder and probed Ivan's face, "Are you okay?"

Ivan knocked his hand away. "Dummkopf! Big funeral in church. Everybody come. Sam sit in front. Write for paper. You open coffin. I alive. Alice have white dress. Sam say I do. Everybody happy." Ivan took a deep breath, and his face paled with the effort it took to explain his plan.

Stormy choked on his coffee, and Jake mumbled, "I, uh, need the ketchup from that other table."

Ade's lips twitched, but he did not laugh. He pulled the pencil from behind Mick's ear as the man bent and poured another round of coffee. "I wrote down your plan, Ivan. We'll keep thinking, and hopefully, we can come up with a few more ideas and then vote for the best one."

The others quickly agreed. Ivan hung his head and muttered through his mustache, "No need vote. Plan is good."

"And so, you see, Alice, Miss Ruth was important to my sister and even more important to her children, especially, Our Firy. I don't know everything that happened. I was still in Ninilchik, and Anna never wanted to talk about her past."

"Sam showed me a letter about your sister. I'm sure he'd let you read it." She shrugged into her coat. "About the other thing..."

Ollyanna's eyes twinkled. "Sam is well-loved in this town. We just want him to be happy."

"He doesn't know how miserable he is," Jake shouted.

"Nothing a good wedding wouldn't cure," Ade added.

Alice swallowed, and her eyes darted around the room, but she stood frozen like a deer caught in the headlights.

"It's just harmless speculation, dear. Nothing will come of it," Ollyanna said.

Alice hurried past the round table, avoiding everyone's eyes, embarrassed that they not only knew about her and Sam but also that they discussed it so freely.

She heard their continued conversation as the Café's door closed behind her. Despite her embarrassment, her heart knew she wanted something to come of it.

Sam reached for his jacket while staring at the sleeping feline. He sighed, wished the animal sweet dreams, and headed to Totem Park. As Sadsack's naps increased, so did Sam's walks. Today he needed the park's tranquility to infuse his soul.

The trail in the park had been a favorite of soldiers and their sweethearts during the war. They called it Lover's Lane. Even the high school kids were regular visitors, more interested in each other than the long-ago battle between the Russians and the Tlingits.

Today Sam's mind drifted toward Alice. Did she know the trail was called Lover's Lane? Would she want to walk it with him?

Sam kicked a broken branch out of his way. The trail turned, the underbrush thinned, and he heard the waters of Indian River tumble into the bay as they had since time began.

Later, Sam headed to town along Lincoln Street. He saw the

sun streak through the clouds and touch the waters of Crescent Bay. Not many big-city editors could walk to work through a forest or next to an ocean.

Once he opened the door to the Sentinel, all the peace and serenity he had absorbed on his morning walk vanished. The linotype clattered, and the phone rang. Two customers stood at the counter, airing their complaints. Chuck dashed in and yelled he had a game after school. "I'll see you tomorrow."

Sam ignored the chaos—he sat at his desk and put his head in his hands. Margaret Mary's words echoed in his mind, "Ask her out on a real date!"

Sam's hand hovered over the telephone, then opened the wooden cigar box. Didn't Alice know he considered their morning meetings dates? Didn't she realize what it meant when he insisted she come more than once a week? Didn't she recognize Agrefena wasn't getting any younger and had to hire an assistant baker because Sam bought so many crullers? And she raised the prices! Didn't Alice know he willingly paid those high prices just so she would keep coming? Sam shook his head and stubbed out his cigar. Obviously, she didn't know.

Sam bit the inside of his lip and stared across the street at the Pioneer's Home. He imagined Alice attending to the old sourdoughs. Her smile would charm them, and her cute nurse's uniform and cap would put a gleam in their eyes.

Her shift ended at six o'clock. What if he happened to be in front of the Pioneer's Home when she came out of the building? What if he casually steered her to the new hotel just a block away? Its elegant dining room overlooked the channel between Sitka and Japonski Island. He'd heard the food was good, and they had live music for dancing.

He rubbed his chin, which was scratchy. He'd take the afternoon off to shower, shave, and maybe shine his shoes. He'd tell Margaret Mary he had a lead on a good story and wouldn't be back until tomorrow. She didn't need to know his plans or superimpose her opinions over them.

Satisfied, Sam leaned back in his chair and closed his eyes. He could see it happening just as he planned.

The fish cannery's whistle blew at precisely six o'clock. Alice came out of the Home several minutes later. She waved goodbye to her co-workers, then noticed Sam. So far, so good. He tugged at his tie and straightened his collar.

"Why, Sam. Don't you look nice? No five o'clock shadow, or should I say six o'clock?"

Did the woman have to notice everything? He rubbed his hand over his cheek.

"Where are you headed, Sam?"

He pointed toward the hotel and mumbled, "Has it occurred to you we've never had a meal together?"

"We had that picnic on the beach, remember?"

"Eating tuna fish sandwiches while sitting on wet sand doesn't count, not like a real date," He mumbled, almost to himself.

What's that?" She leaned closer.

"Nothing, just thinking out loud. Wondering about Miss Ruth walking on Sitka's wooden sidewalks."

"It's always Miss Ruth," she whispered.

"What?"

"Nothing, Sam. I wonder about Miss Ruth too."

Sam breathed a sigh of relief, although he was aggravated as well. All thoughts of the hotel's fine dining room, romantic music, and harbor lights vanished. He grabbed her hand and pulled her away from the hotel. "I have the letters in my office."

She glanced over her shoulder and saw several couples enjoying their intimate dinners. "Didn't you say something about harbor lights and romantic music?"

Sam's face reddened, and he was glad the clouds covered the moon. "Let's order clam chowder from the Café. I can't wait to tell you the latest about Miss Ruth."

"Chuck, have you asked Sarah out yet?"

Chuck scowled and scrunched up his paper and tossed it in the trash. "She keeps talking about the play's leading man. I might have to change my mind about the whole dating thing. Women!"

"You know, Alice Blakely and I meet several times a week to discuss Miss Ruth, but as you say—women!"

"Something wrong with her, Boss?"

Sam tapped a pencil on the space bar of his typewriter and thought about Alice. She was just the right height and nearly came to his shoulder, just the right shape—pert nose, wavy hair, lovely smile, and a good listener.

"Boss?"

"Er, no, nothing wrong with her, just hard to figure out."

"Not like Miss Ruth, eh?"

Sam reached for a cigar. "Actually, Chuck, the more I talk to Alice, the more she reminds me of Miss Ruth."

"In what way?"

"Miss Ruth traveled throughout Southeast Alaska and across

the Gulf for decades; her goal was to help people. She was deep, accommodating, feisty when she needed to be."

"Just like Alice helps all the old dudes at the Pioneer's Home."

Sam quirked his eyebrow.

"I meant all the elderly gentlemen and ladies."

"She hasn't been anywhere in Alaska but Sitka," Sam spoke, almost to himself, "Alice said she would like to trace Miss Ruth's footsteps, see where she worked and lived."

"Are you going to take her, Boss? The word around town is that you two are pretty thick. If you weren't so old, I'd say you were going steady."

Feeling the heat rush to his face, Sam swiveled his chair and faced the window. After taking a breath or two, he turned back to the boy. "Going steady, huh?"

"According to Sarah, whose mom works at the Home, Alice always looks toward your office. She starts every conversation with—Sam says—or—Sam thinks—or—I'll have to ask Sam about that."

Sam sat straighter, stifled his grin, and tried to act serious. "I'm sure you're exaggerating."

"I told you exactly what Sarah said her mother said Alice said, but that's not the embarrassing part." Chuck frowned and folded the spreadsheet. "Women!"

"What do you mean, embarrassing part?"

"According to Sarah, who corners me in the cafeteria every day to report," Chuck muttered, "as if I was even interested, I think she wants me to react in a certain way. She gets all girly and pouty when I don't get it right." Chuck scratched behind his ear and fell silent.

"Embarrassing part?" Sam prodded.

"I'm not embarrassed. It's Alice."

Sam's head jerked up, and he wished the boy would focus.

"The other nurses ask about you daily— what you think of the new exhibit at the museum, the current movie playing, or the menu at the new hotel. And Alice doesn't know because you haven't..."

"Because I haven't taken her any of those places." Sam mopped his face with his crumpled handkerchief.

"Sarah says it sometimes leaves Alice in tears—that's when Sarah tilts her head and stares at me, waiting for me to say something. I don't know what she wants."

Margaret Mary, who had been listening, set a bundle of advertising copy in front of Sam. "You two are just about hopeless. I've told you what to do, Sam, but you haven't got the gumption. And you, young man, it's obvious. Sarah wants you to ask her out."

The middle-aged man and the teenage boy couldn't make eye contact. Margaret Mary tapped her foot and clenched her jaw.

"I tried to take Alice to the new hotel for dinner..." his voice faded.

"What happened?" Chuck asked.

Margaret Mary whirled to face the boy, "They ended up in this very office talking about Miss Ruth. Some date!"

"With Agrefena's clam chowder," Sam added.

"That doesn't count. What I want both of you to do is plan a real date. Alaska Day is not too far away. There's the ball, the parade, the re-enactment. Ask your ladies to these events. You can even go in period costumes."

The two males looked at each other in horror.

Margaret Mary growled, "Men!" and stomped back to her linotype.

Sam grabbed his hat and jacket, "Come on, Chuck, we'll go to the Café for some *dude* time."

Chuck shrugged into his jacket and followed the editor. "If you want to be a professional journalist, Boss, no slang."

FIFTY

SAM, 1963

"You need to eat more, you lousy cat. This is some of the finest crab from Bristol Bay. Come on, Sadsack, just a bite or two."

Sadsack opened his eyes, blinked, licked his paw, and went back to sleep. Sam ate the crab himself, although he didn't enjoy it. Concern for the cat made everything tasteless.

Sam settled on the stone hearth next to Sadsack, "You've had a long and productive life, Sad. You kept my mom company for years, and look how you've taken care of me. You've kept the house free of mice, although I could do with fewer pawprints on the window." Sam looked toward Sadsack's favorite spot on the sill. "Never mind, leave all the prints you want."

He swallowed the lump in his throat and rubbed the cat's head. A deep sadness washed over him. "You know I don't mean it when I call you a lousy cat or a no-good feline. It's my way of saying...I...I love you."

Sam sniffed and berated himself for his emotion. He pulled his handkerchief from his back pocket and blew his nose. Sadsack's tail twitched, and he opened one eye, "I think I'm catching a cold. Nothing to worry about."

Sam believed Sadsack was Sitka's longest-living cat, but the end of that life approached with a steady step. Sam slapped his thigh. Why did death interfere with life, and why was he so maudlin over a stupid cat? What did anything matter anyway?

He leaned against his overstuffed chair, it scooted back a few inches, and he saw the corner of a familiar style of envelope and handwriting. "Look at this, Sad, a letter must have slipped under the chair. It's postmarked 1960. Let's see what Miss Ruth has to say to us."

FIFTY-ONE

Dear Kamalei,

I go to bed early, and when the opportunity presents itself, I sleep late. My energy level is not what it once was. I have all the aches and pains of those approaching ninety, but overall my health is good, and I praise God for that.

My memories of yesterday and last week are not as straightforward as those of past decades. Lately, I have been pondering my past and wondering if I have made a difference.

Some might look at me with pity. I imagine they say Miss Ruth never married. She has no children or grandchildren—just a dried-up old maid. Alone.

You and I have lived through two World Wars, several waves of financial panic and the Great Depression, Spanish influenza, and other traumatic events. I have been involved with the Alaska legislature regarding temperance, integration, women's suffrage, and Native rights.

I am not sure I have made any lasting contribution to these significant historical issues, but I hope I have had some small influence for good in people's lives, or else why have I lived?

I know the people in Alaska have changed me, but I wonder if their lives would be the same if I had never come to this wild, wonderful land.

I turn away from these oppressive thoughts, but they come back to plague me. I have prayed but have not been able to banish them.

I am enclosing a letter that has cheered and encouraged me and has enabled me to finally abandon these negative thoughts...

—MISS RUTH'S LETTERS 1960

Dear Miss Ruth,

It has been many years since you've received a letter from me, and I hope this one reaches you and finds you well. (I do not even know if you are alive.) I beg your forgiveness for my lack of response over the years.

Yesterday, my ten-year-old granddaughter asked me to teach her to sew. We started with handkerchiefs. I showed her how to fold the edge twice and stitch in and out, up and down.

I told her how the woman who taught me to sew arrived via dog-sled in the middle of a blizzard. Her eyes lit up, and she wanted to know everything about the olden days in the frozen North.

After saying good-night and her mother took her home, I sat near my large rain-spattered window. Vancouver's skyline was misted by the rain, as it often is. But I felt the warmth of a small cabin not far from the Chilkat River in wild Alaska.

I slipped to my knees and rested my arms on the windowsill. I thanked God for sending you to me. I remembered our journey to this city, the people, the tall buildings, the automobiles, things I had never seen. I was sad that you could not stay with me forever.

I was a backwoods, ignorant, uneducated child who didn't adjust quickly to the big city of Vancouver or to the woman who claimed to be my mama's mama.

Grandmother let me dictate letters to my father, and I enclosed little pictures I drew. Later, when I could write, she bought me stationery and stamps. She admitted that you insisted communication with my father and brother was necessary for my mental health.

He only occasionally answered. You know how erratic mail service was back then, and they didn't get into Haines very often.

Eventually, he and my brother abandoned the cabin and went further into the interior to trap and prospect. I never heard from them after that.

At first, my grandmother and I hovered around each other. I told her what life was like before my mother died, how much she loved all of us, but how dreadfully she missed her mother.

Grandmother told me stories about my mama when she was young. I begged her to repeat them, sometimes every day. They helped me to know who I was and where I came from.

I believe my grandmother regretted cutting my mother out of her life. Anyway, we became close. She kept her promise to you and read the Bible aloud every night.

We saw your Jesus in those pages and came to know him for ourselves. My husband, children, and grandchildren all love our Savior. That would not have happened if a certain half-frozen and nearly incoherent woman had not stumbled onto the porch of our isolated cabin.

I became a teacher, married a teacher, had two sons and a daughter, and now I have six grandchildren, five boys and a girl.

My dear Miss Ruth, do you realize what an unintended legacy you have left me? You brought me out of the wilderness and into life. Your legacy lives on in my children and grandchildren.

Words of gratitude are insufficient, but I thank you with all of my heart.

Cora May Matthews

P.S. I have enclosed several handkerchiefs my granddaughter made for you.

...And so, my dear Kamalei, my doubts and fears of not living up to my purpose and potential have been banished by Cora May's letter. I have always tried to love the Lord and do what's right. I guess part of that is learning to leave the results to Him.

Yours ever,

Miss Ruth

FIFTY-TWO

SAM, 1963

Sam put the letters in his pocket to share with Alice. Sadsack made a noise somewhere between a growl and a moan. Sam knelt by the cat and promptly forgot about the letters.

Sam wiped away the moisture forming in his eyes and watched the rhythmic rise of Sadsack's chest, slow but steady. He rubbed his own chest and called Margaret Mary.

"Thanks for coming; he's by the fireplace. I really should cancel with Alice. She'd understand."

Margaret Mary threw her coat and hat on the couch. "Sadsack and I will be fine. He's just old, Sam, and you must accept that he won't live forever. None of us will."

"I guess I'm feeling down."

She hugged him and said, "That's okay, my boy. Alice will cheer you up, and if she doesn't, she will be sad with you."

"She's like that, isn't she?"

"She's everything you need, Sam. The whole town knows it."

Sam grabbed his fedora, feeling better already, "I'm beginning to think the whole town is right. I won't be too long."

"We'll be here."

Alice opened her door before Sam had time to knock. "Don't you think it's too chilly for a picnic?"

"The sun is shining, and the sky is blue. For Alaska, that's all you need. And this," he held up a picnic basket. "Fried chicken, French bread and cheese, and a thermos of Agrefena's coffee."

"What? No crullers?"

Sam showed her a white paper sack, "I ordered extra."

"Let me put on a sweater and grab my jacket."

"Don't forget gloves and a hat. The tide is coming in, and it will be colder at Sandy Beach."

"Pour that coffee quickly. My teeth are knocking together." Alice settled herself on the thick wool blanket Sam provided. "Brrr!"

He pulled a scarf from the basket and wrapped it around her neck.

"Why Sam, this is the first time you've given me a gift." She saw his embarrassment and quickly added, "It's the same blue as the water and the sky. It's perfect. Thank you."

He handed her a plate, and they ate in companionable silence, then threw the scraps to the gulls.

"Thank you for lending me Miss Ruth's prayer journal. However, that Judge could have been more careful when he slit the cover."

"It was in Connor's leg along with John Merritt's diary and a few other things. The prayer book didn't make much sense to me."

"John Merritt was her grandfather, right? I'll have to borrow that sometime. I'm not changing the subject, but what happens when Margaret Mary puts those little metal letter things in her linotype machine?"

Sam's cheeks puffed out as he laughed, "Those little letter things are called slugs, and many things happen, but eventually, their image is imprinted on the paper. Why?"

"And when the slugs are corroded?"

"The image is marred."

"Precisely."

Sam threw his last crust to the seagulls and wrapped the chicken bones in his napkin. "You are not making any sense, Alice."

"As near as I can tell from Miss Ruth's book, she believed God made us in His image, and then we corrupted or marred ourselves by not doing things His way."

"And then what, we became slugs?" He laughed and reached for a cruller. "Please, no religious jargon or cliches. They give me a headache."

"When you have a corrupted slug, you have to replace it with one that's clean and pure, right? That's what God had to do."

"Huh?"

"According to Miss Ruth, all of our evil had consequences, and the punishment had to fit the crime. Death."

"We all die, Alice." He sighed and thought about Sadsack.

"Yes, but Miss Ruth said God wants us to live with him forever after dying. So He had to find someone pure, uncorrupted, and unmarred so that he could take our punishment, but there wasn't anyone, so He came himself as Jesus."

Sam snorted, "So Jesus is God? God judged God and punished God, so we get set free. That is the most ridiculous thing I ever heard, illogical."

Alice grabbed his arm and pulled him to face her. She looked into his bewildered face and grinned, "That's the beauty of it, Sam. Nobody would make that stuff up. I don't understand it, but I kind of believe it."

Sam scratched his head and looked across the water to Mount Edgecomb on the edge of Kruzof Island. Alice followed his gaze and said softly. "It's a beautiful mountain. Solid. Strong. Like Miss Ruth's faith."

"Keep talking. I don't get it, but I'm listening."

"Did you go to Sunday School when you were a kid?"

Sam sat up and folded his arms around his knees. He rested his chin on them but kept his gaze on the mountain. "Just enough to get vaccinated against it, I think."

"I never went. All I knew about Christmas and Easter was Santa, bunnies, and eggs. But again, according to Miss Ruth, Christmas and Easter are one story."

Sam closed his eyes and remained silent. Alice leaned close to him and whispered, "Do you have a Bible?"

"An old one of my mother's."

"Can I borrow it? I want to look at the verses Miss Ruth wrote about. She tried to live by the Bible, I think. She wasn't perfect, but she learned to go to God with her struggles."

"That does come through in her letters. What if we look up those verses together?"

"I'd like that. I believe God is working to bring me to life."

Again, Sam was quiet. Alice put her head on his shoulder and silently talked to the God she did not yet know.

Sam smiled and stroked her cheek, "Let's pursue that life together."

"I think that Life is coming after us."

"Even better."

FIFTY-THREE

SAM, 1963

As Sam readied himself for work each morning, he told Sadsack Alice was on her way to his office. In the evening, Sam recounted her visits to the cat. He always ended his report with, "You know, Sadsack, there is nothing I look forward to more than beginning and ending my day with that woman."

Despite the overcast day, Sam whistled as he carried the coffee and crullers toward the newspaper office. His weekly visits with Alice had become an everyday occurrence, either before she started the day shift or early evening if she was on nights. If he was lucky, she came twice a day.

He paused at the corner of Lincoln and Barracks Streets and shifted Agrefena's thermos and crullers to his other arm. Alice sat on the low stone wall that surrounded the Home's grounds.

Something about the bend of her back and stooped shoulders worried Sam. He hurried to his office and rid himself of the crullers. He grabbed two mugs and hustled back to Alice but slowed his approach when he heard her sigh.

Sam shifted his weight from one foot to the other, and the mugs clinked. Alice looked over her shoulder. "I love it," she whispered, indicating the Home. She wiped her wet eyes with her sleeve and sniffed.

He heard the pensive sadness in her voice. It made him uneasy, so he ignored it. "The architect was progressive, and the building works as well now as when it was built in the 1930s."

"I love it all; my patients, the statue of the old sourdough, the landscaping of all three acres. This short cement wall encloses the grounds—like a wrapper around a cupcake. I often see tourists and townspeople sitting on it or leaning against it."

"I like the nasturtiums that flank the main sidewalk all summer," Sam said.

"I like them too, but this is my favorite." Alice touched the hedge of flowering bushes on the inner side of the stone wall. She fingered one of the delicate pink flowers, then bent to breathe in its scent.

"Our Sitka Rose," Sam whispered, but he wasn't thinking of the flower.

"Like me, it's not from here."

"The rose was brought from Japan in the 1930s. I wrote a feature on it years ago."

"It didn't do well, did it, Sam? Poor little rose."

"Once they crossbred it with the Kamchatka rose, it thrived."

Alice lifted her yearning eyes to his. "Yes, it had to be united with something here. Something from Sitka."

Sam swallowed and again felt that pensiveness in her. He poured a cup of coffee, but she shook her head. "The plane to Juneau leaves in two hours, and I haven't finished packing."

"You're going to Juneau?" Sam frowned and flung the contents of the mug into the rose bushes.

"St. Louis. My mother is having surgery. Nothing life-threatening, but she will need care afterward."

Sam dug the toe of his shoe into the sidewalk. "I'm sorry about your mom, but how long will you be gone?"

"A few weeks if there are no complications, maybe longer."

"But you're coming back?"

"I can't think right now, Sam. Alaska was going to be my big adventure. I'm not sure it's my life."

"But, Alice—"

She started toward home, and Sam followed. "Call me when you get to Juneau, Seattle, and St. Louis."

"Long-distance is expensive and just for emergencies."

"Reverse the charges. I don't care, just call me. Better yet, give me your family's telephone number in St Louis and your arrival time. I'll call every fifteen minutes until I know you've arrived safely."

"That would drive my father around the bend. I'll call you as soon as I land in St. Louis."

"You could call me every day to let me know how things are going. Reverse the charges."

Alice laid her arm on Sam's. "I'll be busy, and those phone calls are an unnecessary expense; for you and for me. I need to be practical." She reached into her purse and scribbled on the back of her grocery list. "This is my family's address. You're a writer. Write to me."

Sam stuffed the paper into his pocket and nodded.

She stopped in front of her gate. "Thank you for walking me home, but I have to pack, and you have a newspaper to publish. "Goodbye, Sam." She reached up and gave him a quick kiss on the cheek. Blushing, she ran into the house.

The gate swung closed behind her. Sam stood there, hand to his cheek, eyes suspiciously moist. The door closed behind her as he whispered, "I miss you. You haven't gone yet, and I miss you."

During the next few weeks, Sam poured his heart out in daily letters to Alice. He described the most profound emotions in his heart and soul. He explained how his words were often lodged between his warm heart and thick tongue whenever they were together. He sketched the future he saw for them and asked her if she could ever care for him as he did for her.

And every day, he wadded up the letter and threw it into the fireplace. As he watched it burn, he cursed himself for being an emotional coward and vowed to do better the next day.

The letters he mailed were full of the town's gossip and Sitka history, more tidbits about Miss Ruth and the activities of men at the Café.

He scoured each letter he received from her, but Alice answered in kind. She wrote about her mother's progress, what it was like to be home again, and how fun it was to reconnect with old friends. Sam frowned when he saw the words. What did she mean—old friends? What kind of friends? Men friends?

And just as he did, Alice wrote long descriptive paragraphs about the weather.

"I'm telling you the man is depressed, positively morose," Jake said.

"What is mor...moo...moo-roose?" Ivan sputtered.

"He still picks up the coffee and crullers every morning. Margaret Mary says he gazes at them for hours and then throws them in the trash." Mick shook his head. "I'm not saying I don't mind making money off the man, but I hate to see him so miserable."

"We've got to do something, develop a plan," Ade said.

Stormy Durand salted his steak and sighed, "As you know, I still patrol Sitka's streets, only now I call it my daily walk. I can't tell you how often I looked through the Sentinel's windows and saw Sam staring at nothing."

The Café was not as busy this morning, and the men's voices carried. Agrefena had been going over her menus at a nearby table. She frowned when she heard Ade say, "We cannot leave Sam to his own devices. We have to do something."

Agrefena stood behind Ade. He jumped when she growled, "You will do nothing, Ade, except tell your wife to call me. Margaret Mary has been watching Sam for weeks and already has a plan. She is ready to execute it with Ollyanna and me." She waved her wooden spoon in their direction. "Do not interfere."

"Woman not make good plan. Man must—" Ivan said.

Agrefena tapped him on the head with her wooden spoon. "Quiet, old man."

The others contained their laughter as Ivan rubbed the sore spot on his head. He chewed on his mustache and mumbled Russian curses as Agrefena gathered her menus and returned to the kitchen.

"I don't like this at all." Ollyanna Bunderson wrung her hands. "I don't know what the new Father will say, but Father Alexi, may he rest in peace, would forbid it."

Agrefena came into the storeroom with coffee and frybread. She set the tray on a large box of onions and sat on a five-gallon bucket of dried beans. "You can't let the Fathers dictate your actions. This is too important."

Margaret Mary knew she'd have a headache before this meeting was over. She forced herself to speak softly, "Ollie, we are doing this for their own good."

"But it's not honest."

"We aren't doing anything wrong," the linotype operator insisted.

"Then why are we hiding in the Café's storeroom?"

Agrefena peeked out the door. "So those nosy men don't get wind of our plan—interfering old gossipers."

Ollyanna twisted her wedding ring, "I don't know what Ade would think."

"He'd be all for it," Agrefena said.

"But don't tell him." Margaret Mary shot a look to Agrefena, who grinned back at her. It seemed Ollyanna was the only one who didn't realize that Ade was not above a bit of chicanery when it suited him.

Three heads turned as a fist thudded on the door. "Are you in there, Ma? Why is the door locked?"

"Not now."

"The salt shakers are low."

Opening the door, she pushed a box of salt into his hands and tried to block his view, but at less than five feet tall, she did not succeed.

Mick smiled at the two other women and then noticed their stricken faces. "What's going on?"

Silence.

"Ma?"

"Everything is prepped for the lunch crowd. You can handle it. If anyone complains, give them free fry bread." She closed the door more firmly than she intended.

"Ma?" the door muffled Mick's voice, "Ma?"

"Go away." She turned to the others and said, "Where were we?"

"You were explaining to me why I needed to be a part of this deception."

Margaret Mary hefted her bucket of beans closer to Ollyanna. She sat down on it and took the other woman's hand. "Dear Ollie, everyone knows you are the most honest woman in town."

"Straight as a stick, no one will suspect you," Agrefena said.

"When you talk like that, I want to ask the Father what to do."

Agrefena grabbed a piece of fry bread. She chewed slowly. "Ask yourself, what would Miss Ruth do?"

Margaret Mary watched Ollyanna open and close the latch on her purse in a rhythmic, almost hypnotic way. She could tell the other woman took the question seriously.

"I think Miss Ruth would get Sam and Alice in the same room and convince them to be honest with each other."

"That's hard with Alice in St. Louis," Agrefena said.

"That's what we're attempting to do," Margaret Mary said at the same time.

"But you want me to lie," Ollyanna whined.

Margaret Mary rubbed her head again. "Agrefena and I will do most of the talking. Pull this letter out of its envelope at my signal and read these lines." Margaret Mary held the paper in front of Ollyanna and pointed.

...and so, while I do think Sam cares for me, perhaps a little, he has never said so. I do not know if I shall return to Alaska.

"But Alice didn't write that."

"Sam will think she did. He knows the two of you have become friends." Agrefena topped off everyone's coffee.

"What if he wants to see the rest of the letter? What if he asks me questions? I know I'll mess this up."

"If Sam asks any questions, just tell him you're too upset to talk, stuff the envelope in your purse, and rush out crying or something." Margaret Mary's head pounded. If people would just follow directions.

"No, I can't do it."

"When you see Alice walk down the aisle in a long white dress, you will be glad you helped bring them together." Agrefena patted Ollyanna's shoulder. "Do it for them."

Ollyanna left the storeroom, clutching her purse with both hands, white-knuckled, and with a troubled face.

Margaret Mary's headache was a raging tornado tearing through her head and neck. "This won't work without her. Sam knows I'm not above a bit of subterfuge, you either."

Agrefena picked up the tray. "She'll do it."

Margaret Mary shook her head, and the tornado touched down again. "Do you have any aspirin?"

Agrefena fetched two tablets and a glass of water. "It's just her way. She'll chew on it for a couple of days, then join our next planning session as if everything was settled. Don't ask her if she's committed, or her doubts will rise again."

The meeting with Sam was conducted with the precision of a military operation. Margaret Mary was careful not to meet his eyes. As planned, she let Agrefena do most of the talking.

"Some of the nurses were having lunch at the Café. I overheard one of them say Alice was offered a job at a big St. Louis hospital. What do you think about that, Sam?" Agrefena said.

Ollyanna whipped the page out of the envelope, kept her head down, and read the two lines. Sam held out his hand and asked for the letter.

She dropped her purse, scrambled to cram the scattered items back into it, and ran out of the office with tears in her eyes.

"Good job, Sam. Now you've upset Ollyanna." Margaret Mary turned her head and winked at Agrefena, who nodded with satisfaction.

Agrefena set her coffee mug down and pulled her coat on. "I told her she needed to tell you about the letter. I'll talk to her this afternoon." She gave Sam a long look and winked. "If I had my wooden spoon, I'd knock some sense into you, but I guess what you do with the information is your business. I have to get back to the Café."

Sam poured himself a cup of coffee and sat with his hands cupped around the mug. He stared into the dark liquid. "What do you think, Margaret Mary? What should I do?"

"Do you want Alice in your life?"

Sam stood up, paced the office, sat at the worktable, returned to his desk, sat down, and stood up again. "Of course," he growled, red-faced.

"Don't take that tone with me." Margaret Mary pitied the poor man and gentled her voice. "The whole town knows you love her, but they are taking bets on whether you'll do anything to let her know. The odds aren't in your favor Sam."

Sam's red face grew even redder, and he grabbed his hat and coat. "I'm going home." He walked home the long way, which gave him time to think. He pictured the months and years ahead without Alice and felt physically sick.

"I bought you a can of sardines, Sadsack." As he fed the cat, he said, "What should we do about Alice?" The cat ignored him. "I've asked you several times, and you've never answered."

Sadsack's bright green eyes blinked, and he rubbed himself around Sam's ankles. "She belongs here with us, doesn't she, Sad?"

He spent almost an hour with the long-distance operator. The line seemed continually busy. Finally, the phone was answered. The young boy on the other end of the line had difficulty hearing him. Sam had to shout Alice's name twice before the youngster called her to the phone.

"It sounds like you're having a party."

"Just family and a few friends. Mom's been given a clean bill of health, and we're celebrating. I can't wait to tell you about this man I met..."

What man? "What are you saying, Alice?"

"..chaplain at the hospital. He helped me understand the verses in Miss Ruth's journal. It's all real, and I've become real, renewed."

"Hello? Hello? Alice, are you there?" What man he wanted to ask, and what did you say about Miss Ruth. Instead, he said, "When are you coming home?"

"This is my home, Sam. I grew up here."

"I mean, when are you coming back?"

"Just a minute, let me stretch this phone cord to the hallway. It's a little more private. It's hard to hear you, Sam, speak up."

"The whole town is waiting for you to come back."

Alice laughed. Sam tossed his cigar into the fireplace and said, "Everybody misses you."

"Even you, Sam?"

Sam clenched his jaw and rubbed his hand over his eyes. His heart rate escalated. He knew he needed to get the words out. He opened his mouth. Nothing. He cleared his throat and tried again. Nothing.

"Sam? Sam? Are you still there?"

"I'm here, Alice, but you're not."

"What did you say? I can't hear you."

Sam gulped and pushed the words out of his heart and into his mouth, "Come home, Alice. I...I...I need you."

"What?"

"I need you. I want you to come home," he practically shouted.

FIFTY-FOUR

SAM, 1963

Ivan Mishkin sat on the damp wooden bench outside the Sitka Café; the Café's overhang gave scant protection when the wind drove the rain sideways.

He held a mug of Agrefena's good black coffee in one hand. He smoothed his bushy mustache with the other, releasing the raindrops his facial hair seemed to attract.

The early morning weather chilled his old bones, but he wouldn't complain to his Café cronies lest they chastise him. They each took a turn at their newly established morning ritual, and Ivan couldn't admit the cold and wet aggravated his arthritis. "Hurry, woman. Time is come," he muttered to the empty sidewalk.

Silently, Mick slipped out of the restaurant, patted the old man's shoulder, poured some of the secret ingredient into Ivan's mug, and returned to his duties.

Ivan saw Alice Blakely at the end of the block. She pulled her headscarf tighter and turned up the collar of her heavy winter coat. Like most Sitkans, she didn't carry an umbrella.

"Miss. Miss. I have plan. No need vote."

She stopped when he raised his voice and repeated his strange comments. "What are you talking about, Mr. Mishkin?"

Ivan chewed on his mustache and tried to remember the rules of what he should say. The men at the round table had thrown too many suggestions and orders. He scratched his head and muttered what was at the forefront of his mind. "You marry, Sam. Yes?"

Alice bit her lip and leaned against the telephone pole. She felt her heart knock on the sides of her chest. "Did Sam say something?"

"I not die."

"Do you feel well, Mr. Mishkin?" She took him by the arm and gently pulled him to his feet. "Let me take you to the doctor?"

Ivan chewed on his mustache and raised his voice, "Olga agree."

"Shall I call her to come and get you?"

He pulled his arm away and shouted, "Buy white dress."

"Mr. Mishkin, I..."

He jumped to his feet. "Is good plan."

Alice Blakely, torn between her nurse's instinct to try to help this elderly man and fear that others might hear his ramblings, said, "Let me at least help you inside."

"Marry Sam! No need vote." His voice had attracted the attention of several passers-by who stopped to listen. Alice shifted her weight from one foot to the other. She avoided everyone's eyes and could not answer their questions or react to the teasing comments.

Agrefena came to the door and saw Alice's deer-in-the-headlight-look, "What's going on?"

Ivan pulled on his mustache. "Foolish woman."

Alice gave the old man a gentle tap in Agrefena's direction. "I really must go." She ran the rest of the way to the Sentinel, slammed the door, and leaned against it. "You have to do something, Sam!"

"What?"

"He seemed confused, but he's just like the others."

"What are you talking about, Alice?"

"I can't take it anymore," her voice rose, and she glanced at Chuck, who worked a couple of hours before going to school.

Sam poured her a cup of coffee and set it on the corner of his desk. "Sit down, have a cruller, and tell me what's bothering you," He kept his voice calm.

She took one step forward and flailed her arms at him. "Ever since I came back from St. Louis, they've been at me. I've felt like I've run a gauntlet for weeks just to get to work. I hate them all."

Sam walked around his desk, took Alice by the arm, and guided her to her usual seat. He hung her coat and scarf on the coat rack and said, "I know you, Alice. You couldn't hate anyone. Take a deep breath."

She shuddered, took a sip, then a large gulp, and choked on the coffee, "It's your friends. Every morning I'm waylaid by one or another of them. They make it seem accidental, casual, even providential, but I know it's deliberate." She clenched and unclenched her fists. "Make them stop."

"Has anyone hurt you?" Sam half rose from his chair.

"Yes," she hissed, glancing again at Chuck, who leaned over a sheet of paper and wrote furiously.

"They accosted you?" Sam pulled his jacket off the hook.

She shook her head. "They wink, laugh, make remarks."

Sam threw his coat back over the peg and sat down. "What did they say?"

"You're a man of the world, Sam. Invincible—strong. It's easier for you." She wiped her wet eyes and blotchy face. Her voice tremored, and she whispered the word, "They keep saying—marriage."

Sam blanched, turned away, and ran his hand over his head.

His thinning hair reminded him of his age and all his inadequacies. "I've known those men all of my life. They care about me and love you. Who wouldn't?" Sam scratched his head and met her eyes. "Really, Alice, they're harmless. Here, have a cruller."

She batted the bag away, "Make them leave me alone! This is so embarrassing. You have to do something!"

Margaret Mary put her arm around the distraught woman. "I'm taking her home, and then Sam, you and I will have a little talk."

As the teary-eyed Alice pulled on her coat and snatched her scarf from Sam's outstretched hand, Margaret Mary shook her finger in Chuck's direction. "And don't think I don't know you haven't asked Sarah out yet. You better be here when I get back."

Sam and Chuck ate the last of the crullers in a dreadful silence.

The morning clatter of crockery, the sizzling bacon, and the smell of Agrefena's frybread assaulted Sam as he settled himself at the round table. "I mean it, fellows. You have to leave Alice alone and don't say the word marriage. It embarrasses her."

"Or does that word scare you?" Stormy's eyes twinkled, "I know it would scare me."

Stormy held his mug aloft, and Mick noticed. He made the rounds with his coffee pot.

"We just tried to encourage her, give her some gumption," Ade said.

"Is okay. I friendly." Ivan said

Stormy finished his bacon and snagged a piece from Sam's plate. He waved the crispy thing in front of Sam's face. "I think Sam here is the one who needs some gumption, some matrimonial gumption."

Mick topped off Sam's mug last and quietly asked, "What are you going to do about Alice? I've got fifty bucks on the line that says you won't do anything."

"The odds are really against you, Sam. You need to show this town that you can do more than write about other people's drama," Jake said.

"Ollyanna wants to know when you will make an honest woman of Alice," Ade grinned.

Sam's coffee nearly went down the wrong way. He coughed, cleared his throat, and growled, "You've embarrassed her and hurt her feelings. I'm so mad at you all."

Agrefena prodded him with her ever-present wooden spoon. "Ask yourself why it matters what these foolish old men say?"

Sam fidgeted with his fork. He hadn't eaten anything yet and didn't think he would. He pushed his plate away. "Well, I..that is... I...Alice is..."

Agrefena smiled and whispered in his ear, albeit loud enough for everyone to hear, "Everyone in town can see you love this woman. Open your eyes. Make her happy. Make yourself happy."

"You sure missed this story, some journalist you are," Jake laughed.

"We all thought something would happen when Alice returned from St. Louis, but it's still just coffee and crullers. Neither one of you is getting any younger, Sam." Ade winked at the others.

Stormy Durand leaned back in his chair, balancing on the two back legs. He hooked his thumbs through his belt loops. "We need a new topic of conversation. Marry the woman and put us all out of our misery."

"Love girl. Have wedding." Ivan pounded his fist on the table.

"Is decided."

"Well said, Ivan, well said." Mick splashed an extra measure of the secret ingredient into Ivan's mug.

Sam shook his head and muttered, "I give up."

Stormy chuckled, "Good, these louts will find someone else to harass once you're married."

"I meant I give up trying to talk sense into any of you."

FIFTY-FIVE

SAM AND ALICE, 1963

Alice opened her door and frowned. "Your face tells me it didn't go well."

"I tried, but they are not going to stop."

"The nurses on my shift aren't giving up either. I almost hate going to work."

"I'm sorry." Sam leaned against the door jamb. "Everybody thinks they know what's best for us."

The timer dinged, and Alice opened the door wider, "Come in, Sam. I have cookies in the oven." She put the kettle on. "You have to do something. I can't sleep. All I do is drink coffee and eat cookies. I can't relax."

"Me either. The guys have been harassing me for weeks. It would serve them right if we..." his voice trailed away, and he reached for another cookie.

"If we what, Sam?" She lifted questioning eyes to his while Sam shoved two more cookies into his mouth. Alice pulled another pan of cookies out of the oven.

"Just say it," she snapped.

"We should fly to Juneau and get married. That would show them." He said the words and realized he meant them but averted his gaze.

"I don't think a woman could marry a man just so his friends would stop giving them a hard time," Alice whispered.

"She could if she loved him." Sam focused his gaze over her head to the rain-splattered window.

"She would if he loved her." Alice lifted her hand to his cheek and turned his face toward her.

"Alice, do you..?"

"I do..."

They laughed. He rubbed his knuckles across her cheek and kissed her.

"Will you?" he asked.

"I will."

"I'll buy the tickets," he said.

"I'll pack a bag."

He swung her around, kissed her again, and grabbed his hat.

"Wait, Sam. We have to be clever about this."

"I'll tell Margaret Mary I'm covering a story in Juneau."

"Maybe you should fly there a day or two before me and get everything ready, the preacher or judge, the ring, the hotel."

"Why, soon-to-be Mrs. Sam Mitchell, you are a clever little thing, aren't you? Now we just have to think of a reason for you to go to Juneau."

"Send me a telegram with my cousins' name saying they'd like me to come to Juneau since their cruise ship doesn't stop in Sitka."

"Like I said, clever." He kissed her again and laughed, "I could get used to this."

Her smile faded, "I would have liked my family to be there."

"Do you want to wait? We could get married in St Louis at Christmas."

"I'm not waiting. We'll visit my folks at Christmas."

No one approached the round table without a nod from one of the regulars. Jaws dropped, and silverware clattered when Margaret Mary rushed into the Café, plopped down at the table, and said, "Something is going on. Sam asked me to take care of Sadsack for a few days while he's chasing a big story in Juneau."

"That's not unusual," Jake said.

Margaret Mary signaled Mick to pour her a coffee. "The next day, Maddie called me. Alice got a telegram from her cousin, suggesting Alice fly to Juneau to meet the cousin's cruise ship."

Ade rubbed his chin. "Interesting."

"It's more than that," Margaret Mary gulped her coffee. "Maddie said Alice was unusually excited and blushed when anyone asked her questions about her cousins."

"So, Sam is in Juneau, and Alice is in Juneau. Both for several days." Stormy Durand laced his thumbs through his belt loops and leaned back in his chair. "Are you thinking what I'm thinking, Margaret Mary?"

"I think they are getting married, and none of us are invited."

Agrefena poured another round of coffee and said to the linotype operator, "Come to the kitchen. We need to have a meeting."

"For what?" Ivan asked.

Margaret Mary stood and winked at him. "We have plans to make, a menu to create, people to invite, things to organize."

"Plans? Peoples? Menus?" The old man chewed on his mustache and set his confused eyes on the kitchen door.

"It's okay, Ivan. They will let us know." Ade tried to sound comforting as he threw some bills on the table. "I've got to let Ollyanna know. She'll want to be a part of it."

❧

The men at the Café took credit for the elopement. After all, they had been encouraging Alice and Sam for weeks. The nurses at the Pioneer's Home felt cheated out of a wedding.

Margaret Mary, who believed her little talk with Sam had set the whole project in motion, enlisted their aid for the grandest wedding reception Sitka had ever seen.

❧

Several days later, Rob Nelson did all the pre-flight checks and started the engine. The floatplane bobbed in the calm water. He turned to the couple coming toward him and tipped his cap. "Howdy, Mr. Mitchell, Mrs. Mitchell."

Alice laughed and grabbed Sam's arm. He grinned and said, "I guess the secret is out."

"Are you kidding? The whole town will be waiting on the dock, and you'll be escorted to the Café for what I'm told will be the grandest shindig the town has ever seen."

Sam turned to his new wife. "See, everyone loves you."

"Not only that, they're all taking credit for your marriage. I have orders to radio our arrival time."

They boarded the seaplane, and he radioed his father. When Rob bought the business from Bob Nelles some years ago, he brought his father aboard as partner and office manager.

As predicted, the crowd in Sitka was large and loud. The congratulations and well-wishes flowed, as did the food and drink. Sam did not notice the only one missing was Margaret Mary.

FIFTY-SIX

SADSACK

Margaret Mary opened Sam's back door and waited for Sadsack to greet her. He didn't. She found him on the floor at the foot of Sam's bed. "Poor kitty, you didn't even have the strength to jump onto his bed."

The cat lifted his head, opened one eye, and tried to rise. She fell to her knees. "Oh, Sadsack."

Margaret Mary lined a cardboard box with one of Sam's bath towels and gently lifted the aging feline. She marched with steely eyes and a determined step six blocks to Sitka's only vet.

"Old age. Worn out. His organs are shutting down. I offered to put him to sleep last week, but Sam wouldn't hear of it."

"Of course not. Is he in any pain?"

"Hard to tell. Don't think so."

"Then I'll take him back to Sam's."

The vet gave her a vial and a syringe. "If he's in pain later, squirt this into his mouth."

With a tightness in her chest and a heavy heart, Margaret Mary laid a fire and waited for the hearth to warm, then laid Sadsack on it. She found one of Sam's half-smoked stogies and pulled a shirt out of his laundry basket. "Here you go, Sad, at least it will smell like Sam is here."

Did she hear a faint purr? She bent closer to the cat and decided yes, the cat had definitely thanked her.

"I remember the first day you came to this house. What a frisky little thing you were. Sam's father recently buried, and his mother was so lonely with Sam practically living at the office." Her rhythmic strokes along the cat's back soothed her as much as it did him.

"Sam had to learn the ins and outs of the newspaper business on the job. I helped him as much as I could. Your job was to take care of his mother, and you were diligent. Years later, when she died, you turned all your attention to Sam. Such a good cat."

The cat trembled, and his breathing slowed. Margaret Mary sniffed and said, "Thank you, Sad, for waiting until Sam had Alice to care for him."

The clock on the mantle chimed, and Margaret Mary knew she would miss Sam's reception. She whispered to the cat, "Sam's plane just left Juneau, and the flight will be around 45 minutes depending on the weather. Agrefena will tell Sam and Alice that I'm mad because I couldn't plan the wedding, and so refused to come to the reception. I'd rather have Sam think I'm mad than know you are..."

Sadsack meowed. The sound was thin and tinny.

"Perhaps I should meet his plane and bring him home to you." She scratched his favorite spot behind his right ear. For once, the old linotype operator didn't know what to do.

The cat tried to open his eyes but failed. Margaret Mary scratched behind his ears. "Don't worry, Sad. I won't abandon you." She sniffed and wiped her nose on her shirttail, refusing to leave him, even to get a tissue.

Sadsack paused for several seconds between breaths. Each one seemed to take more effort than the last, and Margaret Mary knew the end would come before the plane. " You've had a good life, Sad, you fulfilled your purpose, and if I'm not mistaken, the cat next door looks ready to deliver. I will see that Sam and Alice have the pick of the litter. Your legacy will live on."

Sadsack took a deep breath and shuddered. Margaret Mary cradled the cat, and her tears fell on his greyed tabby coat. "Sam will be happy with Alice, but he will miss you dreadfully. Your duty is done dear Sadsack. It's okay, you can go."

Sadsack twitched the tip of his tail and stopped breathing.

EPILOGUE

Harbor Mountain, Sitka, Alaska, 1983

Ruth Mitchell, tall and slim, raced up the trail on Sitka's Harbor Mountain. The sun-kissed freckles that popped on her face made her appear younger than her seventeen years.

"Ruthie, wait!"

She laughed as her ponytail swished from side to side but didn't stop until she reached the crest, "What kind of Native are you, can't even climb a little mountain?"

"My grandfather was a Tlingit, his wife from Nebraska, and my mother was white. I'd hardly call myself a Native." He bent over to catch his breath, "It's a good thing that logging road comes almost to the top."

"It's a better thing your old pickup still runs." She turned to face the view from Sitka's Harbor Mountain, "Did you know there was a signal station up here during World War II? They were searching for Japanese submarines. Never saw any, but Dad said they did see something suspicious at the Castle one night."

"Don't start, Ruthie. I agreed to a hike and a picnic, nothing more." He eased his backpack off and handed her a bottle of water.

In mock anger, she frowned at him, "I wish the Castle were still there, the Russian one that burned, not the huge Victorian house that replaced it. Peter, imagine if there were no bridge connecting

Baranof to tiny little Japonski Island. Back in the day, you paid a dime and took a shore boat."

He shrugged.

"I can imagine Japonski without that jet runway crawling out of the sea. During the war, the naval air station on that tiny island was Sitka's only defense. No jet planes, just some PBYs and maybe a, what did they call those old monster planes, a something goose?"

He shrugged again.

"Or before that when it was just the Russians and the Tlingits." She laughed before her mock anger turned real, "Why can't you see the stories, Peter? Do you know our little island town has nine different cemeteries? Every grave once a life, every life a story. Of course, I love the Russian cemetery best."

"I know. I've plodded through it with you enough times. Reading gravestones is an odd thing for a teenage girl to do."

"It's the stories. Don't you wonder about the people that came before us? Those not born in Sitka had to come by sea and, later, air. Don't you wonder?"

"No." But he said it softly so she wouldn't hear. He emptied the contents of his backpack, "Come and eat."

She plopped down, "I was born too late."

"Aww, Ruthie, don't start."

"I'm serious. You know about my namesake, Miss Ruth?"

He shoved his tuna sandwich in his mouth so he wouldn't have to answer and handed her the other sandwich.

"She had adventures—a quest. She helped people too, and I'm going to do the same. But now, there is nowhere left to explore, and it seems the government has taken over helping people." She gnawed on the end of her thumb. "I need a quest, Peter, a huge, wonderful, magnificent quest."

He groaned and started on the other half of his sandwich.

"I'll find one; I know I will." She pulled the wax paper away from the tuna sandwich, took a bite, and laid it on the ground. "I don't really want to go anywhere except the past. I'd like to have known Miss Ruth."

He ripped open a bag of potato chips.

She stared into the waters of Crescent Bay and imagined it without the marina or the Harrigan building. What must it have been like to walk along its gently curving beach? Half a century ago, school kids had recess on that beach. She scanned the town, her eyes resting on the docks near the fish canneries. She didn't see the pleasure boats, water taxis, seiners or trawlers; instead, she saw steamships offloading gold seekers.

Few people knew placer gold had been discovered in the hills behind Sitka and the mountains above Juneau years before the big strike on the Klondike. She mumbled her thoughts aloud, not really speaking to Peter.

"Huh?"

"Didn't you pay attention in history class?"

Peter lay back, put his hands behind his head, and closed his eyes.

She poked his leg with a stick. "Peter! Listen to me. Dad told me hundreds of stories about Miss Ruth. I wrote them down."

The thought of a sun-soaked nap vanished. He reached for an orange.

"And another thing—he's not going to ship me off island for college. He never went. Besides, I've done two years right here in Sitka. It's enough."

"If you hadn't taken all those accelerated courses and night classes, you'd just be graduating high school like the rest of us." He riffled through his backpack, fumbling for the candy bars.

"I couldn't wait. There is too much life to be lived. I can't be stuck in school." She jumped up and stretched her arms wide, "Oh Peter, every island in Sitka Sound has a story, every rock, tree, and wave. He can't make me leave. I won't!" She drew angry circles in the dirt and then tossed the stick away.

Peter wrapped the orange peels in a napkin and stuffed them in his backpack.

"The question is, how do I get him to see my point of view? I've got to have a good reason to stay."

Peter picked up her sandwich. She shook her head, so he ate it.

"He's getting on in years and needs more help at the newspaper, but he won't admit it."

Peter guzzled his root beer.

"I'm a better newspaperman than he was at my age. He even says I'm an all-around better writer too." She gazed beyond Mount Edgecombe and saw Russian fur traders and Aleut otter hunters.

"What would Miss Ruth do?" he asked.

Ruth spun around, "Peter, you're a genius. I could kiss you."

"If only," he mumbled and watched her pull a small notebook from her pack.

She began to make lists. "I'll get old copies of the Sentinel from the state library in Juneau; Dad did a big story on her when she died. I'll also see what information the churches have in their archives. You know all of Dad's material burned in the big fire of 1966. It's romantic, really." Her pencil hovered over the paper as she thought about the past.

Peter mumbled around a mouth full of hard-boiled egg, "How was half the town burning romantic?"

"Not the fire. How could you think that? Dad had set up a writing room in the apartment above the newspaper office, all his notes, and the letters..."

"That's not romantic either," Peter interrupted as he reached for another egg. When she wasn't looking, he threw the yolk in the bushes.

"As the fire got closer, all he could think about was Mom, not Miss Ruth. Everything was engulfed in flames. Ashes!"

"Still not romantic."

"Oh, Peter! You are such a...a...boy!" Ruthie put her hands over her heart and sighed, "That night, Sam Mitchell, Jr., Editor of the Sitka Sentinel, realized he loved Alice Blakely Mitchell more than Miss Ruth. He had to find her and tell her.

"But they were already married. I don't get it."

"Mom wasn't at home or work. He had to find her and make sure she was safe, even if all of Miss Ruth's letters burned; that's the romantic part."

"If you say so, Ruthie."

She bit the end of her pencil, "I'll visit the Pioneer's Home. Some of the residents must have heard stories about Miss Ruth when they were younger. Maybe some of the ancient ones knew her when they were children."

Peter shook his head. When Ruthie made her mind up, all he could do was tag along.

"Mom will be on my side. She's dreading her empty nest. This is going to work."

"Huh?" Peter, a cookie in each hand and one in his mouth, stared at her.

"Don't sound so confused. It was your idea. Dad has wanted to write about Miss Ruth forever. We'll do it together, and he'll think it was his idea."

Peter up-ended the backpack, and empty candy wrappers and water bottles fell out. No more food. Being with Ruthie always made him hungry. Bewildered. Confused, even muddled. But mostly hungry.

Ruthie stuffed the notebook in her pocket, gazed at the view from Harbor Mountain one last time, and ran down the trail.

He scrambled to stuff the trash from their picnic into the backpack when he heard Ruthie call over her shoulder, "Hurry, Peter. We have research to do and stories to write. It's going to be glorious."

Author's Note

I love the characters in My Mama's Mama, and I hope you do as well. It saddens me to think about letting them go. I'm not ready. Are you?

I wrote about Firy for my grandchildren. I wanted them to know my mother's life and times; a world so different from the one they are growing up in.

My fictional characters also have a history and reasons they came to this specific town on this particular island. What are their stories? Why did they choose to settle in Sitka?

We know about Miss Ruth, but what about the others? Father Alexi, Ade Bunderson, Agrefena Evans, Alice Blakely, and others. Their stories must be told.

Coming Soon

THEY SETTLED IN SITKA

THEY SETTLED IN SITKA

Father Dimitri Alexi

The stranger set up his equipment quietly and efficiently. He looked proper and professional in a buttoned-down white shirt. Black framed glasses. Shoes polished. Well-worn leather briefcase. Young. I saw the beginnings of a scruffy beard. Why had I given him permission to come?

The samovar steamed as I turned the spigot, and choice Chinese tea streamed into the glass mug. He seated himself across from me; I handed him the tea and pushed the bowl of sugar cubes toward him. He nodded his thanks.

I looked everywhere except at him, then sighed, "You want to know why I settled in Sitka?"

"My job, as a state archivist, is to collect accounts from our eldest citizens. It's important, Father. You are living history."

There were too many closed and locked doors in my soul—places I had not entered in decades. Rooms abandoned and boarded, almost forgotten. I had no desire to open them.

"Please." He clicked his pen, opened his notebook, and turned on his tape recorder.

The reels on the recorder turned, and I envisioned strangers hearing my pain. I poured a cup of tea to distract myself and looked into the amber liquid. I opened my mouth and then clamped my lips together.

"Are you ready?" he asked.

"I don't know where to start." Did he hear the reluctance in my voice? The fear? Did he care?

"Tell me a little about your family history."

I sat silently for several minutes, then slumped in my chair. The sweat from my brow dripped into my eyes, and they became unfocused.

"Father, are you okay?"

I seemed to hear him from a great distance.

"Is there anyone I can call? The woman who let me in, your wife?"

"House... housekeeper." I sensed he went to the door and hollered, but I did not hear him.

She hurried in with my pills. "The Father needs to rest. Call in a day or two to see how he's doing."

He packed his equipment, awkward, silent, continually glancing in my direction. He looked worried as he left but voiced sympathetic platitudes.

I lay in bed the rest of the day feeling worn-out and old. The memories came, and my heart raced once more. I had barely survived living my life; how could I endure revisiting it?

Made in United States
Troutdale, OR
06/24/2023

10752248R00213